Victo
Ca ,
the Goodreads givea
Hope you enjoy the book!
C.C. Bolick

FEAR JUSTICE

The Fear Chronicles Book 1

C.C. Bolick

FEAR JUSTICE

Dirt Road Books

ISBN 978-1-946-08918-2

Cover Design by Fiona Jayde Media

Edited by EbookEditingPro

Books by C.C. Bolick:

Leftover Girl Series:
Leftover Girl
Secrets Return
Prison of Lies
Illusion of Truth
Fate of War

The Agency Series:
Run Don't Think
Love Don't Wait
Fight Don't Fear

The Fear Chronicles:
Fear Justice

For Christie

Without her help, this book would not have been possible

Prologue

Travis Payne sat in the chair across from the director's desk, tapping his fingers on his knees. Sylvia Greene was never late.

She'd called this meeting only hours before Travis was scheduled to leave for a mission, one with the promise he might finally have the justice he'd been seeking for the last twelve years. He'd finally confront the man who knew what happened to his father. He could almost feel the satisfaction of learning the truth.

Sylvia was the only person in the world with the power to stop his plans. As the second hand spun around the clock on the wall behind him, desperation began to take hold. She'd already asked him to sit out the morning meeting.

All agents attended that meeting, unless they were on an assignment that didn't allow communication. Travis couldn't help but think of a time before he wore the black suit that now clung to his skin, making him feel as if he didn't belong here or anywhere else. With the pride of a police officer or firefighter, he followed the agency's dress code as if this was his uniform. He'd fight in this suit, protect innocent people, or die if the ultimate sacrifice was ever required.

The door opened and a young intern stepped in, holding a cup of coffee which she placed on Sylvia's desk. The smiling girl with glasses hadn't been on assignment more than a few days if she thought Sylvia would drink anything but the coffee she made herself.

"Sylvia has been delayed by a meeting with a senator. She asked that you wait."

"No problem." It was worse than Travis had thought. He knew exactly which senator and he didn't want to face her wrath after the meeting was over.

The intern left and Travis shifted in the chair as ten minutes passed and then twenty. Sylvia's phone rang four times. He watched the aquarium to one side of her desk. Blue and yellow fish were meant to be soothing.

Travis felt anything but comfort.

He'd been in trouble often over the years, enough to visit this office on more occasions than he'd like to admit. Losing his mom and dad had left a gaping hole in his life, a hole Sylvia tried to fill by allowing him to remain at the agency in her care. He'd grown up within the walls of this underground base. From the age of nine to twenty-one, she'd always been there. He owed her everything.

And yet he'd kept the biggest secret of his life from her.

The agency was founded as a government project to keep U.S. citizens safe from people with powers. As a kid, he'd read comic books late into the night. Unlike most people his age, he'd known the truth. People with special abilities not only existed, they sometimes threatened the safety of others. A secret government agency protected the people of Earth from these threats.

When Travis realized he had the power to teleport himself anywhere in the world at thirteen, hiding the truth from everyone seemed like the only way to have a normal life. He'd almost died in his efforts to hide. Now, his secret was out and there was no going back to being a 'normal' agent. All the respect he'd built with the other agents vanished with his admission to Sylvia.

Would Sylvia change his orders now that she knew he was no normal human? With a deep breath, he resolved to complete this mission with or without her blessing.

The door opened behind him. Travis didn't move, only stared at the gold nameplate on her desk. From the way Sylvia's heels clicked as she circled the desk, he felt sure she had bad news. The room filled with the soft smell of roses. Her smell. For as long as he'd known Sylvia Greene, she'd worn this same perfume. Despite being in her sixties, Sylvia had a fierce inner strength and was known to others as a deadly agent who got results. He relaxed slightly as a warm feeling grew within him.

No, he couldn't afford to drop his guard. This woman raised him and he naturally felt at home around her. Travis schooled his features. The mission to find his dad meant everything.

"You look almost recovered," she said.

"Almost?" His eyes rose to meet hers. "I'm fine."

"On the outside." She sat behind the desk, her eyes slowly raking over him. "You were under that water for thirty minutes. Logic suggests we shouldn't be having this conversation. How do you feel inside?"

Travis laughed. "In the last twelve years, you've never asked how I felt inside."

"Before you were just an agent. Now—"

He leaned forward. "I'm still an agent. I've spent years training for this job. No one can take that away from me."

"Agreed. No one can take your place at this agency, but I was going to say that since you now have powers…"

"I've had powers for years."

"But no one knew of your powers. You hid your secret well."

"This agency was formed to control people with special abilities. Inhuman abilities. The government sees anyone with a power they can't control as a threat. Why would I tell anyone here about my powers? I never wanted to be locked in a cell or studied like some science experiment."

"I've read the various reports regarding your powers. Can I see a demonstration?"

Travis rose from the chair with a rush of anger. "You mentioned a case. I thought you brought me here to discuss a lead."

She linked her hands on the desk in front of her. "Sit down, Agent Payne. I have information on a case you worked a few months ago."

The caution in her voice knocked the wind out of him. He sat. "Have you changed your mind about me going to Florida? It won't take long for me to confront Mason and make him give me answers."

"You've become obsessed in this search for the truth."

"Donald Mason and my dad were partners. He knows what happened the night my dad disappeared."

"Possibly." Sylvia opened her desk drawer and pulled out a manila folder. She slid the folder across the desk, but he didn't reach for it. The tab was marked with a single word.

Firebird.

Travis thought of the young woman who once bore that name. In the pictures, she always kept her black hair braided down her back. At first the nickname was a joke, something an agent pulled from a comic book. After almost two decades, the name had come to define her.

He'd followed every lead in the case of this missing woman, but with no success. Eighteen years ago, she'd disappeared, presumably died while on assignment for the agency. Five months ago, she was captured on a security camera halfway around the world. His mission then had been to find her and secure her return to the agency. He'd soon realized that every path this case took led to a dead end. Travis was not one to admit defeat.

"You remember the case?" Sylvia asked.

"How could I forget Rosanna?" His throat burned as he spat out the words. "Another person with a power this agency employed—or forced her to use—depending on how you look at it."

"The view might be different from your side of this desk. Either way, she was extremely powerful. The power to stop a nuclear bomb changes the scope of war for the entire human race."

"That's not all she could do, is it?"

"She could also *start* a nuclear explosion."

"Which made her a threat to the human race. It also proves my point—I hid my powers because I didn't want to be seen as a threat."

Sylvia drummed her fingers on the desk as she watched him. "When she first appeared on the agency's radar, our best agents were sent to bring her in."

"My father and his partner; I've read everything the agency has on Rosanna."

She pointed to the file. "You've never read this."

Travis raised an eyebrow and opened the file. A picture of Rosanna was attached to the top of a report. The look on her face showed what some might mistake as fear, but he knew better. Her hands gripped a small suitcase tightly in her lap; her white dress and lace-up shoes made this girl seem as if she'd been born a hundred years ago. His fingers slid across the picture while his eyes fixed on the long golden hair. Her name and a date were written on a white strip along the bottom of the picture. "This was taken when she was first discovered?"

"Yes."

"Her hair isn't black like in the other pictures. Why haven't I seen this before?"

"Because I buried the file. There are some advantages to being director."

"Do you know what happened the night she disappeared?"

"She worked at this agency for three months—her power first appeared just after her eighteenth birthday. Our doctors studied this power and tried to find a way to control her. Basically, they did their jobs."

"You kept her at this agency against her will."

"There was nowhere on this planet she could go without another government or terrorist group seeking her power for their use. We also had a bigger problem."

Travis looked up at her. "What could be bigger than being hunted by every terrorist group on the planet?"

"Being in love with one of our agents."

His eyes widened.

"She and your father's partner had an affair. No one realized what was going on between them. Mason and your father were tasked with keeping her safe, but she disappeared when the terrorist group Black Dawn tried to kidnap her." Sylvia let out a long sigh. "I believe her disappearance was a cover-up."

Anger rose within him. "You think my dad helped his partner betray this agency?"

Her lips formed a thin smile. "Your father was a mystery and I have no doubt he helped Mason make her disappear."

"What happened after she disappeared?"

"Your father and Mason took on a new assignment. Years passed."

"Mason never contacted her?"

"Not that I could find. You know the rest of the story. A few months before your father disappeared, Mason resigned from the agency. He'd had enough of the politics and decided to move back to his hometown. He settled down and married an old girlfriend who had a child."

"And turned into a drunk." It was the hardest aspect of Mason's life for Travis to understand. He remembered the agent who taught him magic tricks as a kid, who would sometimes talk with Travis's dad late into the night. Would Donald Mason recognize Travis when they finally came face-to-face?

"That wasn't until years later, after his wife died in a wreck that he blamed himself for."

"I've seen how he's wasted his life. It's not cool."

"Remember, it was his life to waste. I stayed away and let him have his peace. He'd served this country and saved countless lives over the years. He deserved to be left alone." She laid a picture on the desk next to the folder. "I went to see Mason years later. He never knew I was there, but I managed to snap this picture of his wife."

Travis stared at the picture of a woman with golden hair and a young girl clinging to her side with the same golden hair. He put her picture next to the picture from the folder. The woman in the newer picture wore sunglasses and her hair was shorter, but the way her head tilted to the side looked similar. "The same woman?"

"I think it might be."

"You never told anyone?"

Sylvia shook her head. "They were safe and they were happy. You might not think I have a heart, but I assure you I do."

"You really think Mason changed her identity and they lived happily ever after?"

"For a while. Three years ago, his wife died in a collision with a drunk driver. Oddly enough, he couldn't deal with her loss and started drinking as a way to numb the pain."

A small flash of hope spread through Travis, causing his pulse to speed. "They captured her on a security camera five months ago. Are you saying his wife is still alive?"

"I'm saying I don't know." Her eyes drifted past him, to the far wall. "I visited Mason a month after she died. He was beside himself with grief."

"You talked to him?"

"I wanted to bring him comfort."

"I thought your allegiance was to this agency."

"Mason saved my life on two occasions." She looked at him. "He played the part of agent seamlessly and now I wonder if he also played me."

Travis sat back in shock. Sylvia Greene never showed weakness. "Let me go down to Florida and talk to Mason. I'll make him tell me the truth."

"Your mission is not Donald Mason."

"He was the last person to see my dad alive. I want to hear what he knows."

"That will have to wait. Your mission is to bring in their daughter, Regina Mason."

Travis shivered. He'd seen the girl on a previous visit but never approached her or her father. Her hair was longer now, but still the same shade of gold as Rosanna's.

"You think she has this Firebird power?"

"If she does, your job is to find out. Everything you need to know about how her mother's power worked is in that file."

"This isn't going to be a quick mission, is it?"

She shook her head. "Regina is about to start her senior year in high school. I want you at that school. Become her friend and gain her trust."

"What do I know about friendship or gaining anyone's trust?"

"You're an expert at manipulation."

Travis swallowed the bitter taste in his mouth. "She'll have no idea what she's getting into."

"If anyone can find a way to get her on our side, you can. If she has the power, better that we find out before she accidentally sets off a nuclear event."

He stood. "Any more advice?"

"Be careful. We're not the only ones watching Mason. Members of the Black Dawn may have found his location. They tried to exploit Rosanna's power then and they'll do the same to young Miss Mason if she indeed has this power."

"That will complicate my job."

Sylvia smiled. "Good thing you're more than a normal agent."

CHAPTER ONE

Dad wasn't supposed to disappear.

Yes, he often drank more than he could handle for one night and came home as the horizon beyond the lake started to glow. He also claimed he forgot my cell number on more than one occasion. But he always came home.

Until the morning he didn't.

That morning, I climbed down the ladder at the foot of my bed, careful not to wake Alfie in the bunk below. I washed my face at the kitchen sink like I did every morning and marked another day off the calendar. "Things get better when they can't get worse," I whispered. It was Mama's favorite saying. Two hundred and twenty-five days of school left.

My senior year started a week ago and already I spent my days thinking of what would happen when I turned eighteen and graduated. I flipped up the cabinet door to my right and pulled down two bowls. I'd make me and Alfie a bowl of cereal, check on Dad, and then…

I realized the only sound in the camper was Alfie's labored breathing. With his asthma, he sometimes struggled to catch his breath. I'd have to make sure his inhaler got packed before we left for school.

Shoving aside the curtain that separated the front bedroom from the rest of the camper, I peeked inside at the empty bed. Dad never made it home. A feeling of disgust settled in my stomach as I returned to the calendar and circled the day with my black sharpie. I'd always known this day would come. He'd beg and plead with me to forgive him and I would for Mama's sake.

I felt no fear for him, only disgust.

Why worry when no one could kill someone meaner than a snake? It was like that Johnny Cash song he always listened to. The kid's dad made sure he was mean enough to survive in the world without him. Well, he'd made sure Rena Mason was strong enough to survive.

Jacob Andrews, a friend who'd grown up with Dad, insisted I let him know if Dad ever failed to come home. I'd promised years ago, but Coach Andrews was now principal of the school. How would he react if I showed up in his office?

He'd be furious with Dad. Most of the staff at Palm County High would probably be shocked to know about Dad's drinking. Coach Andrews hid the truth well, which was fine with me. I didn't need their pity and I didn't look forward to the entire school whispering behind my back.

I'd spent three years mastering the art of invisibility. The last thing I needed was child services taking a look around our camper. We'd lived on this lake since before Alfie was born. Other people might raise an eyebrow at our tight living space, but I wasn't about to let Dad screw up our home.

Mama would never have let things get this bad.

I wiped my eyes as I cursed myself for thinking of her. The accident was years ago and yet…

"Rena," said a voice behind me.

Alfie yawned as he sat up on the lower bunk. Our beds filled one-half of the back part of the camper; a small bathroom with a stand-up shower took up the other half. Between the back of the camper and Dad's bed at the front was the kitchen area with a table that could fold into a bed. The kitchen had everything a normal kitchen would except at a third of the size.

My friend Piper, who I'd known since she moved to Wynder six years ago, called this a micro-kitchen. She was from a small town in Wisconsin where it snowed enough in the winter to close the schools. It never snowed in Florida. Piper's eyes had doubled in size the first time she saw our home. Her parents had taken her camping growing up, but she had no idea people actually lived in campers.

Thankfully, she hadn't run when I finally told her my secret. I'd refused to invite her over for six months, only to feel a mixture of relief and embarrassment when she learned we didn't have a real house. At least not one with a foundation. She even knew about Dad's drinking, though I tried not to mention how he forgot things like award ceremonies and meet-the-teacher nights at school. Or the late nights when I made sure Alfie got dinner and a bath before taking his medicine.

My eight-year-old brother crawled into a bench-seat of the table. Since we had no family to visit, I couldn't remember the last time the table top had been lowered and the cushions spread across to make a bed. Above the table, I pulled a gold box from a row of cabinets.

Things will get better, I told myself.

"No," he said. "I want the cinnamon kind."

Sighing, I reached for the red box instead and filled his bowl with cereal. I opened the fridge to the right of the counter and pulled out the milk. We really should buy more milk at a time, but only half-gallons would fit in the door. I drowned the cereal and Alfie smiled as he took the first bite.

I'd do anything for my brother, which included raising him for the last three years. After the accident, Dad seemed to check out of reality. The drinking wasn't as bad in the beginning. He'd held Alfie and wiped his tears. Dad had even tried to discuss the facts of life Mama usually addressed. Embarrassing? Yes, but I loved him for trying.

As the months without Mama grew, he came home later and later. He wasn't the same man who raised us. The happy sparkle in his eyes had faded to the bleak gray of survival.

Alfie stopped chewing and stared up at me. "Where is Dad? He's usually here for breakfast."

"He's passed out," I lied, with a glance toward his bedroom. "Don't worry."

"He came home late?" Staring at the curtain that blocked off his room, Alfie started to rise. "Maybe I should—"

"Don't wake him. Just finish eating so we can get going."

Alfie looked at the clock on the microwave which hung above the stove. "School is a hour away."

"*An* hour. I need to get there early." Inside, I groaned at the thought of lying again. It was getting so easy these days.

"Okay." He finished the cereal and opened the small closet between the bathroom and kitchen. His clothes had been folded and stacked next to mine. Alfie reached for a red shirt and a pair of shorts. "Did Dad wash clothes? He must have since these weren't here last night."

"Sure," I said, marking my third lie. My fourth if I counted telling myself things would get better.

* * * * *

As I waited in the line of traffic near the elementary school office, I thought of what I'd say to Coach Andrews. I barely focused on tapping the brakes of Dad's truck each time the car before me crawled forward. The car moved through a light—we were only two intersections from the school—and I slid forward when the car cleared the intersection and left enough room for me to safely pass through.

"Rena," Alfie screamed in terror.

I slammed on the brakes as a screeching sound cut through the air and became the only noise I heard. A truck stopped only inches from our side. My hands tingled where I gripped the steering wheel. In the mirror, Alfie's eyes were squeezed tight and his body shook. The smell of rubber burning stung my nose.

The next sound I heard was a horn, but I wasn't sure where it came from. The man driving the truck to my side waved in apology and backed out of the intersection. We'd almost been slammed, but I pushed the bad thoughts to the back of my mind. Dad had always insisted I control my fear, especially when driving. Controlling fear meant not worrying about all of the bad things that could have happened but didn't.

"Rena," Alfie said again.

"Are you okay?" I asked.

He nodded. "That truck didn't hit us."

"No." I hit the gas and finished my path through the intersection, falling in behind the vehicle that was now several car-lengths ahead of me. "Everything is fine. Don't worry."

After dropping Alfie off in front of the elementary school office, I fought the single lane of traffic between me and the high school. Flipping through the radio, I hoped to find a station with actual music. The up button wouldn't… I cursed as the plastic broke beneath my finger. The down button would have to be it today.

A news update, a joke about drinking beer that wasn't funny… I slammed my hand against the wheel. Music, I just needed music. Whatever beat came out of the speakers didn't matter, but I needed something to calm me down and fast. I had to focus on anything other than almost getting hit.

Cars ahead were stopped as far as I could see. In the distance, blue lights flashed with a warning to slow down, but who was moving? At this point, I'd be happy crawling past the black and white car. According to the dash, the pickup had less than a quarter of a tank. That should be plenty of gas for me to reach the parking lot across the road from the school.

Being a senior this year meant I got to park in one of the first two rows, which would be useless if all those spots filled up before the traffic moved. I needed to reach the office before the first bell rang and talk to Coach Andrews. *Principal Andrews.*

I groaned. The man had been around as long as I could remember. He coached my soccer team long before he became principal of the school. Back then, he'd covered a variety of sports at the rec center—anything the community needed. He and Dad had graduated together, from the same school I couldn't get out of fast enough.

Straight As, a scholarship… I'd put my plan into motion the day I walked through the front doors of Palm County High. It would be my escape from this town. The only downside was leaving Alfie. Who would take care of him with me gone?

I shook my head. Better not to think of that day.

Instead, I'd think of what to say when I reached the office. Coach Andrews had made me promise to let him know if Dad ever left for the night and didn't return before sunrise. I'd be in his office the next morning.

Why did it matter if Dad didn't come home before sunrise? Maybe he couldn't find a way home this time. He was probably somewhere sleeping off a hangover… yeah, it wasn't bad. Surely, he wasn't lying in ditch somewhere or in a hospital bed. I bit my lip as thoughts of Mama's trip to the hospital surfaced. After the accident, she'd never come home.

No, he wasn't hurt. He'd left the camper yesterday, before Alfie and I got home from school. I had the truck so he wasn't out driving. He hadn't made it home, and I'd been too angry to call. I should have dialed his number on my walk to the campsite's laundry building instead of listening to music on my phone. Alfie had fallen asleep and I needed that hour and a half alone. One call and Dad could have given me some dumb excuse about why he couldn't make it home.

Coach Andrews swore he'd never let anything happen to Dad. I had his number; he'd vowed to answer my call anytime. When he'd asked for my word about helping him keep tabs on Dad, I'd nodded my head like a good girl and made the promise. This was Dad's best friend. He could be trusted.

Why did the thought of talking to him make my skin crawl?

A familiar song came on, one with a fast beat, and I turned up the music. Finally. I laid my head back and sighed. This day would be like any other. I'd make it through until the last bell and then—

The blare of a horn made me jump. My eyes flew open. Up ahead, the traffic had cleared, which allowed me to reach the parking lot without stopping again. I pulled into an empty spot and checked to make sure my senior pass hung from the mirror.

With a long sigh, I made up my mind to face Coach Andrews and killed the engine. No running away today. I only had ten dollars in my purse and that would barely get me to a gas station in this gas-guzzling pickup, much less back to the camper. I grabbed my purse and my backpack from the seat beside me.

On the walk to the office, I kept my head down to avoid making eye contact with anyone. At the door to the office, someone stepped in front of me.

"Rena," said a confident voice.

I glanced up at Robbie Masters, captain of the football team. Not to mention the wrestling team, and he ran track… "Hey, Robbie," I mumbled.

"What do you think about going out this weekend?" A smile stretched across his tanned face, showing perfect teeth. The orange-and white-striped polo shirt fit snug around his huge arms.

If nothing else, Robbie was direct, and I liked that about him. Not enough to climb into his red mustang, but he did get points for not wasting my time. "No."

He raised an eyebrow. "No? That's it?"

"I'll be working this weekend."

"You got a job? Where?"

I gripped the strap of my backpack. "I'm always working, Robbie. Every weekend."

"Oh."

Usually he left at this point. People rushed around us, trying to get to class, but he didn't move. Why was he still staring at me?

Robbie frowned and rubbed the back of his neck. "Thought maybe after the summer you'd changed your mind about us."

"You've seen my place," I said. "You know I pick up all the chores around the house. I don't have time for dating." Nine months and I'd be watching this town fade in a rear-view mirror. He couldn't understand why I had no intention of planting roots here. This wasn't the day to explain.

"Even for me?" Robbie's smile returned. "I'll buy you dinner and a movie. Any other girl wouldn't tell me no."

The sadness in his voice tugged at my insides, but I managed to keep my emotions in check. "Look on the bright side. You'll never be lonely."

He stepped closer. "If it's because of your brother, I can find a babysitter. My mom would—"

"It's not."

"I could help with your chores sometime."

Robbie had me close to breaking. Other guys had offered to take me out, but never with the friendship he showed. I fought to keep the smile fixed on my face. "That's actually nice of you to offer, but it wouldn't be right. You've got way too much to do with football and wrestling." And I didn't trust myself not to fall for him.

"Rena," he said with a lowered voice, "I get it. You've told me 'no' so many times I've lost count."

"I'm sorry. I don't get why you want to date me."

He clenched his fists. "You're the prettiest girl in school."

My smile died. Our conversations had never gotten this serious. "Don't."

Robbie leaned close. "Inside and out. Ask any of the other guys on the football team. If anyone tells you differently, I'll make them sorry."

With a laugh, I touched his arm. "Robbie, I'm not the girl for you. As soon as we walk across that stage at graduation, I'm out of this town. Out of this life."

He narrowed his eyes as he stared into mine. Heat charged through my veins. I didn't want to date Robbie, one of the most popular guys in school… or did I? I'd made a habit of avoiding anyone labeled 'popular.'

His face changed back to the grin he used for the popular girls. "You'll be sorry you turned me down."

Stepping away from Robbie felt right, though I knew he was teasing me. "I'm sure I will be."

Robbie was probably the nicest about me turning him down—other guys got an eye roll and a flip of my hand as I walked away. His family had money, but not the kind that made them ignore the people who didn't live in their fancy neighborhood. He'd asked me out for the last two years. Though his attention secretly made me warm inside, it didn't change the fact that any thoughts of dating would derail my plans for the future.

Mama always called me pretty when I was younger. After the accident, I never wanted to hear those words again.

I sighed as Robbie walked away from the office with the same rock-star smile he used for everyone else in school. He winked as he gave me one last look.

This was for the best. Robbie was a great guy, I knew inside, but I couldn't let him know how I felt. It wouldn't be fair to string him along.

I'd never dated anyone at this school, even though this town had been my home for as far back as I could remember. It was the only place I'd ever really known. Before Alfie was born, I remembered how my parents sat up laughing as they talked about growing old together. All those nights they thought I was asleep in my bunk, I'd lay under the sheet and stare at the tiny window, glowing with the moon's light, and listen. They'd whisper 'love you' and

I'd grin with happiness.

A shudder passed over me as I remembered why I'd stopped at this office. Turning for the door, I gasped as a guy I'd never seen opened the door and waved me forward. His eyes lowered to the floor when I stepped past him, but I caught the brief flash of green.

"Thanks," I mumbled as I walked to the counter. The secretary, Mrs. Yale, sat talking on her phone. She nodded at me, said a few more words, and placed the phone in its cradle on her desk.

"Can I help you?" she asked.

"I need to see him. Coach… sorry, *Principal* Andrews."

"He's in a meeting, Rena. Maybe you can leave a message."

I took a deep breath. "This is important."

Her eyes moved over me and filled with pity as she nodded. "Take a seat. I'll let you know when he's available."

"Thanks." Tears burned in my eyes, but I spun around before she could see. If she'd turned me away, I'd have walked out of the office with my head held high. This was just about me fulfilling a promise. I didn't need her pity and I definitely didn't want to think about what others here would say about my family. If Coach Andrews wasn't available to talk…

I took another breath and turned to a row of seats along the wall. Some part of me wanted to talk to Coach Andrews. Some part of me needed to tell him Dad's drinking had finally become the most important part of his life.

Dad needed help. If only I could figure out how to make him stop. Maybe we all needed help.

Along the wall, only one seat was empty. I dropped

down next to the guy who'd opened the door for me. With a long sigh, I closed my eyes and attempted to block out laughter from a group of girls outside of the office door. They were cheerleaders and seniors; the stuck-up sound of their voices made me wish I'd never climbed out of bed this morning.

"You should have said yes." The soft words were almost lost in the other voices around us.

"Excuse me?" I opened my eyes and looked at the guy sitting beside me.

He stared ahead. "Robbie Masters asked you out. You should have said yes."

I glanced over him. Short brown hair and a clean face, black long-sleeved t-shirt that hugged muscular arms, black jeans. This guy had to be burning up with the long sleeves. His body wasn't built quite like Robbie's, but I wouldn't pick a fight with him. My eyes stopped on his hands. Both were covered with black gloves. Glancing over him again, I realized the only visible skin on his body was his face.

"Aren't you hot?" I asked. "It's ninety-five degrees outside."

He shook his head. "Aren't you going to ask why I said that about Robbie?"

"I could tell you I don't care and save us both the trouble of talking about it."

A smile tugged at the corners of his mouth as he turned to me. "Robbie's a nice guy. What a shocker for a rich boy and a jock."

I glared at him, though it was hard to stare into his green eyes without a look of bewilderment. Something about those eyes put me at ease, when I should have felt anything but relief after what he said about Robbie. "How would you know?"

"I checked him out."

"Checked him out?" Laughter burst from deep inside of me, a rolling laughter I hadn't felt since the last time Dad spent a whole week sober and drove me and Alfie up to the mountains for the weekend. I so needed this laughter. "What did you find when you 'checked him out'?"

"Like I said, he's a nice guy."

"Most guys around here are. Probably even you, though I've never seen you at this school before."

"That's because I started last week." He smiled and held out a hand. "I'm Tony and no, I've never thought of myself as a nice guy."

Staring at his outstretched hand, I hesitated. "Rena."

Tony moved his hand closer and his eyes took on a look of intensity, as if daring me to shake his hand.

"What's with the gloves?" I asked.

"Skin allergies. What's with the hesitation?"

"Hesitation?" With defiance, I reached forward. "I'm not afraid of you."

"What *are* you afraid of?"

As his hand gripped mine, my breathing sped and I fought to control my voice. Our skin wasn't even touching. Hiding my feelings with Robbie had been easy, but this was… weird. "Why are you worried about who I date? You don't even know me."

"I know your name is Rena Mason. We've got physics together."

A twinge of guilt caught me off-guard. "I haven't noticed you before."

"My dad taught me to blend in with my surroundings, like camouflage."

"He was a hunter?"

"Not exactly, but he did teach me how to shoot before he left."

"Left?" The instant his words were out, I felt a connection to him. It was a sadness that welled from deep inside, the knowledge that we were alike in a terrible way.

Tony cleared his throat. "Sorry, I don't know why I said that. You don't want to know anything about me."

"Regina," said a voice from behind the counter.

I glanced up, into our principal's worried eyes. Without giving Tony another look, I stumbled to my feet and approached the counter. Coach Andrews opened a door at the end of the counter and waved me into his office.

"Regina," he said when I'd taken the seat across from his desk. He gently closed the door behind him.

Why did he have to call me Regina? Only my mother had used that name. "Dad didn't come home last night."

Coach Andrews walked around the desk and sat in his old-fashioned leather chair. His huge arms leaned against the desk as he watched me. Taller than Robbie, he wore his Palm County polo shirt in much the same confident manner, proving that even a man in his forties could keep up with our wrestling star. He leaned back to stretch his arms across the tailored armrests. "Are you sure?"

Instead of staring at his eyes, which were probably filled with pity, I glanced at all of the plaques and awards he'd accumulated over the years. He was obviously proud of the framed newspaper clippings of students that went on to state, and even one boy who now played major league baseball. Old habits die hard, and I wasn't the only one who still thought of him as the patient man who spent twenty years introducing kids to sports. Many still called him Coach in a voice filled with pride.

Above the bookshelf next to his desk was a small framed picture of him and my dad. They'd entered the Army together after high school. Two years in, Coach

Andrews had taken a bullet for a fellow soldier and still had a slight limp to prove it.

"Dad wasn't there when we left for school."

He sighed. "Has the drinking gotten worse?"

"Yes."

"How often does he come home after midnight?"

"Every night for the last three months." My eyes met his and I felt shock at the red-hot anger in his eyes. Where was the pity?

Coach Andrews leaned forward. "I'm sorry, Regina, you and Alfred deserve more than having to fend for yourselves. I thought after the last time Donald and I talked… He didn't want you taken away; I knew that would destroy him."

"Maybe you can try again. Maybe he will listen."

He reached for the phone. "My duty is to keep you safe. I think it's time to make this official."

"Calling child services won't keep us safe."

His hand hesitated over the phone. "What do you know about your father's past?"

"What do you mean, his past? He grew up here in Wynder with you. He was in the Army."

"What about after the Army? Do you know where he worked when he met your mother?"

I shook my head. "I was six when Mama moved us to Florida. He lived in a campground like where we live now. They got married. His job was maintenance for the campground, like now."

"Do you remember anything before you moved here?"

Why was he asking these questions? "Mama moved a lot. One day she told me she was going to get married. I'd finally have a dad."

"She loved you and so does Donald. Don't ever doubt

that."

"I don't."

Coach Andrews eyed me with a look of surprise. "Your strength never ceases to amaze me. I know you provide the bulk of Alfred's care—"

"Try all of it."

"Who takes care of you?"

It was a simple question. Unfortunately, tears formed in my eyes and I turned to wipe them away. "Can you find him?"

Sighing, he stood and walked around the desk. I grabbed my bag from the floor and stood, backing away.

"Are you afraid of me, after all these years?"

"I'm not afraid of anything. This is me wanting to hit something."

"I should have known—Regina Mason has no fear."

I wiped my cheek. "That's not funny."

"I'm not joking, merely making an observation. I know about your visits to the counselor's office. You're driving Mrs. Howard crazy over scholarships you want to apply for. As of current standings, you're in the top five for GPA."

"Top three," I said.

"You want out; I get it. Maybe another home would be best for you. If we could find a couple to take you both—"

"I can take care of Alfie."

"I'd offer to take you in myself, but my lifestyle isn't for kids. I'm not married and… there's a lot you don't know about me."

"Then find my dad. Make him understand that drinking isn't more important than us."

He put a hand on my shoulder. "Is that what you think? What has Donald said?"

"He doesn't have to *say* anything. He shows us how he feels by staying away."

"I'll find him. Give me until tonight, okay? I promise to make this right somehow."

As I left Coach Andrews' office, I felt better. At the end of the counter, I noticed Tony's seat was empty. I'd forgotten about him during the meeting with Coach. Those green eyes—I'd have to look for him in physics. I thought of how my breathing had sped as we talked. And the way he teased me about Robbie.

It defied any logic left in my messed-up life, but I actually looked forward to seeing him again.

CHAPTER TWO

At lunch, I grabbed a salad box from the cafeteria and joined Piper at a table along the back wall. People rushed around us in the crowded room, but no one spoke to me or Piper. Most of them knew better.

"Hey," she said as I sat across from her. "Bad day?"

I shrugged. "Just another day."

"And what are we down to?"

"Two hundred and twenty-five days until graduation."

"Can't come fast enough, right?" She glanced at my salad. "Since when are you into eating healthy?"

"I don't really feel like eating anything. At least if I waste half of a salad, I won't worry about it later."

Piper stood. "I'll get you a slice of pizza."

"Sit down and forget about the food. Dad didn't come home last night."

Her eyes widened as she dropped onto the seat and leaned across to whisper. "You came to school and he was still gone? Have you tried his cell?"

"I've been too angry," I said. "There's no point in trying to whisper. No one can hear you with all the noise in here."

"Did you talk to Coach?"

"I told him first thing. He said not to worry because he'd find Dad." Rubbing my arms, I wondered how the school always kept this cafeteria so cold compared to the blistering heat outside. "Since they're friends, I'm hoping he'll get Dad straight."

"Maybe he can scare your dad into not drinking anymore."

"Not likely." I opened the box in front of me and slid a piece of brown lettuce aside. Only two cucumbers. The rest of the leaves soon drowned in ranch dressing. With a frown, I took a bite of the salad. "This tastes worse than it looks."

"Okay, miss allergic to healthy." Piper opened the zipper of her lunch bag. "Want me to get my mom to start packing you a lunch?"

And bring more attention to the fact I needed help managing my life? "Thanks, but Dad does give me money. After our trip to the grocery store, he gives me forty dollars every week."

"Half of that goes into your gas-guzzling truck."

"His gas-guzzling truck."

She snickered. "You're the only one who ever drives it." As soon as the words were out, her face tensed with a look of apology. "I'm sorry, but you know what I mean. Your dad hasn't driven since—"

"Just leave it alone, okay? You don't need to remind me how backwards my life is."

The lights flickered as they often did when the heat outside reached a hundred degrees. "Hope Palm County paid the power bill."

As we laughed, a vision of Tony laughing with me flashed through my mind. "Robbie asked me out again."

"Let me guess—you said no for the thousandth time."

"He offered to get a babysitter for Alfie so he can take me to dinner and a movie."

"That's actually kind of sweet. Why can't someone like Robbie ask me out a thousand times?"

"So you can turn him down too?"

Piper laughed. "I knew it. You turned him down again."

"Probably for the last time, if he's got any sense." I hesitated while watching her face. Like me, she wore no makeup and hadn't bothered to do more than throw her hair into a ponytail that morning. She'd never complained about guys asking me out or seemed remotely jealous. "Do you want Robbie to ask you out?"

"Robbie Masters is a jock and you know I don't date jocks."

But she'd dated plenty of other guys in our high school. "You never said anything bad about Robbie before."

"That was when I still had hope you might…" Her voice lowered. "Taking care of your brother doesn't mean sacrificing any chance at fun. I think for once you should say yes."

"I don't like Robbie."

"No," she said, "you don't trust yourself around Robbie. He might mess up your perfect plan to leave this town after graduation."

"I've got to get out of here. You know I want to go to college."

"So do I, but you don't see me ignoring everyone and everything around me just to get a 4.0."

"I don't ignore everyone. After I turned Robbie down, I met a new guy in the office."

Her eyes narrowed. "I haven't heard of any new guy. What does he look like?"

"Tall with light brown hair—it wasn't much more than fuzz, but he had a cute smile. He wore all black including his gloves."

"Gloves?" Piper brightened. "Does he ride a motorcycle?"

"I didn't ask. All I know is that Tony is his name he wears gloves because of a skin allergy."

"Joey Buckingham said the same thing back in ninth grade. Remember Joey?"

"Yeah," I said. "Everything he touched made his skin break out in a red rash."

"You would know," Piper said. "Remember when Joey almost got beat up and you took up for him?"

Groaning, I pictured the day I stood up to four football players and threatened to turn all of them in for bullying Joey.

"He followed you around like a puppy for months afterward."

"Joey was a nice guy."

"Like Robbie?"

"Seems like I remember someone had a crush on Joey."

She rolled her eyes. "That didn't matter when he only had eyes for you."

Guilt rose at the hint of jealousy in her voice. "Robbie did make those other guys leave Joey alone. It was nice of him to help."

"He helped Joey to get your attention and you still turned him down. Tell me about this new guy."

"I don't think he has a skin allergy."

Piper laughed. "Is he in the cafeteria? Can you point him out?"

I glanced around, surprised by the way my heart began to race. No guy had ever made me feel as if my stomach had been tied in knots. If Tony was in here, I couldn't let him see me stare.

At the far end of the room, I spotted him at the register. His head was down as he paid the cashier.

"That's him?" she asked.

"Yes," I whispered as my heart pounded in my chest.

"Rena," she squealed. "He's cute."

The way she said my name reminded of Alfie, of when he cried out in terror as the truck almost hit us. I'd pushed the thoughts away but now they came rushing back. My hands shook as I thought of what could have happened to my brother.

"Holy crap."

"What?" I swung around to meet her huge eyes.

"Your hands… Rena, your hands are glowing."

Startled, I looked down at my hands. Blue sparkles danced along my palms.

"What's going on?" Piper shoved her lunch aside and reached over the table for my arm.

I spun away from her and jumped to my feet. Leaving my salad box on the table, I put my hands together and ran for the exit. Behind me, Piper yelled my name. People stared, their eyes boring into me as laughter filled the room. Near the door, I met Tony's eyes before exploding into a hallway packed with people.

What was happening to me? I didn't stop running until I reached the bathroom, where I threw open the door to a stall and quickly locked myself inside. My heart pounded as I examined my palms.

There was no blue. No sparkles. My skin felt as normal as it did on any other boring day at Palm County High. Only 225 more, I reminded myself.

"Rena," Piper called into the restroom. "I saw you come in here. Are you okay?"

Reluctantly, I opened the door. "I don't know what happened."

Piper glanced under each of the stalls before taking my hand and inspecting my palm. "I could have sworn…" Her eyes raised to mine. "Tell me you saw the glowing blue sparkles."

I pulled my hand away. "I don't know what you saw, but my palms couldn't have been glowing."

"There's a logical explanation. I saw this movie last night—"

"There's no logic to my hands glowing."

"Not logic—magic." Her voice rose with excitement. "You've got some kind of special power. We've got to figure out how to activate it. I wonder if you can—"

"There is no magic and I don't have any power."

"Are you saying you didn't see the blue sparkles?"

With a long sigh, I walked around her and headed for the bathroom door. "I'm not crazy."

Piper ran behind me. "And I am?"

I stepped into the hall, which was booming with voices and laughter. "I didn't say that."

She grabbed my arm. "Tell me what you saw."

"Nothing," I shouted, loud enough people stopped and stared.

"Fight," someone yelled. "Mason's going to beat someone up."

Again, Piper looked down at my hands. The painful way she glanced up shook me inside, but I couldn't admit to seeing what she had. People would think we were both crazy. Going over our conversation in my mind sounded crazy. My hands couldn't glow with blue sparkles.

A circle of laughter broke out around us, which reminded me that Piper was waiting. "I didn't see anything," I said, holding up my hands. "I hate to break it to you, but there's nothing special about me."

With a scowl, she turned and stomped in the direction of the cafeteria. "You really are a bitch sometimes," she called back, "just like everyone says."

I didn't go back for my salad.

* * * * *

By the time I reached my last class of the day, AP physics, I'd convinced myself that what happened at lunch was just a figment of Piper's imagination. She thought she saw blue sparkles on my hands and then she'd managed to convince me it was the truth. I never saw the glowing blue because it wasn't possible. Piper might believe in magic or witchcraft—she once bought a book of spells at a thrift store and swore it was the real deal—but I wouldn't be fooled into believing.

If magic were real, her dad wouldn't have left her mom for the secretary at his law office. She could have made sure her parents stayed in love. Maybe she could have made my dad forget about alcohol.

At least she didn't get the chance to ask more questions about Tony.

As I dropped into my seat at the front of class, a figure in black passed me with his eyes averted. I glanced up in time to see Tony take a seat at the back of my row. He still wore the black gloves, but I turned around before he could notice me looking.

Tony. Life had seemed like total crap only minutes before we met and he'd managed to brighten my day. Then at lunch life turned to crap again because of him. If I hadn't been trying to point him out to Piper, she never would have—

The door slammed and I jerked to attention. Our

teacher, Mr. Miles, had entered in one of his bad moods. Only a week of school had passed and already he'd shown enough mood swings to make my head spin. Yes, this was supposed to be a hard class. It would count toward college credit. But did he have to be so harsh to everyone?

"Homework, please," he said in an angry tone. "Pass it to the front—that is if anyone solved problems four and five. If not, keep your papers until you figure out the answers."

I glanced around. No one moved to pass up their papers.

"Did I mention I grade on a bell curve?" Mr. Miles turned to the board and drew what looked like a large hill. He drew a line to chop off the beginning of the hill and the end. "Do you see this center section? That's where most of you will fall—in the average range because that's what you are." He pointed to the first part of the curve. "The rest of you will be here, in the red zone."

The girl next to me raised her hand.

"Yes, Miss Aiken?"

"Aren't you going to give some As?"

He laughed. "You do remember this is AP physics? Now, pass up your papers."

I opened my notebook and looked at the sheet of homework. I'd worked through all of the problems while I fumed about Dad not coming home, including four and five. Until now I'd been sure my answers were correct.

Maybe signing up for AP physics had been a bad idea. I needed an A in this class—any engineering program would require physics, including the aerospace program I'd asked our counselor to help me apply for. There was an easier version of physics with a teacher who wasn't a college professor at night… No, I wasn't taking the easy way out. I'd pass this class without messing up my 4.0.

A tap on my shoulder brought me back to class. I reached for the paper that someone shoved over my shoulder. The single page was folded in half with the name Tony Price written on the outside. I folded my paper and put it under Tony's.

Mr. Miles raised an eyebrow as he noticed the papers. "So, we do have some takers." He took the papers from my hand, gently, which felt odd since his tone left me expecting him to rip the homework from my hands. "Mr. Price and Miss Mason."

When no one else offered their homework, he opened Tony's page and looked over the answers while the clock ticked away a full minute. He then gave a cursory glance over my answers and put both pages on his desk. "Where did we leave off yesterday?" Strangely, his tone was no longer filled with anger. "Can anyone explain the possible values of the angular momentum vector, in the non-inertial body frame, for a free asymmetric top?"

No one raised their hand. "Miss Mason?" he asked, glancing down at me. "Were you going to ask for an A?"

"No sir." I gritted my teeth. Yesterday we were talking about gravitational forces, not any kind of vectors. Definitely made a bad choice by signing up for this class.

"Well," he said, "could you answer… Mr. Price, do you have something to say?"

"No sir," came the frigid voice behind me.

"Well, you raised your hand. Who raises their hand without something to say?"

"I think you've said enough for everyone," Tony said.

Laughter sounded from several of the other students. It took every bit of willpower not to turn around and look at Tony.

Mr. Miles went to the board and dragged his arm across the bell curve to wipe away the marker. His white shirt had a huge black stain beneath his elbow. He swiped a hand through his hair and rapidly wrote an equation that had more letters than numbers. I decided it must be some advanced form of Calculus.

"Can you solve this equation, Mr. Price?"

"No sir," Tony said.

"When you can," Mr. Miles stressed each word by slamming the marker against the board, "this class will be yours to teach." He spun around to face me. "Now, Rena, explain what we discussed yesterday."

I groaned, reminding myself how badly I needed this A, and did my best to explain what he'd taught us about gravitational forces.

Mr. Miles cleared his throat. "Good. Week one was for the basics. Now we'll tackle the real problems." He glanced to the back of the row. "Anything you'd like to add?"

When no one said a word, Mr. Miles gave a contented smile and began writing another equation on the board. For the first week of class, his emotions had flip-flopped from anger to humor and then to a sadness that almost left the man in tears. Yesterday, someone had joked about him being on drugs, but I didn't find that funny.

I wondered if Tony would face his wrath for trying to stick up for me. At least, that's what it seemed like. Had Tony been sticking up for me by raising his hand and distracting our teacher?

The rest of the class went by without another outburst. Mr. Miles passed out a quiz in the last ten minutes and sat as his desk until the bell rang. "Stay behind, Mr. Price."

I froze at his words. Would he punish Tony? As I stood and grabbed my bag, I looked back at Tony, who remained in his desk. He studied my face and gave me a slight smile, as if to reassure me he had everything under control. Tony tilted his head to the door.

Outside, I wondered if I should wait for him. But what would I say? School was over and I needed to pick up Alfie. My brother worried if I was late—he'd once freaked out when I was thirty minutes late because of backed-up traffic from a wreck. The stress aggravated his asthma.

I'd have to talk with Tony another time.

If I ever figured out what to say.

* * * * *

Despite backed-up traffic, I reached the pick-up line at my normal time.

"How was your day?" I asked as Alfie climbed into the backseat of the truck. He sighed with frustration as he maneuvered himself into the booster seat and pulled the seat belt over his shoulder. Mama always joked that I'd be the tallest in the family. I'd outgrown her at twelve, but was still shorter than half of the girls at school. Poor Alfie was shorter than *all* of the kids in his class.

"Okay," he finally said.

"That's it?" I asked. "What did you have for lunch?" When he didn't answer, I glanced in the mirror.

Alfie stared out of his window. "Barbecue sandwiches."

I sighed and slowed down for a four-way stop. He hated BBQ. Even though I was the first at the stop, I paused to make sure the other truck wasn't going to go. The man behind the wheel waved me on.

"Do you think Dad's home?" Alfie asked.

"I hope so." It wasn't fair to get Alfie's hopes up, but I'd covered for Dad that morning. He didn't know about Dad staying out all night. Maybe Coach Andrews had found Dad and brought him home.

The clock on the radio showed it was four. That meant school had only been out for thirty minutes, which wasn't enough time for Coach to find Dad and bring him home.

"What's for dinner?"

I thought about the money left in my purse after I'd bought lunch. Less than ten dollars wasn't enough to buy dinner for both of us, unless we had fast-food and bought off the dollar menu. The idea of eating greasy chicken nuggets and fries turned my stomach. A yellow light flashed on the dash and I swore under my breath. I'd forgotten about needing gas.

What was left of my ten was quickly guzzled by the truck when I stopped at the next gas station. "Sorry, Alfie," I said and climbed back into the truck. "That was the last of my money. Looks like we're having something from the fridge at home."

"Maybe Dad will be there to cook dinner."

Maybe we'd have a bag soup—just add water and heat the noodles in the microwave—or maybe I'd heat up a can of spaghetti with meatballs. But we'd had that last night. I thought of all the homework I needed to do. Mr. Miles had given us another assignment, along with the problems I'd marked for honors calculus.

At the entrance to the campground, I was still going over the homework assignments in my head. I slowed the truck and nearly coasted through the speed zone that protected campers as they walked and rode bikes along the narrow pavement. The woman at the campground office stepped into my path with arms waving. Everyone called her Birdie, but I'd never learned her real name.

I rolled down my window and felt the sticky afternoon heat. "Is everything okay, Ms. Birdie?"

She wiped her forehead where sweat tricked from under the straw hat she wore. Her sunglasses showed my reflection. "I've been looking for your father."

Haven't we all, I thought. "He isn't home?"

"I haven't been to the other end of the park since lunch, but he wasn't there then. I knocked on the door for ten minutes." She pointed behind the office, to the pool with still blue water. Usually the pool overflowed with people by this time of day. "The pump isn't working again. I need Donald to get this fixed A.S.A.P. Our campers need relief from this heat."

Dad was responsible for the campground's maintenance, which is why we were allowed to stay in the campground year-round while most visitors were restricted to camping no longer than a month. We'd lived here rent-free for years. Until recent months, Dad always kept the pool and four bath houses functioning perfectly, along with anything else the owners asked him to do. I wondered if his drinking would finally get us kicked out.

"I'll let him know," I said.

Ms. Birdie lifted her sunglasses and wiped the sweat from under her eyes. "Tell him I'll be waiting." She turned and walked back to the office.

I rolled my window up and took a deep breath of the cold air rushing from the vents to either side of me. The truck might be an old gas-guzzler with a rusted bed, but at least the air worked.

"Where do you think Dad went?" Alfie asked. "He was home this morning."

"Don't know." Why did I have to lie to Alfie that morning? He was the one person in the world who deserved so much better. I hit the gas and drove to the camper at thirty miles per hour instead of the signs that warned a speed limit of fifteen. With the extreme heat and the pool not working, most people weren't out walking.

Better to get this over with. I passed two bathhouses, along with the laundry building, and made the loop at the end of the campground. Our camper was at the last campsite in a circle that lined the edge of the lake. In the yard next to ours, an older couple reclining in canvas chairs waved. A flag hung beside them—with the red and gold colors of a football team—and a dog at their feet flapped his tail around but didn't rise. I didn't know their names; most of the guests stayed for a week or less so I'd given up on getting to know people years ago.

I stopped the truck next to the door of our camper and climbed out. Alfie dropped to the ground next to me and slammed his door. Before I could get on to him for slamming the truck's door, he ran up the steps and reached for the camper's door.

"It's locked," I said.

"No, it isn't." He turned the handle and raced inside, slamming that door behind him.

"Alfie!" Prepared to yell at him for slamming yet another door, I froze as I stepped into the camper. The smell of bacon frying took me by surprise, along with the dull radio which hummed an old country song.

In front of the stove, Dad put down the spatula he held and turned to me with a smile. "Hello, Rena."

"You're home," is all I managed.

Alfie sat at the table and began to tell Dad what he'd learned in science class about metamorphosis. "It's the special way a caterpillar turns into a butterfly," he said.

Dad leaned against the counter. With his good hand, he cracked an egg into a metal bowl. "The caterpillar isn't the only thing that changes. Other animals like frogs change, too."

"What about people?" my brother asked. "Can people

turn into a butterfly?"

"Maybe not a butterfly," Dad said, "but people do change. Sometimes for the better…" his eyes met mine, "and sometimes for the worse. That's one thing I can promise you about life, son, everything changes constantly."

I laughed as I dropped my backpack in front of the couch and sat down. "What are you cooking?"

"Breakfast." Dad turned back to the stove. "Can't you smell the bacon? I figured since I missed breakfast this morning, I'd make a special breakfast tonight. Eggs, grits, and whatever else you might want. This is my apology for not seeing you off to school."

"You were sleeping," Alfie said. "Rena told me not to wake you. Besides, she made us cereal and we can't have breakfast for dinner."

Dad gave me a strange look. "We can have whatever you want for dinner."

Alfie shrugged. "Even waffles?"

"Even waffles. What do you think, Rena?"

"Sounds good," I said. "Oh, Ms. Birdie stopped us on the way in. She said the pump for the pool isn't working so no one can swim."

"I'll check it out when I'm done with breakfast. Can't have the guests stuck in their campers and unable to swim in this heat."

"Dad?"

He raised an eyebrow. "Yes?"

"Is everything okay?"

Dad's serious expression melted into a smile. "Of course. I'm here now and everyone is safe."

"We weren't safe this morning?"

Laughing, he pulled the bacon from the pan, one strip at a time, and laid it on a plate covered with paper towels to catch the grease. "Don't worry, Rena. Just do your homework while I make waffles."

"But, last night—"

"I've given up drinking," Dad said firmly. "This time for good."

"Woo-hoo," Alfie said.

I wanted to ask about Coach Andrews, but Dad began to hum along with a song on the radio. Alfie pulled out a graded test and showed Dad, obviously enjoying every minute of attention from the man he'd never stopped adoring. It didn't matter that Dad came home at all hours of the night and I took care of everything for Alfie. What mattered is Dad loved him and he wanted to make Dad proud.

No way could Alfie understand that trusting Dad would only end in more pain. Not only would telling him be a waste, I didn't want my brother to hurt like that. Maybe in a few years he'd understand the truth. At least for now he could live in the bliss of not knowing.

Dad was an alcoholic.

If I'd learned anything for the past three years, alcoholics only cared about one thing.

* * * * *

That night, I placed a folding chair a few feet from the edge of the lake and watched as the last slice of orange disappeared from the sky. I rubbed mosquito repellent over my skin to fight the constant assault from the bug-filled night. The smell of the repellent barely covered the rank smell of the water before me. A halo of insects swarmed around the light next to the door of the camper. Across the water, a splash sounded above the croaking frogs. From the way the water rippled, I figured that must be one of the two gators living in this lake. Neither came close to people unless there was an offering of food.

The sound of a branch breaking came from the woods next to me and I jumped from the chair. For a second, I thought I saw a shadow, as if someone stood along the edge of the woods. After a few moments of blinking, my eyes adjusted to the darkness and I realized it had to be the light playing tricks on me. No one ever came near our camper.

"Rena," Dad said. "Are you okay?"

I turned to where he stood, a few feet from the camper's door. "It's nothing. Thought I heard a noise in the woods."

He walked to the edge of trees and peered into the darkness beyond. In his right hand, he held a bottle of water. His left hand, bent and scarred making his fingers barely able to move, hung at his side. "There's nothing here but a squirrel. Surely you're not afraid of a squirrel."

"I'm not afraid of anything," I said.

Dad smiled and walked toward the water's edge. "I believe you on that one."

I moved to stand by his side. "Did you fix the pool?"

"Good as new or until someone else loses a retainer and stops it up. Are you thinking of going swimming?"

"Not tonight."

"What *are* you thinking of, Rena?"

"Where did Coach Andrews find you?"

"Sleeping off a hangover in the back room of a bar down on Railroad Street. Jacob told me you were worried, and with good reason. I promise not to let that happen again."

"I thought something might have happened to you. I should have called you when—"

Dad put an arm around my shoulders. "No, I should

have called. I let my demons take over and I wasn't here to look after you and Alfie."

"We were fine."

"Because of you. I never imagined you growing up without your mother. I always knew the day would come when you realized what I really am inside. Your brother still has a way to go." He looked down at me. "Thank you for not making him hate me yet."

"No one hates you, Dad. We just want you to be here. Really here, with us all the time, not out drinking."

"I deserved that." Pulling away, Dad moved closer to the water. "You're strong, Rena, like your mother. And smart. Thank goodness you didn't turn out like me."

"I've been applying for scholarships. My counselor thinks I've got a good shot at getting money for school. I've kept a 4.0 in every class and I want to get into a school that teaches aerospace engineering."

"You want to be an engineer?" His eyes stayed on the water. "That would make your mother proud."

"What about you?"

"Everything you do makes me proud."

"I want out of this town," I said, barely above a whisper. "I don't want to live like this."

Dad turned to me, his eyes glistening in the light from the camper. "I thought we were safe here, that people forgot who I once was."

"Who you were?" I thought of Coach Andrews' strange way of questioning me about Dad's past. "You've worked in this campground for years."

"But before that, I wasn't the same person."

"You mean you didn't drink?" I asked sarcastically.

His face fell as he moved closer. "I never drank, at least not like I have since your mother died. I can't live in this world without her."

"What about me? What about Alfie?"

"You both deserve better. If only she were here. I can't help you when… There are things about you, questions I can't answer as you grow up."

"Mama told me about growing up years ago. Dad, I'm good. I just want to get a scholarship to college and…"

"Get out of here?"

I waved my hand around the yard that was barely big enough to park the truck. "Who would want to stay here?"

"You'll get your chance soon enough." Dad pulled his wallet from his back pocket and opened it. With shaking hands, he withdrew a white card with a name written in black ink. Sylvia Greene.

"Who is Sylvia Greene?"

"I've heard chatter that someone from my old life has plans to track me down."

"Why would anyone?"

"What matters now is that I keep you safe. If anything happens to me, I need you to get Alfie and head to Atlanta."

"Atlanta? What's going to happen to you?"

"When Jacob found me at lunch, he gave me the sit-down that I deserved. He insisted I hadn't prepared you for the future and he was right. I have enemies from years before you were born—people who might come after my family if they ever find us."

"Enemies? Like you were in the mafia?"

He smiled. "No, but the people I crossed weren't forgiving and they never forget. If I ever disappear for real… if you don't see me again for twenty-four hours—"

"You said you were going to quit drinking. You promised Alfie."

"Rena," he said in a pleading voice, "if I ever don't come home again, drive to the airport in Atlanta. There's a car rental office painted with green and white. Go to the desk and ask for Sylvia. Don't leave until they let you see her."

"What about school?"

"This is important. Promise me you'll go and promise me you won't trust anyone with this secret."

"What secret? I don't understand."

"Do what I ask and you'll be safe." Dad pulled me into a hug. "Don't tell anyone your name or mine. Just get in the truck and drive until you reach the airport."

I choked back my anger. Despite the lingering smell of alcohol, I felt the surge of love in his embrace. It had been months since he'd hugged me and I didn't want him to release me yet. "I promise."

"Good." After a few deep breaths, he pulled away and wiped his eyes. "I always knew I could count on you."

Why did I get the feeling I could no longer count on him?

CHAPTER THREE

Dad made breakfast again the next morning, this time French toast with powdered sugar and maple syrup. Alfie ate four slices. I ate only two, which prompted Dad to insist I should eat another slice and 'put more meat on my bones.' Instead, I grabbed my backpack and walked outside, leaving Alfie at the table. When they emerged, Dad lifted Alfie into the backseat and pulled the seatbelt over his shoulder.

Even though Alfie could take care of himself, he kept his mouth shut as Dad clicked the buckle in place. I sighed as Dad waved and we pulled out of the driveway. The last twenty-four hours had been nerve-wrecking. First our dad was missing and then he turned into a model-parent with the right to question what I ate.

Part of me felt thrilled. The other part felt like telling him what I thought of his absence for the last three years.

At least Dad had mentioned a list of jobs around the campsite. Ms. Birdie had stopped by early with several items needing maintenance, enough to keep Dad busy for at least two weeks. Maybe that meant he'd also stay sober for two weeks.

I didn't think about yesterday's lunch drama during my first two classes. All I thought about was the potential

Dad might stay sober. He'd never made that promise before. I knew better than to get my hopes up, but I couldn't stop the warm feeling that grew inside of me.

It wasn't until I reached the cafeteria that I thought about Piper's anger. She'd avoided me after school, but I never imagined her seat would be empty at lunch. I dropped my backpack at the table and got in line while hoping Piper was simply running late.

On the far wall, a blue light flickered and then made an arc across the ceiling. I craned my neck to find the source, which turned out to be a senior with a laser pointer. Holden from history class—I grinned as I realized how dumb the thought of my hands glowing blue sounded.

The blue light flashed across the face of a younger guy carrying a tray. He dropped the tray and tried to hide his face as he bent to pick up the remainder of his lunch. Laughter exploded from the nearest table.

I fought the urge to walk across the cafeteria and shove my fist into Holden's face. At least he'd never tried to ask me out. If he ever did… The thought of hitting Holden actually made me feel better. Picking on someone who couldn't weigh more than a hundred pounds, whose clothes hung from his arms in anticipation of puberty, didn't make Holden look cool.

The line moved and I stepped closer to the entrance. At least I knew why my hands were blue. Holden must have been pranking me. Everyone at his table probably laughed as I ran from the cafeteria, again making me want to hit Holden. He'd caused the fight between me and Piper. With all the drama of Dad coming home last night, I'd forgotten my plans to call and make things right with Piper. It wasn't the first time she'd acted weird about something I knew was impossible.

Blue glowing in my hands? Definitely impossible.

Most people stopped believing in elves and witches by the time they reached junior high but not Piper. Anything magical caught her attention. She'd become an outcast at school around seventh grade because of her ideas. I didn't see anything wrong with being different. Even though her beliefs weren't the same as mine, she'd always been a good friend, though her magical notions typically didn't involve me.

The line moved again. The smell of cheeseburgers made my stomach growl. Maybe they wouldn't serve the wheat buns that made me think of eating a cardboard box. Again, I glanced at the table but no Piper.

If I didn't hang around Piper, I could probably sit at one of the 'popular' tables. But that would mean listening as those girls complained about the size of their mansions or how their lives might end if some football player didn't ask them out. Piper had stood by me as I recovered from the accident—she checked on me every day until my hip healed and I could walk again. Most of the other students stayed away as if I'd returned from the hospital with some horrible disease. I guess they couldn't stand the thought of Mama dying any more than I could.

Because of Piper, I knew every detail of the latest wizard movie or how some archaeologist had uncovered proof of magic in an ancient civilization halfway around the world. Some people sneered at the dream-catcher that hung inside the door of the locker we shared, but I thought the web with feathers looked cool.

I grabbed a tray and cringed when I looked over the row of cheeseburgers with wheat buns. All the same. I placed one of the cheeseburgers and a container of fries on my tray. With a carton of chocolate milk—the same brand Mama always bought—I approached the cashier.

The cashier held out a hand and I froze, remembering my wallet was empty. Some students put money on accounts, but I usually paid daily. I had a secret stash where I saved any dollars left after the week was over, but I always tried to avoid spending that money. If only I'd slipped out a few dollars to get me through the day. Maybe if I'd asked Dad, he could have spared some money.

"Is something wrong?" she asked.

"I forgot my money."

The woman smiled and her netted gray hair bobbed as she nodded. "I can help you out if I need to, Rena. Your dad really should apply for discounted lunches, maybe even free. I'm sure with his financial situation…" Her cheeks turned red. "I mean I'm sure you would qualify."

"I can pay you back tomorrow." Dad would be furious if he knew I took a handout. He always insisted people stay out of our business, especially the government. "We don't owe the government and they don't owe us," he often said.

"Take it out of this," said a voice to my side.

I looked up into Tony's green eyes. He handed the cashier a twenty and she counted his change before I could say a word. "It's not necessary," I finally said.

He exchanged a glance with the cashier. 'Of course it was necessary' was their silent communication.

"I'll pay you back," I said.

"Not necessary," he replied.

He'd thrown my words back in an almost silky tone that made my heart speed. I owed him a smile or thanks, but I couldn't meet his eyes. With the tray in my hands, I walked to my seat while trying not to make eye contact with anyone. People had filled the table around me but left the two seats to either side of my backpack and across from me open. I dropped into my normal seat and lowered my head.

"Can I sit?"

With a jolt, I looked up as Tony stared at me from across the table. "Excuse me?"

"Here. Can I sit with you for lunch?"

I glanced at the empty seats around me and reluctantly opened my mouth. "Sure."

"Good." He dropped into the seat across from me and lifted one of two cheeseburgers from his tray. Tony took a large bite and watched me as he chewed.

I took a smaller bite.

"What's wrong?" he asked.

"I hate wheat bread." How could I possibly say *he* was the one making my stomach flip?

Tony looked over his burger. "Never paid any attention to the bread."

"You're new here, right? They started a healthy eating program at the end of last year. All bread has to be wheat and I hate it. At least last year we had a choice."

He lowered the burger and gave me a strange look. "You're serious."

"I'm rambling. Sorry. If you want, you can sit somewhere else."

"But I'm already sitting here."

Laughter tickled my throat. "Thanks for buying my lunch. I've never had a guy… That sounds so dumb. I usually have money."

"I've got money. It's not a problem." Tony took another bite of the burger. "Where's your friend?"

"Who?"

"The girl you sit with at lunch. Where is she?"

Stunned, I sat back and stared at Tony. How did he know who I sat with at lunch? "What are you doing, stalking me?"

"Do I look like a stalker?"

The teasing in his voice made me want to know more about Tony Price. Or punch him out, which made me consider hitting him just to find out how he'd react. Most people left me alone because I'd proved my ability to fight over the years, especially in the case of bullies. I hated anyone who picked on someone who couldn't defend themselves, but Tony was new. He probably knew nothing about how I'd given up picking fights to stay out of trouble. How else would I get a scholarship out of here?

I glanced over his black clothes and shrugged. "Seems like every time I turn around, you're there."

"Get used to it," he said with a smile that made my stomach flutter. "I thought since you were alone for lunch, I'd keep you company. I'm not stalking you."

Thoughts of Piper dampened the warmth that grew as I watched him. "She's mad at me."

Tony opened a pack of mayo and squeezed it on the tray next to his fries. He swiped a couple of fries through the mayo and took a bite.

"You don't eat ketchup?" I asked.

"Is that a deal breaker?"

I stared into his green eyes and smiled. Something about that shade of green, exactly like the diamond-shaped emerald ring Mama gave me, and the way he smiled calmed my stomach. I looked down at my right hand, to the antique silver that never came off. "No."

"That's a cool ring."

With my free hand, I covered the ring and Tony narrowed his eyes. He opened his mouth, but someone stopped behind me before he could speak.

"Hey, Rena." Robbie Masters put a hand on my shoulder.

I felt like shrugging away from him but didn't want to

make a scene. Instead of looking up at Robbie, I stared at Tony. "Hey, Robbie."

"Is this jerk bothering you?" Robbie asked, in a tone he'd never used around me.

Tony raised an eyebrow and I shook my head slightly. "Just hanging out," Tony said.

Robbie's grip on my shoulder tightened. "How about not hanging so close to Rena? She doesn't like guys coming on to her. What's your name?"

"Tony."

"Tony. You're new and I get it. Still learning your way around here."

"That's enough." I pulled away from Robbie's grip. "Don't ever touch me like that again."

Anger flashed in Robbie's eyes as he looked from me to Tony.

"You play football," Tony said. "I saw the video of that play you made last season with eight seconds to go."

Robbie controlled his voice. "That was a great night."

"You don't have anything to worry about," Tony said. "I'm not after your girl."

My fists clenched. "I'm not his—"

"Good," Robbie said. "Rena's special. I want to make sure she's taken care of."

The conviction in Robbie's voice reminded me he was a nice guy most of the time. I looked up at him. "I can take care of myself."

Robbie smiled. "Just shout if this guy gets any ideas."

Ideas? Like how Robbie was trying to make me look like his girl? I turned back to Tony and this time he gave a slight shake of his head.

"Robbie," someone yelled.

"Okay Rena," Robbie said before heading for his usual table, which never had an empty seat. "I'll be watching out for you."

"Thanks," I said under my breath.

"I told you," Tony said when Robbie was gone.

Anger burned inside of me. Robbie had no right to claim me as his girl and embarrass me in front of Tony. "Told me what?"

"You should have told Robbie yes."

"I'm not into being treated like property."

"That was just a show." Tony finished his burger and the last of his fries. "He's really into you. I should be worried, but I'm not."

I laughed. "Robbie doesn't have a chance."

"What happened yesterday—with your friend? I saw you run out of the cafeteria."

Embarrassment settled in my stomach and I shifted on the seat. "Nothing. We had an argument. I really don't want to talk about it."

"Then don't."

With a sigh, I took a bite of my burger. Maybe the wheat bread wasn't so bad. "Thanks for backing me up in physics class."

"That man is an ass."

"I heard he also teaches college at night. Did you finish his homework?"

"With some help."

"Help?" I asked.

Tony shrugged. "Just keeping it real. We all need help sometimes."

"I don't like asking for help. My dad taught me how to take care of myself."

"What about your mom?"

I grabbed the tray and my backpack and stood. "She's dead. Don't ever ask about her again."

He scrambled to stand. "I'm sorry. I didn't mean—"

Before he could finish, the bell rang and I rushed into a crowd of people leaving the cafeteria. Tony didn't follow.

*****

When I walked into physics class, Tony's desk sat empty at the back of my row. I slid into my usual desk and pulled out my homework. I barely heard Tony shuffle past me and I kept my head down until our teacher arrived.

Mr. Miles placed a stack of papers on my desk. "Find yours and pass the rest back."

Buried in the stack was my graded quiz from the day before. As I searched for my name, I stopped on Tony's paper, which was marked with a red fifty-seven. Heat rose in my cheeks as I quickly flipped to the next quiz. At the bottom of the stack was my ninety-six.

Although I sighed with relief while passing the remaining pages over my shoulder, I felt a nagging feeling that I should have looked over Tony's paper longer. Maybe figure out what he missed. If I could help him… Maybe my anger from lunch was misplaced.

No, I told myself. Tony would be a distraction. The way my stomach swirled at the thought of having lunch with him again was a huge red flag. I'd turned Robbie down for a reason.

After class, I rushed into the hall. Someone said my name, maybe Tony, but I never turned to see who called after me.

At the last corner before I reached the locker, I paused because Piper stood next to the open door. Joey Buckingham stood to her other side, gazing into her eyes. He stood maybe a few inches above her and his hand rested on her arm.

I smiled as I wondered if Joey had stopped to ask her

out. Piper grinned up at him, her mouth moving excitedly. Although I couldn't make out her words, I could feel Piper's embarrassment as she tried to push a stubborn strand of hair behind her ears only to have the brown lock fall back against her cheek. I'd warned Piper about cutting her hair short enough she couldn't keep all of the thick strands tied back.

Joey moved closer as if he planned to share a secret with my friend. Excitement for her fluttered in my stomach. She'd been so coy when Joey once tried to ask me out. Something inside told me she had a crush on him. I'd been able to change his mind about wanting to date me with one conversation. All I had to say is how I wasn't interested in guys.

He took me literally, which brought the horrible thought I'd somehow ruined Piper's chances. The two of us were always together. Before he could ask the question, I'd changed my statement to not being interested in anyone at Palm County. What a sigh of relief when he stopped following me around and stuck to simply waving as we passed in the hall.

"Rena, what's up?"

I spun around to face Carolyn Waters, head of the student council and one of the most popular girls in school. Her arms were folded over her chest and her head leaned to one side. "Not much," I said.

Her nose seemed to turn up as she watched me. "I saw Robbie by your table at lunch."

"And?"

"I thought I told you to stay away from him. You don't remember our conversation on the last day of class?"

I shrugged, which made her drop both arms and stand her full height. "I can't remember what happened last week. Forget before the summer."

Carolyn put her hands on her hips. "You're lying."

Anger flashed within me as I put my hands on my hips. "What does it matter? I don't want to date Robbie."

"Then you should tell him."

"I have."

She leaned closer until our faces were inches apart. "I don't believe you."

Hitting Carolyn would be too easy. She'd moved to Palm County after I gave up shoving my fist in the face of those who harassed me. No one had ever picked a fight with me twice. Could it be that no one filled her in on my lack of willpower before high school? "I suggest you get out of my face."

"Or what?"

I looked down at my open palms. To the right was my potential scholarships. To the left was Carolyn stumbling back after I showed her I knew more than a little about how to throw a punch. My fists balled at my sides. "Do you really want me to make your face blue?"

Her look of contempt wavered. "Would you really hit me?"

"No," I said. "You're not worth getting suspended over. I don't care about Robbie Masters. I only care about getting out of this town after graduation."

She spun on her platform wooden heels and stomped toward my friend. She flashed those sandals like they were the height of fashion, but I wouldn't give up my stained sneakers to look like her. Piper and Joey glanced up in surprise.

"Carolyn?" Piper asked. "What's going on?"

Carolyn shoved her against the locker. I rushed forward as Joey pushed Carolyn away from Piper. Carolyn reached over his arm and slammed her fist into Piper's cheek.

"What are you doing?" I asked, shoving between Carolyn and Piper.

"Making her face blue," Carolyn said. "She'll be fine. Piper can use her magic to heal the awful bruise that should leave."

"Get away from her," Joey said. "I'll tell—"

"Who?" Carolyn laughed. "You'll tell who that I did what? No one will believe you." Before any of us could say another word, Carolyn left us standing by the locker.

Piper held her cheek. "What was that all about?"

"I'm sorry," I said. "Carolyn's mad because she wants me to stay away from Robbie."

"Robbie Masters?" Joey asked. I nodded and he shook his head. "Robbie doesn't want to date her. He wants to date you. Everyone knows."

"Therein lies the problem." Piper looked at me. "She better be glad you didn't rearrange her face."

Joey raised an eyebrow. "You thought about punching her. Admit it."

"That's not me anymore," I said.

"You hit four people that day," Joey said. "Knocked all of them to the ground for jumping me from behind. Remember?"

"Yeah, but I haven't hit anyone in three years. Getting in trouble could mean no scholarship. I can't take that chance."

Piper turned to Joey and smiled. "Could you give us a few minutes?"

He smiled. "Sure. I'll be outside."

I gripped the strap of my backpack as Joey walked to the door and into the heated afternoon. "Are you okay?"

"She didn't hit me that hard," Piper said. "It was just the shock that caught me off-guard. I can't believe she hit me in front of Joey. That's so embarrassing."

"He looked worried about you."

"What about you? Are you okay?"

I sighed. "I'm sorry about yesterday. About the blue we saw—"

"It was Holden's laser pointer. I know because he flashed it in my eyes after class."

"It was wrong of me to lie."

"Rena, fitting in isn't everything. It's okay to be different."

"I know."

"Sometimes I wonder if you do. I've never cared what people think of me."

With a glance over her sad eyes, I dropped mine to the floor. "You're my friend, Piper. No matter what happens." When I looked up, she was smiling.

"I also don't mind taking punches for you."

"Please don't be mad at me. I should have told you I saw the flash of blue."

"I don't care if you can't see magic in the world like I can. That wasn't what made me mad."

"Then what's the problem?"

"The problem is how you're always scheming to get out of this school. Scholarships are great and a lot of people dream of college. You've got the future all planned out, don't you?"

"What's wrong with planning?"

Her voice shook. "What about us?"

"Us?"

"When you're gone, where do you think I'll be? My grades are okay, but I have no interest in those advanced placement classes you take. I'm going to cosmetology school like my mom, if I get in."

I rubbed the back of my neck. It wasn't my fault Piper had chosen not to take classes that would prepare her for a four-year college. "I hadn't thought about where you would go."

She sighed. "That's my point. When you see the future, you only see yourself. I need more than that from you. I need a friend who's here with me now."

Gripping her arm, I pulled Piper to me. "I am here with you now."

She shook off my grip. "For how long? The minute your opportunity out of here magically appears, you'll be gone. Will you even call me?"

I'd never thought that far ahead. Scholarship… college… out of this town… but Piper? What would happen to her? "You know I'll call."

"I'm not so sure."

"Piper, I—"

She held up a hand. "Just think about what I said." With that, she turned and walked toward the door where Joey stood outside.

* * * * *

That afternoon, Dad stood by the camper when I pulled into the driveway with Alfie. He opened the door for Alfie to jump out and placed the cap from on old bottle in his hand.

"Wow," Alfie said. "How did this get bent in half?"

"That's what a dryer can do when the wrong thing falls inside. You wouldn't believe what else I found when I took the back off."

"You fixed one of the dryers?" I asked.

He nodded. "You always clean out the lint trap, right?"

"Sure." I tried to think back a few nights. I'd washed and dried clothes, but had I cleaned the gobs of lint that usually lined the trap?

Alfie ran up the stairs. "Did you make dinner?"

"The baked potatoes are almost done." Dad pointed to where smoke rose from the coals of his grill. "I made steaks."

"Steaks?" I asked. "We didn't buy steaks at the store this week."

He placed a memory stick in my hand. The case was purple and the initials R.M. were carved into the side.

How had I missed cleaning out the pockets of my jeans? "Thanks. I didn't realize I lost this."

"Don't worry about the steaks. From now on, I'll have a little extra money. Me not drinking means we can splurge a little more."

"Speaking of money," I said. "I put the last of my money into the gas tank yesterday."

Dad reached into his back pocket and pulled out his wallet. He handed me two twenties. "This should keep you going for a while. On second thought…" Dad handed me another twenty. "I'm sure Alfie needs money for lunch."

On Monday, I'd given Alfie enough money for the week. "I'll make sure he puts this on his account."

Dad smiled. "What would we do without you?"

His question took me by surprise. "You'd be fine."

"You know what I mean. Ever since your mother…" His eyes drifted over the lake. "Let's go check on the potatoes. There's nothing worse than having to microwave steak."

"I'll be there in a minute. Got to get my backpack."

As Dad stepped into the camper and closed the door behind him, a black car with dark tinted windows crept along the pavement and made the loop which included our campsite. The front passenger's window had been rolled down a few inches. The sweet smell of a cigar swirled from the gap like two white arms reaching for the sky.

The soft sounds of classical music came from the speakers. Through the cracked window, I made out gray hair and a thick gray beard. The man's face never turned my way. His eyes, protected by black sunglasses, faced straight ahead as the car passed and disappeared around the curve. The music faded from the air along with the soft purring of an engine.

Guests sometimes drove around the entire campground out of boredom or genuine curiosity. Sometimes they knew Dad had the mechanical ability to fix issues with their campers and hoped to either buy his services or guilt him into helping. How successful they were usually depended on how much Dad had to drink the night before. A few times random visitors stopped with cameras and wanted to check out our view of the lake. But this felt different.

This man wasn't looking for a lake or a repair job. A shiver passed over me as I hurried into the camper.

CHAPTER FOUR

The next morning, I marked another day off the calendar next to the sink. Friday had finally come. Dad made omelets that morning, stuffed with bacon, cheese, and mushrooms. He laughed when I asked for seconds.

Just before the first bell rang, I found Piper standing around back of the gym. Carolyn was in her face, pressing closer as Piper refused to yield and take a step back. A circle of students had formed around them. My feet sank in a layer of mud when I stepped off the sidewalk.

Piper shrank back as the voices around her began to cheer for Carolyn. Two of Carolyn's friends held her arms when she gave up and turned, refusing to let her run away.

"We don't need any more freaks in this school," Carolyn said. "You and your freaking friend Rena need to get out of here."

It was time to put an end to Carolyn's plans to hurt me. If she wanted to fight, she needed to face me instead of picking on Piper. Although the top of Piper's head barely reached her opponent's chin, I'd stare Carolyn in the eye with no problem.

Piper was the first to notice me stomping toward

Carolyn. She shrugged off the girls who held her arms and, leaning over, barreled head first into Carolyn's stomach.

Carolyn stumbled back and landed on her butt in the grass. Mud covered her hands as she tried to fight her way up to stand. The momentum of Piper's charge carried my friend forward and she landed on her knees next to Carolyn in the mud.

The circle of students moved back as Carolyn's friends pulled Piper to her feet. One girl gripped a huge patch of Piper's short hair and pulled her head backward. Carolyn lurched forward with a streak of red in her eyes.

In that moment, I didn't think about a scholarship or how my hands would throb afterward. I punched the two girls holding Piper, hard enough they stumbled backward in shock. My fist was aimed for Carolyn's face when someone gripped my arms and spun me around.

"Rena?" shouted Coach Andrews. "What the hell were you thinking?"

"She was helping me," Piper said from my side. "Carolyn tried to beat me up."

Coach Andrews released my arms. "Go to the office. All of you." He spun to where Tony had stopped a few feet away. "Stay out of this."

Carolyn laughed as she walked off. "Guess we'll all be suspended now. See what happens when you don't listen, Rena?"

Tony gripped the strap of his backpack with his black gloves. From his expression, I imagined his knuckles turning white as he stared at Coach Andrews.

Although I should have felt embarrassment knowing Tony saw me fight, a calm settled inside. Now he knew the real me.

I'd been an idiot to let Carolyn turn my dreams of college into a nightmare.

* * * * *

"Tell me what happened," Coach Andrews said as I dropped into the seat across from his desk. "I've heard everyone else's account and now I want to hear yours."

I glanced at the clock on the wall of his office. What a wasted day—I'd already missed my first class and half of the second. My stomach growled, reminding me lunch would start soon. Piper had gone home with a pink slip for three days' suspension. Carolyn followed shortly after with a pink slip of her own. She gave me an evil look as she left the office.

"I'm listening."

"Carolyn attacked Piper. Her friends were holding Piper's arms."

"Go on."

"I couldn't let Carolyn beat up Piper, not after I…"

"What did you do, Regina?"

I sank lower in the chair. "Carolyn wants to date Robbie Masters. She's jealous because Robbie wants to date me."

Coach Andrews hesitated as he watched me. "All this is over Robbie Masters?"

"I told Carolyn I didn't want Robbie, but she's determined to hurt me."

"And hurting you isn't as easy as it sounds."

I shrugged. "I didn't plan to hit anyone. Yesterday I asked Carolyn to stay away from us. She didn't get the message."

"When you saw them fighting, you should have told a teacher. The penalty for fighting is suspension. You know that. I thought we came to an understanding years ago, back when you protected that Buckingham kid."

"He didn't stand a chance."

"But one of the boys you beat up—his dad was superintendent of our school system. Do you know how hard it was for me to keep you off the suspension list?"

"Is that what you're going to do now? Suspend me?"

He ran a hand through his hair. "Most of these kids would love three days to sit at home and play video games. I happen to know staying home would be a stringent punishment for you. It could also affect your quest for a scholarship."

I closed my eyes. "Piper is my friend. They would have hurt her."

"Yes." He sighed. "If nothing else, you've been a good friend to that strange girl."

My eyes flew open. "She was there for me after the accident."

Coach Andrews rolled his chair back and walked to the window. He opened the blinds and light spilled into the room. Beyond the window were rows of cars. "When I walked up, those girls were holding Piper's arms. I know you were protecting her." He spun around. "If I keep this off the books, can you stay out of trouble?"

"But Piper—"

"You can't save everyone. Right now, you need to let Piper serve her punishment and stay away from future fights. Do you understand?"

Piper was still in trouble, but this fight wouldn't be on my record. I still had a chance with those scholarship applications. Despite an ache for Piper, a feeling of relief sent me to my feet. "Yes sir."

"Get out of my office."

I smiled at him. "Thank you."

"Hey," he said as I reached the door. "Has Donald been out late again?"

"No. He's made breakfast three times. He's caught up

on fixing most of what's broken around the campground."

"Good. I hope things will be better for you and Alfred."

With another 'thanks', I ran from the office to finish what was left of my second class.

* * * * *

At lunch, I took my usual seat and stared at the plate of pizza. Friday was always pizza day, but someone had the bright idea that wheat bread might make good pizza dough. I was far from convinced.

"Can I sit with you?"

I looked up at Tony and waved for him to take the seat across from me. He wore black jeans and a long-sleeved black shirt, which he'd rolled up to his elbows.

"I'm sorry about yesterday," he said.

"For what?" I asked, pointing to one of his bare arms. "So, you do get hot."

He slid both sleeves down to his wrists and dropped into the seat. "For whatever made you run out of here. Unless that's normal."

Laughing, I took a bite of the pizza. The crust felt like I'd bitten into a wad of paper, but the pepperoni was real at least. "This isn't so bad. And no, me running out of the cafeteria isn't normal."

"I'm glad you didn't get suspended."

I almost dropped the pizza. "I was able to forget about that until now. Thanks a lot," I said in a teasing tone.

"Sorry."

"Does anyone else know about me fighting?"

"Everyone knows because everyone around here talks."

"That's Palm County for you—a thousand students

with nothing better to do than talk. How big was your last school?"

"Nothing like this. It's kind of unnerving. Some things should really be kept secret."

"Can't argue with that." I finished my pizza while he ate a slice and watched me in silence. "What are people saying about the fight?"

He shrugged. "There are lots of stories, but I know the truth so why does it matter?"

"Did you see me—"

"Hit those girls? Yep."

"You probably think I'm crazy."

"They were bullying your friend. Kind of cool the way you knocked them down."

I reached for the carton of milk on the corner of my tray. "I thought Coach Andrews would suspend me. I'm glad he didn't."

"Well, you didn't start the fight."

"I know, but everyone here knows he looks after me. Not suspending me might make him look bad."

Tony sat back and smiled. "Why don't you stop worrying about everyone else and think about yourself? What are you doing this weekend?"

"That's the last thing I want to think about."

"Okay." He shifted on the plastic seat. "Where do you live?"

"In a campground on Gator Lake."

"You live in a campground?"

For a moment, I felt embarrassed at the revelation, but then I realized Tony had asked with nothing more than honest curiosity. "Yeah. My dad's the maintenance manager."

"That sounds cool. My dad took me camping when I was a kid, but you get to camp all the time."

"It's not as fun as it sounds. Where do you live?"

"On State Street."

I checked the clock on the wall. Almost time for the bell. "That doesn't tell me much. State Street runs all the way through town."

"Then you'll have to guess where I live."

"I'm not good with guessing games," I said. "Just tell me and don't waste my time."

He laughed. "Which is exactly why I won't tell you. When you know all my secrets, you won't want to hang out anymore."

"Is that what we're doing?" The bell rang and I stood with my backpack.

Tony reached for my tray. "I'll get that. Like I said before, you should let people help you."

I thought about his grade on the physics quiz. "Before I passed back the quizzes in physics, I saw your grade."

"It sucked. Science was never my best subject."

"Why sign up for AP physics?"

"I didn't have a choice. My schedule was chosen for me."

"I know how that feels. What college are you trying to get into?"

He looked around the room. "I'm thinking I might work for the government."

Students headed for the hall and he fell in beside me as I followed. "My dad was in the Army. He's told me all about missions in Iraq."

Tony dumped the trays at a trashcan near the door. "Have you ever thought of joining the military instead of college?"

"I want to be an engineer."

"You could get a job as a nuke engineer on a sub. The Navy would pay for your school."

"And I'd have to work underwater—no thanks. I want to be an aerospace engineer."

His eyebrows rose. "You want to fly?"

"I was thinking more like designing planes so other people could fly. If I could get into the space program…" I laughed. "Yeah, there's a dream that will never come true."

"Why not?"

"My dad barely has enough money for me and my brother to live in a camper. His job as maintenance for the campground is the only reason we've got beds to sleep in. He can't afford to send me to college."

"Why is college such a big deal?"

Outside the cafeteria, I turned to him. "My mom wanted me to go to college. She said I'd have opportunities she never did. Looking back now, I don't understand why she thought I'd have opportunities. Only rich people get the kind of jobs they want."

"Your dad doesn't enjoy doing maintenance?"

The crowd of students was thinning and I didn't want to be late. As I walked toward my next class, Tony stayed by my side. "He likes fixing things, I guess."

"He's probably great at it. You might think that being an engineer is important, but keeping the world working—that's important. Everything that someone designs must be maintained. Do you have a car?"

"I drive Dad's F-150."

"Who changes the oil?"

"Dad does."

"What do you think would happen if he didn't change the oil?"

"I guess I would."

"But what if you didn't? How long do you think that truck would run before the motor locked up?"

"I'd pay someone to change the oil before that happened."

"Money is useless if no one does the work."

Tony continued to talk, but I tuned out the rest of his bid to convince me. The harder he tried, the more I realized some part of me was falling for Tony. Maybe it was the way his lips curved when I knew he wasn't trying to smile. When he ran a gloved hand over his hair, which had clearly been shaved a few months before, I realized Tony was cute. He was weird with the gloves and how much he talked, but he seemed real and full of mystery… more so than any other guy I'd met at Palm County High.

If only I could deny the looming truth—having feelings for him this soon made Tony dangerous.

"Did your mom like science?" he asked.

I nodded. "She could recite the number pi out to fifty decimal places."

"What was her name?"

"Jackie Mason."

"Jackie?" He stopped when we reached the door to my class. "Did your dad ever call her anything different?"

"That's a weird thing to ask."

He shrugged. "My mom's name was Emily but my dad always called her Em."

Thinking back to the time of wondrous beauty and happiness that was my childhood—late nights with Mama making up bedtime stories and Dad spinning me around and around in his arms, laughing—I really didn't care to think of that time anymore. My mother was dead and she was never coming back.

"When did she die?"

I reached for Tony's arm. "Your listening skills are crap."

With his gloved hand, he shoved me away. "I'm

actually a great listener."

"Which is why you asked about my mom. Again." Despite how I'd warned him, Tony's smile warmed me inside. I never talked about Mama with anyone but Piper, and she rarely brought up the subject anymore. "Do you want to come over after school?"

Tony's face twisted with shock but he recovered almost too fast for me to notice. "Are you asking me out?"

"Maybe."

"Wow, I'm better than I thought."

I shoved an elbow into his side and he bent over in mock pain. "At what?"

"Making you like me, of course."

"I thought maybe I could help you study for the physics test next week."

"You're offering to tutor me?"

"Why else would I invite you over?" Maybe Dad would still be sober. If our tight living space didn't scare Tony off, he might be worth hanging out with. Most other guys at school would run the other way. Tony, however, didn't seem to be afraid of anything, especially not me. "Do you have a car? I can give you directions to the campground."

"Nah," he said after a brief pause. "I'm sure your dad will be sitting by the door with a three-fifty-seven in his hands."

I laughed. "My dad doesn't have a gun."

"You might be surprised."

"Well, I don't know. He *was* in the Army. You're not afraid of him, are you?"

Tony's phone buzzed and he checked a text. "Sorry, gotta go." He ran down the hall and disappeared through the double doors at the other end.

Another bell rang, which meant I was now late. Still, I

couldn't shake the surprise of Tony's quick exit.

What did I say wrong?

* * * * *

That afternoon, the camper was empty when I pulled onto the gravel next to the door. Dad had waved to us from near the pool behind the office. He'd stood by a fence talking to Ms. Birdie.

"Hurry up," Alfie said as I closed the folding door to our bathroom.

"I can't change with you watching me." Quickly, I changed out of the t-shirt that was drenched with sweat and into a tank top. "Get your bathing suit on." When I stepped out of the bathroom, he stood near the door with his towel and a float that would be big enough for him to lay across.

Alfie took a deep breath and blew into the tube. After the third breath, he erupted in a fit of coughs.

I ripped the float from his hands. "You shouldn't be blowing this up. Where's your inhaler?"

"I'm fine," he said between coughs.

How could I stay mad when his chest heaved and his face turned pale? "Let me try." I blew until the yellow plastic bulged at the seams.

With Alfie's change of clothes in an old grocery bag, I grabbed my purse and led him back to the truck. I lifted the float onto the bed of the truck and dropped Alfie's bag next to it. At fifteen miles per hour, the float wouldn't fly out.

Dad sat in a chair near the pool when I parked next to the office. He glanced up as I opened the gate and let Alfie inside the fence. Alfie ran by and launched into a cannon ball over the deepest end of the pool.

"You didn't suit up," he said.

I shook my head. "I don't feel like swimming today."

He patted the folding chair next to him. "Jacob called about the fight."

Lowering into the chair, I kicked off my flip-flops. The hot plastic scorched my skin, but I didn't move as dad watched me. "He didn't suspend me."

"Which is great, but I thought you'd gotten over your fighting streak about the time your mother—"

"Don't say it."

"Is there something going on I need to know about?"

"You've spent the last three months drinking for most of the night. Coming home for three days doesn't give you the right to judge me."

He watched Alfie climb from the pool and get a running start. "Don't run on this concrete."

Instead of slowing down, Alfie laughed and continued to the edge of the pool.

"Alfie," I yelled.

My brother slowed and looked at me before jumping into the water.

Dad turned to me. "I deserved that. And yes, you're right about me being gone."

"Can we not talk about the fight?" Leaning back, I closed my eyes and tried to take a nap as the sun lowered in the sky. Dad yelled at Alfie, but his words faded as I drifted further from the pool and the dreaded heat, not to mention the mosquitoes.

"Rena," called a voice from the gate.

I jerked and wiped my eyes. The sun had dropped to gleam along the horizon.

"Bout time you woke up," Dad said. "Maybe you shouldn't have taken all honors classes this semester. You look worn out."

Swinging my legs around the seat, I stood as Ms. Birdie opened the gate and stepped onto the concrete. "Yes ma'am?"

"Rena, honey, could you make a trip to the store for me?" She held out a list with items scrawled in cursive.

I squinted at the grocery list. "Does this say tomatoes?"

"Four of them at least and two packs of the spring mix. I've got a taste for salad tonight, but we've been busy today and I haven't had a free minute to leave the campground."

"People are coming in for the holiday weekend," Dad said. "You don't mind making the trip, do you?"

Shaking my head, I started for the gate. "I'll be back in an hour."

"Take your time," Dad said. "Traffic is backed up all the way to the bank on second avenue."

Ms. Birdie pulled a set of keys from her pocket. "Take my car. There's no reason for you to waste your gas for me."

"It's not a problem," Dad said.

"Donald," she said, "you just sit there and mind your own business. Rena's a great driver and I insist she drive my car."

"She is a good driver, but it's only five miles to the store."

Ms. Bridie followed me through the gate and shoved her keys into my hand before I reached the truck. "Go before you start an argument. Your dad's been in an odd mood today."

"But he said—"

"Nonsense. Take my car." She placed a stack of twenties in my hand. "After you get the groceries, would you please fill the tank? You can grab a drink from the gas station if you'd like."

She clicked the remote and the doors of her blue car unlocked. I happily breathed in the new-car smell as I got in behind the wheel. Maybe Dad was right to say I shouldn't drive this car, but Ms. Birdie insisted… "I'd say be careful, but honey you're always careful."

"Thanks, Ms. Birdie." I buckled the seat belt and took my time pulling out into traffic. I'd never driven any vehicle that sat this close to the ground. Around me, trucks flew by and shook the car. My hands gripped the wheel as I glanced up, barely able to make out the drivers while I tried to stay inside the lines.

Maybe driving this car wasn't a good idea.

When I pulled into the store's parking lot, I realized I never even touched the radio. I'd complained about Dad's gas-guzzling truck to Piper, but for once I longed for our pile of rust. At least driving that truck made me feel like I shared the road with the other trucks. In this two-door car, the other vehicles took up as much of the road as they wanted.

After I filled the small backseat with grocery bags, I crossed the street and pulled into a gas station. I paid the clerk a twenty, which included an ice-cold coke. As the gas filled the tank, I wiped the cold drink across my face. Even at seven-thirty, the heat still threatened to smother me. Fumes from the gas made me cough and I stepped back.

From where I stood between the car and pump, I noticed the green sign at the intersection labeled 'State Street.' I opened the cap of my drink and took a swig, which burned my throat. Didn't Tony say he lived on State Street? Somewhere along the miles of street that cut through the center of town?

He'd probably made up an address on State Street. It had to be a joke. As I thought of our weird conversation from earlier, before he ran from the building, a gray car cut across the front of the store and pulled up to a pump on the opposite end of the lot.

The four-door hunk of metal wasn't a car I'd usually notice except for the fact Dad drove one like it when Mama first moved us to Florida. A Nova. Dad's had been gold, but this car was the same shape, even had the same metal wheels. The tag on the back would fold down to reveal the opening for the gas tank; I remembered Dad pumping gas when I'd unbuckle my belt and turn to wave at him through the back window.

The pump clicked off and I hung up the handle. I replaced the gas cap and reached for the driver's door, but froze when I heard a familiar voice. Up ahead, Tony crossed the lot, headed for the store with a phone to his ear. Even if I'd missed the sound of his voice, the black gloves and long-sleeved black shirt looked weird when people walked by him in shorts and tanks.

"We're still on schedule," he yelled into the phone, "but I need another week." Tony stopped in front of a car that slammed on brakes and laid on the horn. He laughed as the car sped around him, never making eye contact with the driver. "Tell them we need more heat until I get back. I'll see you tomorrow night."

Heat? If Tony wasn't hot enough in his all-black outfit, he needed to move somewhere warmer than Florida. I slid into the driver's seat and watched as Tony disappeared inside the store, reappearing moments later with a drink in his hand.

To my surprise, he climbed into the Nova and pulled away from the pump. I cranked Ms. Birdie's car and followed, keeping my head low so he wouldn't notice me. Tony knew I drove a truck instead of a small blue car.

He drove down State Street, keeping his speed below

the limit. At every light, I stayed two cars behind him. I glanced at the clock on the radio. I'd been gone over an hour. Would Dad worry yet?

At a light near the edge of town, he turned into the parking lot of a motel. Twin Pines Motel flashed on the sign. I'd passed this green and yellow sign a hundred times but never paid attention to the old building or the red vacancy sign with only the last four letters lit. I parked at an auto parts store next to the motel and killed the engine, with a view of the motel between two large palm trees. The sun had set, leaving only a faint orange stripe across the sky.

The motel had two stories of rooms that opened to the outside, overlooking a pool with a tree growing out of the center and chains around the gates. At the other end of the parking lot, a restaurant that served only breakfast had more cars parked out front than the entire motel.

Tony parked halfway down from the office, in front of one of fifteen white doors. The window next to the door showed only darkness between the open curtains. He climbed out of the car and spun around as if studying the other cars in the lot. He'd removed the long-sleeve shirt and gloves, leaving his skin exposed with the white tank.

He slammed the Nova's door and withdrew what appeared to be a key from his pocket. Not a card as I'd seen when Mama was alive and we took a trip to the beach, but an actual key. With one last look around, Tony unlocked the door and disappeared inside. He pulled the curtains over the double window until only a sliver of light glowed at the center.

Tony's outline had been the only form in the window after the lights came on. Was he meeting someone at this motel?

I glanced at the street sign hanging from the nearby

intersection. State Street. Tony had said he lived on State Street. Maybe I wasn't the only person in school with strange living arrangements. He'd mentioned his dad on that first day; the man had taught him how to blend in. And then today he'd mentioned his mom. I'd been so busy trying to fight off Tony's questions about my parents that I never gave him the third degree over his situation at home.

At lunch he'd said her name was Emily, but his dad 'always called her Em.' He'd used the word called instead of calls. Did that mean his dad was no longer in the picture, or his mom? Could one of them be dead?

My phone buzzed and I jumped. Dad's number appeared on the screen, no doubt wondering if I'd lost my way home. I gave Tony ten more minutes before cranking the car, but no one emerged from the room.

Figuring out the mystery of Tony Price would have to wait until Monday.

CHAPTER FIVE

I spent Saturday cleaning up around the campground, which earned me forty dollars from Ms. Birdie. Strangely, I didn't think about Tony again until I pulled on the latex gloves before cleaning the bathrooms. Alfie watched the door and kept campers out while I washed down the sinks and scrubbed the toilets and showers. I filled a bucket with a mixture of water and bleach to mop the floors.

If only I had Tony's number… No, I probably wouldn't have the nerve to call him. If his family really lived in a motel, the two of us had more in common than I ever imagined. Lunch on Monday would mean an interesting conversation, if he sat with me again. If not, I'd be alone until Piper returned from her suspension.

That night, my arms ached from the scrubbing, but I climbed into my bunk with a smile on my face. I'd earned enough money to take the upcoming ACT test without having to touch my secret stash; this test was a must for college entry. When I'd asked Dad for the money a month ago, he'd become agitated and quickly changed the subject.

"Maybe you can take the test next time around," he'd said, before leaving the camper and not returning until around midnight.

With Dad taking steps to prove he'd quit drinking, I didn't want to bring up anything for us to argue about. I had the money—I'd kept my stash a secret and only touched that money in the most extreme emergency. I'd take care of the payment myself and he didn't have to know when I took the test.

On Sunday, Piper came over after her family left church. Dad showed up a few minutes later with sandwiches from the sub shop across the street from the campground. Alfie sat at the kitchen table and picked the pepperoni off his mini-pizza.

"Sorry, Piper," he said, "I didn't realize you were stopping by."

"I've already eaten, but thanks." Piper dropped down next to me on the couch.

"I heard you got in a little skirmish at school," Dad said.

"Carolyn Waters and her friends tried to beat me up. I was only defending myself."

"Jacob said you knocked her to the ground. From what I heard, she's twice your size."

Piper shrugged. "That's why I went low to take her down."

Dad held up a hand and gave Piper a high-five. "Great job. Center of gravity is always the most important part of any fight. Unless you have a gun."

I did a double take. "What did you just say?"

Smiling, Dad pulled a coke from the fridge and popped the can open. "I was complimenting Piper on her fighting skills."

"Yeah," I said, "but what was that stuff about a gun?"

His smile disappeared. "You've lived a sheltered life, Rena."

With a roll of my eyes, I turned to Piper, who'd covered her mouth. "Don't encourage him."

She let out a laugh. "You're cool, Mr. Mason. Did you learn to fight in the Army?"

"Something like that. Why was this Carolyn Waters trying to beat you up?"

"Well," Piper said, "she got pissed when Rena said—"

I hit Piper's arm and she slapped a hand over her mouth. "Carolyn just doesn't like Rena."

Dad's eyes shifted to me. "What did you do?"

"Nothing. She's popular and she hates everyone who's not. Standard high school B.S. You went to Palm County. You should know."

His smile returned. "I imagine that school is nothing like when I went." He took a sip of the drink. "I thought maybe you had some boy problems. It's about time since you've never brought one home."

My cheeks reddened. "We live in a camper that's smaller than the bathrooms at school. I try not to bring anyone home."

Piper frowned. "Thanks a lot."

Dad waved a hand. "No, she's right. We live in a small space. Maybe my daughter not bringing home any boys is one advantage."

"Dad," I said through gritted teeth, "stop embarrassing me."

"I've been seventeen," he said. "I know what boys your age are thinking. My job as your father is to protect you."

Protect me? Like he'd protected me and Alfie every night he'd stayed out drinking? "With what, your three-fifty-seven?"

Dad slammed his drink on the counter and all joking left his voice. "What do you know about guns?"

"Nothing," I said. "It was a joke. You know how a dad sits by the door and waits for his daughter to come home—"

"You could have asked 'with what, your gun?', but you said three-fifty-seven. That's pretty specific."

I thought back to what Tony said. "Someone probably said three-fifty-seven in a movie."

"Have you been in my lock-box?" he asked in a tone that made my hair rise.

"What lock-box?" I asked.

"If you know I have a three-fifty-seven, you've been going through my personal things. Rena, I don't like secrets."

"Dad," I said, "you're the only one in this camper with secrets."

The hard-core look disappeared. "Why don't you girls go to Piper's house and hang out? You haven't had an afternoon to yourself since before the summer."

Alfie finished his pizza. "That would be great. Then you and I could hang out."

"Sure." Dad tousled his hair. "You could go swimming while I trim some branches over the pool."

Trimming branches seemed normal enough, but I couldn't shake the way he'd flipped personalities from this stranger with fury in his eyes to the man who showed kindness and love when he wasn't drunk. "Piper is still on suspension."

"My parents aren't mad about the fight," Piper said. "They know it was self-defense."

"Then it's settled." Dad picked up Alfie's plate and cleaned off the table. He placed my sandwich on the slim counter next to the sink. "You girls are burning daylight."

Just when I'd started to figure Dad out, he left me wondering who was the real Donald Mason.

* * * * *

Piper lived about fifteen minutes from the campground, in a small subdivision with manicured shrubs and houses made of red brick. She parked along the street in front of the house since her mom's car and her stepdad's work van took up the entire driveway.

Her mom gave me a hug after we walked into their living room. She ran a hand through the uneven ends of my hair. "You need a trim."

"Are you open today?" I asked, remembering the stylists' chair in their garage. Piper's mom had her own salon set up and saw clients throughout the week.

"I'm always open for you, Rena."

Almost a year had passed since my last haircut, also by Piper's mom. After she trimmed the ends of the blond hair that fell past my shoulders, she offered us food and drinks, even suggested I take home anything I might need. I wanted to tell her not to worry, that she didn't have to look after me. However, having someone care enough to try felt like a weight off of my shoulders.

Piper and I talked the afternoon away while watching two movies on pay-per-view. I avoided the topic of Tony, which turned out easier than I expected since Joey had asked her out. She wanted me to be the first to hear how her fighting skills impressed him. Piper nearly had a meltdown while waiting for Sunday so she could come over and tell me the news in person.

The sun set and Piper's mom served dinner, which was chicken she'd baked in the oven for most of the afternoon. Yes, I felt strange eating two helpings of everything she served, but the chicken fell off the bone and the mashed potatoes… Piper's mom used real butter and cream. The kind of potatoes I cooked for me and Alfie came in a box and mixed with water.

As I helped Piper clear the table, my phone buzzed with a text from Dad.

Stay the night at Piper's. Don't call.

"What's up?" Piper asked. "You look upset."

My pulse sped as I gripped the phone in my sweaty hands and read the text again. Something wasn't right. I'd never stayed the night away from home, even when Mama was still alive.

"Nothing," I said.

"When do you need to be home?"

After reading the text a third time, I slid my phone in my purse. "As soon as you're ready to leave. I've got homework to finish."

Piper laughed. "Do you ever quit thinking about school?"

"No." Maybe I'd feel guilty about lying to Piper, but not until after making sure nothing had happened at the camper.

* * * * *

"Something *is* wrong." Piper squinted as she navigated the dark road between her house and the campground. "You're being too quiet."

Her red Honda felt like a cage as I alternated between watching the time on the radio slowly tick up and staring at the lights of the few cars we passed. "It's nothing. I just have a feeling I need to get home."

She flipped on her bright lights. "You're freaking me out."

"Dad promised to quit drinking, but I haven't been away from Alfie this long in months. I want to check on them."

"Are you sure that's all?"

"Like I said, just a bad feeling."

"No," she said with a sharp intake of breath, "you said you had a feeling, not a bad feeling. There's a difference."

"Just drop it, okay?"

Piper turned into the campground's main entrance. "I'm the one who's supposed to have feelings, remember? You don't believe in anything supernatural."

"Because it goes against science. I guess I'm okay with ghosts and premonitions, but not wizards and wands. That's a little outside of my comfort zone."

She gave a dry laugh and slammed the brakes as Ms. Birdie stepped into our path. "Is that woman crazy?"

Ms. Birdie made a circle with her hand.

"She wants something," I whispered and reached for my door. "Cover for me."

Piper turned to me. "What? I thought I was taking you home."

"It's quicker this way, trust me."

"But that's a long…"

Again, Ms. Birdie motioned for Piper to roll the window down. When Piper didn't move, she tapped on Piper's window.

With a look of surprise, Piper scrambled for the switch on her door. The window whined as it lowered.

"Rena," Ms. Birdie said, peering into the car, "your timing is brilliant. Come inside and help me with a box on the top shelf, please."

"Not tonight," I said. "Dad wants me home."

Before Piper could argue, I climbed from the car and slammed the door. Ms. Birdie opened her mouth, but I turned and ran for our camper. I didn't look back as Piper's headlights lit my way down the cracked pavement. Lights reached out from some of the campers as I passed, but this was Sunday night. Quiet time started at eight.

Smoke rose from the burn pits at some of the sites. I'd often wondered why people insisted on starting a fire with the temperature outside in the nineties. A woman walked with her two dogs, both barking as I passed.

Thick air clung to my skin as my sneakers bounded along the road. My heart slammed in my chest. I took a deep breath. What a mistake.

Before I passed the laundry building and reached the last section of road near our camper, I stopped and leaned over, coughing. Gnats caught in my eyes. I tossed the strap of my purse over my head to keep it from sliding down my arm as I ran.

Up ahead, the camper came into view. The spot next to us was empty. The older couple with the dog must have left. Barely any light escaped the blinds which were closed tight over all our windows. The bad feeling hit me again. Dad always kept the lower part of one window clear so he could see who was coming down the road. He'd always insisted the reason had to do with his time in the Army.

I took a deep breath and ran the rest of the way. My feet slid on the gravel next to the camper's door. By grabbing the metal steps, I kept myself from falling. Without a second thought, I jumped onto the steps and opened the door.

A single light burned over the stove. Dad stood next to the table, which was covered with a stack of papers including what looked like a passport. Next to the passport was a gun.

"Is that a passport?"

"That's the first thing you ask about?" Shock crossed his face as he glanced from the table to me. "How would you know what a passport looks like?"

"Everyone at school who wants to take the senior trip

needs one."

"What are you doing home?"

"I wanted to make sure Alfie's okay."

"He's not here," Dad said.

My insides shook, but he wouldn't see fear from me. "Where is Alfie?"

"Rena, I told you not to come home."

I approached the table. "Is that your gun? The one from your lock box?"

"My three-fifty-seven revolver. How did you know I had this gun?"

"I didn't." My hand passed over the metal barrel and black handle, but didn't touch the smooth surface. "If Alfie's not home, where is he?"

"Somewhere safe. Same place you should be."

I looked up at his face, split by lines that I couldn't remember. How had he aged years since this afternoon?

His hands shook. "They're coming for me."

It was finally happening. Either Dad had lost his mind or he owed more money than he could afford to pay and someone was coming to collect.

"What's wrong? Do you need money?" I went to my bed and opened the small compartment at the corner of the ceiling. Below me, Alfie's bed sat empty. Behind the tiny wooden door was a hard-bound book Mama bought after our move to Florida. She once read the dozen or so fairy tale stories at bedtime—a different one for each night.

Pressed between worn pages of *The Little Mermaid* were bills ranging from dollars up to twenties. I breathed in the smell of this old book, along with the fresh smell of money.

Dad sounded hoarse. "I don't think…"

I held out the book, opened to a crisp twenty. "I've saved for a long time. Whenever I had a little extra money,

I put it away here. Take this money and pay off whatever you owe."

Moisture hinted at the corners of his eyes. "Rena, you are the most amazing child I've ever known. I don't deserve you."

"Take the money," I said.

"Money won't help us this time. These people can't be bought."

"I don't understand."

"I never wanted you to find out about my past like this. They've offered me a job and given us an out; I must take them up on the deal."

I swallowed the lump in my throat. "What kind of job?"

Instead of answering, Dad opened a cabinet above the couch and pulled out a roll of silver tape. Duct tape, he'd called it when wrapping the vent pipe on the back of one of the dryers in the laundry building. "Do you know what this is?"

"Yeah," I said. "You fix everything with that tape."

He watched me as he tore off a piece of tape and placed it along the edge of the counter. His hands moved slowly since the fingers on his left hand struggled to hold the roll. "Not everything, but it will help us tonight. Sit down."

Without arguing, I dropped onto the couch and sank into the cushions. "What are you going to do?"

Dad reached in his back pocket and held out his favorite multi-tool. The tool had three fold-out knives, a file, a screwdriver, and a miniature pair of scissors. "I want you to have this."

My eyes widened. "Your MacGyver knife?"

"You remember watching that show? I didn't think you paid attention to those old reruns."

"Mama said you loved that show."

"I don't know if I'd use the word love. Some of the disasters hit a little close to home." He chuckled, but the humor faded as he leaned close and tucked the tool into a pocket of my jeans. "You might need this one day."

I rubbed my hand over the cold metal in my pocket. "You're talking like I won't see you again."

"You might not."

"Where is Alfie?"

"I told you, somewhere safe." He placed the tape on the table and held up a folded piece of paper. "I was planning to leave this letter so when you came home you'd know where to find the truck."

I thought about how the driveway had been empty. "Where is your truck?"

"Parked behind the gas station that makes the pizza with the banana peppers you like. In the morning, I want you to get the truck and drive to Atlanta. Go to the airport like I said before and ask for Sylvia Greene."

"That sounds crazy. Just walk into a car rental office and ask for her by name?"

He smiled. "You say that name and someone will come for you. You tell Sylvia who you are and that Donald Mason is your father. Ask for her protection."

"What makes you think she'll protect me?"

Dad caught my hand. "Show Sylvia your ring and tell her it belonged to your mother. Whatever happens, don't take that ring off your finger and don't tell anyone you're looking for Sylvia until you reach the airport. Promise me you'll do those two things."

I pulled away from him. "Did you kill someone?"

"Promise me."

"I promise."

"I've had more kills than you can imagine, all in the

name of this country." He grabbed my arm, pulling me to him with a grip that tightened until I let out a whelp of pain. "Don't trust anyone, especially not a man by the name of Louis Castillo."

"Who?"

He released me and reached for a glass that sat on the stove. With one gulp, he swallowed the dark liquid.

"You promised to quit drinking."

"Listen to me, Rena. That man has a way about him—he can convince people to do anything. People steal for him and they don't hesitate to kill. Don't let him get in your head."

"Is this a friend of yours?"

"Louis is someone from my old life. He's not here to help you, no matter what he says. As soon as I'm gone—"

"Gone?"

Dad gripped my shoulders. "He's coming for me, which is why I've got to go. He's the leader of a terrorist group called the Black Dawn."

"You mean like people who blow up buildings?"

He nodded.

"Why would a terrorist group want you?" I thought for a few seconds. "Does this have something to do with you being in the Army? Is he someone you met in another country?"

"Yes and no. We're out of time. When they take me, you must stay hidden. Not a sound to let them know you're here. At six a.m., walk to the gas station and drive to Atlanta, but keep under the speed limit and try not to get pulled over. You've got to stay off the radar."

"Of who?"

"Everyone."

Tears filled my eyes, stubborn tears that burned with anger. "Why won't you tell me where Alfie is?"

"Because they're not after Alfie. Don't call any of your friends and don't speak to that twit that runs this park. She couldn't keep her mouth shut if her life depended on it. I don't care if it takes three hours for you to get to the gas station. Atlanta will be a six-hour drive. Get there by tomorrow night. If you follow my instructions exactly, you'll see your brother again soon."

The shift in his voice to cool and calculating made me straighten. Maybe Dad wasn't the caring person I remembered from the time before Mama died. "What about you? When will I see you again?"

Dad removed the cushion from one of the seats at the table. He pulled away the wood panel beneath and grabbed a stack of sheets and towels from underneath. "You'll have to bend your knees, but there's enough room here for you to hide."

"Hide?" I stood and stared down at the jagged boards that would bite into my sides. A roach the size of my thumb scurried across the boards. "I can't do this."

"Rena, you're tougher than nails. I raised you strong enough to protect yourself. Don't give into fear now."

"I'm not afraid."

"That's what I'm counting on." He sighed. "Hold out your hands." Dad grabbed my wrists in one hand and wrapped the tape around my arms, below where his fingers dug into my skin. At first, the shock held me in place. When I began to fight, Dad's grip only tightened.

"You're going to force me in there?"

"I don't have a choice. You can't be here when my ride arrives." He released my arms and grabbed the section of tape from the counter's edge. "Rena, I'm sorry for this."

"Sorry for—"

Before I finished, Dad slapped the sliver tape over my mouth. Light flashed across the window, spilling through the smallest of gaps around the blinds.

"They're here." His fingers twitched as he reached for the gun and tucked the metal barrel into his pants. He pulled on his camouflage Army jacket and slid the stack of papers into a pocket out of view.

Trying to rip my hands apart made my shoulders throb. I rubbed the tape along my shoulder, unable to get a grip along the edge to tear the tape away. Removing the tape would sting, but not being able to move my lips or breath through my mouth… or scream at Dad was already eating away at my insides.

Sounds of a motor approached the camper, slowly invading the darkness outside of my tiny world. Glancing around the camper, I realized this was the only life I'd ever known. Maybe I should have felt fear, but all I felt was sadness. I'd lost Mama and now Alfie was gone. After Dad left, I'd be all alone.

I'd never been alone.

As if reading my mind, Dad put an arm around my waist and lifted me into the compartment that smelled of moth balls. I bucked and kicked at his legs, but his strength was more than I could fight. He bent my knees, folding my legs so that my entire body could fit. Then he pulled the multi-tool from my pocket and placed it in one of my hands.

"This will get you out." He disappeared and returned with my phone. "I'm setting the alarm for six. You don't climb out until then, understand?"

I nodded.

Dad tossed the phone in beside me and piled a stack of sheets on top of me before sliding the wood seat into place.

Again, I fought the tape on my hands and mouth, this time by kicking the walls around me. Walls I couldn't see no matter how many times I blinked. Tiny fingers crawled through my hair and I cringed.

"Please Rena, you've got to stay quiet. It's the only way we all might come out of this alive."

A banging came from the door and then the sounds of Dad opening the door and welcoming his visitors. Most of the voices were muffled until they approached the table. A weight seemed to press down from above.

"Coffee?" Dad asked. "Something stronger, perhaps?"

"We're here for business, Donald." The man drawled as if English wasn't his first language, extending his words longer than necessary, and accenting all of the wrong syllables.

"I was told you have a job for me. I'm good for the work."

"So good you avoided my men for years. I expected to see your daughter here."

"Stay away from her," Dad said in a frigid voice.

The seat shifted above me and the voice softened. "Do you often think of Rosanna?"

"She died a long time ago."

"By your hands."

Dad cleared his voice. "I was not responsible for her death. I never wanted to hurt her."

"Your job was to protect her."

"From you," Dad said. "You were the greatest danger to her life."

The man talked faster. "You reported she fell from a cliff into the ocean, that she *chose* this end to the life I provided. I gave her everything. You understand, of course, why I could not stop looking for her."

"That was eighteen years ago."

"And one week later we found her body. The ocean returned her to us."

"I'm sorry for your loss," Dad said, his voice firm but sad.

"No. The woman who washed up on that beach was not Rosanna. She wore the same clothes and even the dental work matched, but you forgot one important detail. She had a tattoo on her left ankle, that of a purple rose. The pattern didn't match the original. Yes, I found the pattern she used."

"I don't remember a tattoo," Dad said.

"After all these years, I've finally caught you in a lie."

"Why did you come here? I never imagined the great Louis Castillo might lower himself by visiting a camping trailer in a remote area of the United States. Surely someone from the embassy could have done your dirty work."

"I wanted to see your daughter, to know if she bears any resemblance to her mother."

"She bears no resemblance," Dad said.

"That I will determine myself. Where is she?"

"I have a house in Portland. She's on her way there as we speak."

The camper shook as I imagined massive fists slamming the table above. "You planned to run away from me? You're not the agent I once knew. Do you want to know how I discovered your real name?"

"Who did you kill?"

Laughter echoed through the camper. "I spent almost twenty years searching for a man who didn't exist. You did special ops for the U.S. government. You took down those with the power to destroy whole cities."

"Like you?" Dad asked.

"As I look at the lines of your face and your crippled hand, I wonder what happened to that fiery young agent who never hesitated to protect those who couldn't protect themselves. Despite the price on your head—"

"Issued by you."

"You left me no choice. When I received the call that my men had located you, I boarded a plane within the hour. Now I find a shadow of the man I once admired. What was your plan?"

"To do whatever it took to keep my children safe," Dad said. "You understand, of course."

"Of course. Will you run from me now?"

"Jacob said you promised me a job that will settle any outstanding debts."

Coach Andrews was involved with this? And what was all this talk about killing people?

"You fool. I merely made the offer to draw you out. If I'd known you were hidden away in this *campground*, I would have come to this country and killed you years ago."

"Then kill me now and all of this will be over."

"First I get a look at your daughter. I've seen pictures but I want to sit before her. I need to see if fear lingers in her eyes. Then we negotiate."

"Sounds like we're going to Portland."

"If you've lied to me, you're as good as dead."

This time Dad laughed. The nervous sound rang in my ears, along with his words. "Wouldn't be the first time."

Feet shuffled and the camper rocked as the door opened and then slammed. After two car doors closed and an engine roared to life, the commotion outside faded into the darkness. The only sound for the rest of the night was the dull hum every time the air clicked on.

CHAPTER SIX

"Regina."

I opened my eyes to a world of sunshine. "Mama?"

A strong arm went around me, pulling me up to stand and then swinging me around as if I weighed no more than my Cabbage Patch doll. "Come and feed the ducks, Regina."

Reaching for the bread in her free hand, I raced to the edge of the lake and tossed pieces of the bread at the approaching ducks. They stormed the shore and waddled straight for me, stealing the remaining bread from my hands.

Mama pulled me out of the way. "My fearless girl, you must learn when to stand your ground and when to run. Not feeling fear won't keep you safe."

"They're just ducks," I said. "Hungry ducks."

She kneeled beside me and laughed. "You are too much like your mother; you cannot hide the strength in your eyes." Mama folded me tight within her arms. "You'll always be my little star."

Together we sang *Twinkle Twinkle Little Star* as she rocked me back and forth.

I opened my eyes, this time to darkness. The cramps in my legs reminded me I'd fallen asleep with my knees shoved into my stomach and my hands above my head. I tried to move my lips, only to remember my mouth had been taped shut. In one hand, I felt the multi-tool. In the other was my phone. Sometime during the night, before I'd drifted off to a land I never wanted to leave, I'd managed to find my phone between the sheets Dad had used to cushion my skin from the jagged wood.

With my arms still bound at the wrists and stretched before me, I managed to hit a button on the phone. Five-forty-five. Still time before the alarm went off. Despite the stiffness in my legs, I forced myself higher. The board above felt heavy against my shoulder. I took a deep breath and heaved upwards. The board bounced and fell back into place. With a second shove of my shoulder, the board bounced and fell sideways, leaving a gap of light. A third hit shifted the board enough that it slid over the edge of the seat frame and crashed onto the floor.

Sitting up, I stretched my legs and shook my right foot, which had fallen asleep. My foot began to tingle and then throb as pain shot through it. Slowly, prickles of feeling, piercing my skin like a hundred tiny needles, came back as the pain subsided.

The air felt cool against my skin. My shirt stuck to beads of sweat along my arms and neck. The seam of my jeans dug into my hip and the length of my leg that was pressed against the boards beneath me—I'd never slept in jeans and probably never would again. I took a deep breath, thrilled to no longer feel as if moth balls had been shoved up my nose.

I had to get out of this box.

What would MacGyver do? Using both of my hands, I loosened the tool until one of the knives folded out. I then cut at the tape with one hand. The knife slipped a few times and cut into the flesh around the tape twice. Drops of blood fell on the white sheets around me. It took longer than I thought, but the tape eventually loosened and one layer split apart. I sighed with relief as I began to peel back the rest of the layers.

Ripping off the last layer took nearly all the hair off my arm, but the pain didn't stop me. I reached for the tape over my mouth and tore the strip in one swift movement. Dad always said the quicker the better when it came to tape, but thinking of him brought a wave of anger and hurt. Why did he leave me here?

And how would I find Alfie? Could this Sylvia be the key to finding my brother? Would she appear at the airport as Dad had suggested?

The more I thought about the night before, the less I realized I knew about my dad. He had a history with this Louis Castillo. The smooth, almost poetic flow of his voice intrigued me. This man wasn't from the U.S.—that much was certain from their conversation. He blamed Dad for the death of a woman named Rosanna.

Dad wasn't a killer. He was a drunk and he'd made our life miserable since Mama died, but I couldn't picture him killing anyone. Now this man with the accent was another story. Without seeing his face, I'd felt the pain and anger from his words, along with an evil that knew no limits, but for what? Revenge for the death of someone he cared about?

Had he really been looking for Dad for twenty years? Dad suggested Louis kill him and this would all be over. And then they'd left together.

I thought of when Dad mentioned Coach Andrews. He'd called his friend by name. Jacob had set up a meeting, a job. Coach Andrews knew all about Dad's past. They'd been in the Army together; this strange man had to be someone Dad met in the Army. No way did he meet an international killer in the small town of Wynder.

But something in the way the man spoke had my full attention from the first syllable. He'd threatened Dad and insisted on meeting me. I should have felt fear, but what I felt was more of a guilty fascination. In the last three years, Dad rarely showed his love for me. He'd never communicated the raw sadness and loss he felt for Mama beyond drowning at the bottom of a bottle. This man sounded both broken and filled with an infinite hope. An impossible combination from a voice that would haunt me.

I licked my lips which burned from the tape. The residue stuck to my fingers as I pressed them against my lips. I stumbled to my feet and grabbed a bottle of water from the fridge. The water chilled my throat as I drank the entire bottle, unable to wash the taste of glue from my mouth.

An engine revved outside the camper and I peered through the blinds. The road was quiet; a wisp of smoke twirled into the waning dark at the closest occupied lot. Light trickled through the trees and reflected off of the still water. Again, an engine revved, this time sending ripples across the water as a boat parted the lake.

The gravel of our drive sat empty, leaving a stark reminder that I was alone. If only Dad had given me some hints on how to find Alfie. He'd insisted I go to Atlanta to find a mysterious woman.

But not yet. Someone in Wynder knew what was going on with Dad. I'd see Jacob Andrews before leaving town, despite what Dad said. All I had to do was reach the truck, drive to school, and then…

I released the blinds and changed out of the damp clothes. The phone chimed and I cleared the alarm.

Running around the camper while trying not to make a sound, I emptied the folders from my backpack and tossed in a change of clothes, my phone charger, and a bag of chips from the basket that hung next to the stove.

On my bunk, I found the book from Mama. I held open the pages and shook until money rained on the floor around me. With care, I stacked the money, counting over two hundred dollars. The stack easily fit into a zippered pocket of my purse.

Six-eleven. It was time to move. I opened the door and stepped into the humid air. Birds chirped. Something splashed across the lake. I slid on my sunglasses.

The sounds of an engine cut into the tranquil morning, this time from a black SUV that was creeping past the laundry building, heading for the curve where I stood next to the camper. Gripping my backpack and my purse, I ran between the camper and the lake, my body hugged up against the metal side. I lowered my head and ran along the trees between the camper and the next lot, which was open, and then on to the next lot with a long black RV that reminded me of a mansion.

The smell of sausage frying in a skillet made my stomach growl as if I hadn't eaten in a week. Voices came from inside the camper, but no one stood by the outside kitchen. A plate of sausage links sat to the side of the stove. Maybe they had a large group of people and wouldn't miss a few sausages. I reached for the sausages, grabbing three and knocking one to the ground, and then ducked behind the RV as the black SUV rolled past. Dark tinted windows concealed whoever was inside. Could they work for Louis? The sausage tasted almost as good as the food at Piper's house.

Piper. Dad told me not to call my friends. Some part of me wished Piper could be involved in my disappearance, but it was safer to keep her out of this. Piper wasn't a fighter. She'd been a good friend, but she didn't deserve to get caught up in whatever Dad did to make these people want to kill him.

I cut through the woods along one side of the campground and down a driveway with grass up to my waist. A metal gate blocked my path to the road, but I climbed the bars like a ladder and threw my legs over the top, landing on both feet. Not many people knew of this entrance to the campground; Ms. Birdie made sure no one could get a car past the front entrance without paying.

As soon as I reached the four-lane road filled with traffic racing in both directions, I grasped my bag and purse tight and began to run along the sidewalk. My heels ached while I ran, not stopping for a single light on my way to the gas station. A car honked, almost in my face, but I never stopped or looked back.

Each breath made my chest feel like exploding. With each mile marker I passed, I felt closer to either laughing or crying. I wasn't sure which until I reached the truck, parked at the back of the gas station as Dad promised.

I unlocked the door and climbed inside. Hot tears filled my eyes and spilled down my cheeks before I knew what had happened. Instead of throwing my bags in the backseat, I laid them next to me in the front. If I needed to run again… No, this truck would get me to Atlanta. I wiped my face with the collar of my shirt—my favorite yellow shirt that reminded me of a dress Mama wore—and cranked the truck.

Dad had filled the tank. All I had to do was reach the interstate and then point the truck in the direction of Atlanta. My phone would detail the route seamlessly. I glanced in the mirror above. If only Alfie sat in the backseat.

Why had Dad wanted me to make this trip without him? He could have packed all three of us up and drove to Atlanta himself. He'd been mysterious about his past and what all of this meant. What was waiting for me at the airport?

One more stop and I'd be on my way to finding out.

* * * * *

At the school parking lot, I found an open spot where the sophomores parked, which meant I'd have to walk farther to reach the office. No one stood in the lot or walked along the sidewalk on my way to the office. I gripped the straps of my backpack as if someone might step from the shadows at any moment and steal all I had left in the world.

Except there were barely any shadows with the sun already high in the sky and beating down on anyone dumb enough to be outside at nine a.m. Maybe someone in the office would take pity and get me into Coach Andrews' office without me having to beg.

At the door to the office, a gloved hand caught my arm.

Tony's green eyes cut into me. "Is everything okay?"

I shrugged off his hand. "Couldn't be better."

Although his eyebrows shot up with a clear question, Tony stepped aside as I reached for the door. "Thought maybe I'd caught you on a good day for once."

Fighting the urge to shove him aside, I shook my head. "Yeah, right."

He grabbed the door and held it open as I crossed the office. Two people behind the counter watched me with incredulity. Yes, I was storming into Coach Andrews' office. No, they didn't have the power to stop me.

"Rena," someone said.

"I've got to see him." Without looking back, I twisted the handle to his door.

Inside, Coach Andrews glanced up from his desk and stopped speaking mid-sentence. "Get out."

The man sitting before him turned around and smiled. His crisp gray suit seemed like prime attire for the funeral of someone he'd rather see dead than alive. With one leg crossed over the other, the pattern of his snake-skinned boots stood out against the rest of his outfit. The sunglasses he wore flashed my reflection. He removed the sunglasses and sat them on the desk. His soft blue eyes, almost a gray like his suit, shined with a dangerous glint. His spiked hair, a thick mass of silver with enough grease to reflect the light around us, completed the 'don't mess with me' look. "No reason she can't join our meeting. Thought you'd be halfway to Portland by now."

"Do you work for Louis?" I asked.

"I said go," Coach Andrews growled. "Can't you take a hint?"

The man in gray reached into his jacket and withdrew a gun with a chrome barrel, similar to the one Dad had on the table last night.

I moved closer to see the handle and breathed a sigh of relief. This wasn't Dad's gun.

He stood and waved the gun, ushering me to sit in the chair he'd vacated. When I didn't move, he pointed the gun at my face. "You should be shaking in fear. Where are your manners?"

"I'm not scared of you." I glared past him to Coach Andrews. "Where is my brother?"

Coach Andrews shook his head. "You don't follow orders well." He stood and reached across the desk before I could speak. He grabbed the man's arms, forcing him to drop the gun, which clanked on the floor. Coach stepped around the desk to stand before his opponent.

The man laughed. "You're stronger than you look, but I'm faster." He flipped his hands over and gripped Coach's arm.

Coach fought the grip on his arm as the man twisted him around. With a laugh, the man dealt a blow to the back of Coach's right leg, just below the knee, that brought the two-hundred-and-eighty-pound ex-Ranger crashing to the floor. On his way down, Coach reached for the bookcase next to his desk. The picture of him and Dad toppled from the bookcase and shattered on the floor next to his feet.

The man reached for his gun and leaned over Coach Andrews.

"Don't kill him," I said.

Laughter came from the man holding the gun, along with a look of surprise. "You think I'm an idiot? Agent Mason would hang me by my boots and gut my insides." He kicked one of Coach's shoes. "Still might if I don't get this mess cleaned up soon."

Agent Mason would… was he talking about Dad? "Who are you?"

"You really have no fear." He pointed the gun at me. "Call me Max. I've been waiting to meet you."

"Meet me?" I asked. "Why?"

"Because most people would run when faced with the possibility of death. Instead, you stand and ask questions as if armed men visit your principal here on a daily basis. What if I told you he deserved that beating?"

Coach Andrews groaned.

"I don't believe you," I said.

"Because they've lied to you," he said. "For years, nothing but lies about who you really are. Your father, his friend—"

"Are you going to hurt me?"

"Still you keep a straight face." Laughing again, he leaned closer and used the cold barrel of the gun to slide a lock of hair from my shoulder. "If I harmed a hair on this pretty head, your father would kill me. No, I plan to enlighten you. That would hurt him far worse."

"Mr.—"

"You can call me Max. Others call me The Detonator."

With a roll of my eyes, I took a step forward. "That sounds dumb. What did this Louis person do with my dad?"

Max's face filled with the glow of excitement. "It's been a long time since I got to do the dirty work." He placed his gun inside the gray jacket and pulled another gun from his waist, offering the handle to me as if it were a gift. This gun was solid black without the revolving part like Dad's. "I'll give you a head start. Let's see… five minutes… ten? I want to make this fair."

"Fair?" I stared at the gun. "I've never held a gun."

His eyes lit up. "All the more reason to take this slow. Like opening a bottle from my grandmother's cellar, aged to a crisp yet sweet red." Max closed his eyes and let out a long sigh. "You will have the lead. Then I hunt you down."

"Rena," Coach Andrews moaned. "Please, if you've ever listened to me…"

The pain in Coach Andrews' voice brought the scene before me into perspective. His eyes barely opened as he tried to move and Max kicked him in the stomach. Who was this strange guy, watching me like a hunter ready to attack?

Max laid the gun on the desk and pulled a phone from his pocket. He hit the screen until a stopwatch appeared, which he held in my face. "I've decided not to underestimate you. Five minutes and then I strike."

A scream filled the room. I spun to see the secretary, Mrs. Yale, holding her face as she stumbled backward. Another cry sounded and then the word 'gun.' I backed away from Max and nearly stumbled over Mrs. Yale.

She pulled me out of Coach's office. "Are you okay?"

Instead of answering, I pushed past her and ran around the counter, not meeting anyone's eyes as I left the office and sprinted toward the main doors.

Angry tears burned in my eyes. Dad was right. I should have listened and left town like he asked instead of coming here. I'd promised to run and not tell anyone about going to Atlanta. Stupid me thought Coach would have answers, that maybe I'd find my brother.

But Max had come here. For me? I wondered if Coach knew this man in gray. He must if Dad knew him. Max certainly didn't hesitate to deal blow after blow to a man twice his size. He'd called my dad Agent Mason. I wondered how long they'd known each other. Max seemed intent on hurting Dad by way of me. He'd threatened to enlighten me, whatever that meant. Since when was knowledge something to fear?

As if I knew about fear. Something must really be wrong with me. I'd just faced a man with a gun and he'd praised me for having no fear.

No fear. I'd never faced a bully I couldn't take down. Or been that close to a gun other than in a movie. I'd never been in a situation I couldn't control except for the night Mama died. I remembered the accident and reaching the hospital, but after that…

I should have been shaking like any other normal person when Max beat up Coach Andrews and held out the gun. How did he know I felt no fear?

I slammed both hands against one of the doors. As it opened and I shoved my way outside, I cursed the heat while wiping away the tears. Hopefully, Alfie would never see me like this. If I ever saw Dad again… I thought about Coach Andrews lying on the floor of his office. Would he be okay?

Behind me, a man yelled and I spun around, thinking Max had followed me. Had it been five minutes already? Without slowing, I turned back to face the parking lot. A gray car spun tires as it rounded a curve and sped along the sidewalk, screeching to a stop before me. Dumbfounded, I stared at the dark tinted windows.

A Nova. No, it couldn't be.

The driver's window rolled down. Peering inside, I realized it could be. Tony's face became visible as the window lowered, his arm steadily cranking a handle inside the door.

"No power windows?" I asked.

His green eyes raked over me. "That's the best you can do? Get in."

"Where are you going?"

Someone yelled my name from behind. Tony leaned forward and craned his neck to see around me. "Should I kill the engine while I wait?" The annoyance in his voice didn't send me into motion, but the sounds of a siren approaching did. He gripped the wheel. "Well?"

I ran around the front of the car, to the passenger's door. Tony leaned across the bench seat and opened the door for me. That's when I realized I still had my backpack. I dropped the bag on the red carpet and jumped in the car, slamming the door at my side. With one hand, I reached for the seatbelt. With the other, I braced myself against the dash.

Tony shifted the car into gear and slammed on the

gas. At the parking lot's exit, he slid the car to the right in front of another car that swerved to miss us. The smell of exhaust fumes from the car made me cough. In the mirror to my side, blue flashing lights turned in front of the school. Cars behind us pulled off the road as wailing sirens approached. A car in front of us slowed and Tony went around the car, cutting into the other lane and nearly getting us slammed head-on.

"That was close," I yelled. Thoughts of the accident surfaced and I twisted the radio dial in an attempt to block out the painful screaming. It didn't matter if Tony couldn't hear the cries. "Where's the music?"

"Radio doesn't work."

Great. I leaned my head back against the seat. "Where are we going?"

He glanced in the rear-view mirror. "You can start with thanks." Tony's black-gloved hands gripped the steering wheel as he came to a light and turned right without slowing. He cut the turn wide enough he took up both lanes. Thankfully no one occupied the other lane. "I think it's time we disappear."

"Thanks." I took a deep breath and closed my eyes. "I have no idea what just happened."

"You ran out of the school. Who was after you?"

"A man who beat up Coach Andrews. Knocked him to the floor with one kick. I think this man is working for another man who kidnapped my dad." When Tony didn't speak, I opened my eyes. "I just said he knocked our principal to the floor. He also had a gun. Why aren't you freaking out?"

"Why aren't you?"

"I don't freak out," I said. "It's not me."

Tony's eyes stayed on the road. "Me either."

I turned to stare at the signs we passed. He'd aimed

the car for the center of town. "Why did you pick me up?"

"Something was wrong, I could feel it. I saw the man with the silver hair go into the office. He was packing inside his jacket with another gun in his pants. When you went in, I grabbed the car."

"How did you know that man had a gun?"

"I told you before—my dad was a hunter. He taught me things about people like how to look for danger and when to run. It was definitely time to run."

"I shouldn't have left Coach Andrews, but he told me to run."

Tony cleared his throat. "You said your dad was kidnapped?"

"Last night. Coach and my dad were friends. They joined the Army together." Why was I babbling? Tony didn't need to know my life story. "I showed up this morning because I thought he might know why these people were after my dad."

"Did either of them tell you?"

I shook my head and looked at Tony. "The man who beat up Coach Andrews—he said he'd give me a head start before hunting me down."

Again, Tony glanced in the mirror. "He didn't happen to say he drives a black Lincoln, did he?"

As I spun in the seat and leaned over the headrest to see, the belt cut into my neck. Behind us, a black car crept closer with every second. Someone in the passenger seat leaned out of the window with a gun. "There's a man with a gun following us and I'm not freaking out. At least, I don't think I am."

"No, you're cool."

With a bitter laugh, I turned back around and dropped down on the red vinyl seat. "Cool? When are you going to ask why I'm not afraid?"

Tony hit the brakes and made a turn that left me choking from the belt's grip. "Right after you ask why I picked you up."

CHAPTER SEVEN

We raced through six intersections while I considered how to answer, each turning green as we approached. "That's convenient." My breathing sped. "Would you stop if the light doesn't turn?"

"Probably not," Tony said.

In the mirror to my side, the black car shortened the gap between us. A cracking sound came from behind and I spun to see two holes in the back window.

"They're shooting at us," I screamed.

"That's usually what happens when someone wants you to stop."

"Not where I come from. Aren't you wondering why someone is shooting at us?"

Tony swerved to miss a truck that cut into our lane. Like a pro, he corrected and pulled us into another lane, passing the truck with a roar of the accelerator.

"Wow," I said, "this car has power. My dad once drove one of these."

"That's why I borrowed it."

"Because it has power? Or because my dad drove one?"

He turned to me with a look of surprise. "This car can outrun many of the newer cars. The engine's been updated to be sixty-seven percent more efficient—at least that's what I was told. The carb was holding us back—"

A car turned in front of us and I barely whispered Tony's name before he swung us to the left into oncoming traffic. He turned the wheel and made us spin in a three-sixty. The cars blurred around me. Sounds of screeching brakes and blasting horns became a musical barrage as I prepared for metal-on-metal at any moment. When Tony recovered the car, we were back in the same lane moving forward, but now the black car was in front of us.

"Reach in the glove box," Tony said. "Hand me the gun inside, but don't touch the trigger. It's loaded."

The door in front of me creaked as it opened. There was no paperwork jammed inside, like in Dad's truck, only a black gun, similar to what Max had offered me.

"Is anything wrong?"

"Wrong? You just asked me to hand you a gun. Why are you driving around with a gun in your glove box?"

"To keep people like you from getting us killed." He reached over me and grabbed the gun. "Let's try this again. How about holding the wheel?"

Startled, I reached over and grabbed the wheel. "What are you doing?"

"Getting rid of our tail." He leaned out of his window and fired a shot at the black car. The car next to us swerved and hit the brakes. Again, Tony fired, this time hitting one of the black car's tires. A cloud of smoke and rubber exploded from the back tire on the left. He fired a third shot and hit the right back tire.

I gripped the wheel until my knuckles turned white. The Nova swerved to the edge of the road and I pushed the wheel to the left to miss the black car. The right front of our bumper clipped the back left of theirs, causing the black car to spin.

Tony landed back in his seat and swore as he grabbed the wheel. "What the hell were you doing?"

"Trying to keep us from wrecking." I glanced in the side mirror and other cars were slowing to check on the black car, which was now pointed nose-first in a ditch. "I'm sorry if I damaged your car."

To my surprise, Tony laughed. "That was pretty good driving. And no, this isn't my car. I borrowed it, remember?" He handed me the gun. "Can you put this back?"

I stared at the gun. Why was everyone wanting to get a gun in my hand today? "I've never held one of those."

"Never?" His eyebrows rose. "I thought that, given who your dad was… I mean, you said he was kidnapped."

"I don't know who my dad is." I reached for the gun and pinched the handle in two of my fingers, holding it as far away as possible. After I placed the gun back in the dash, I closed the door tight. I thought about our conversation from earlier. "What do you know about my dad?"

"Well, you said he was kidnapped. Any idea of who took him?"

In the mirror, a car and a truck pulled over to check on the black car. No one seemed to be rushing to get out. "Do you think they're okay?"

"Do you want to turn around and check?"

"No." I focused on the road as Tony turned onto State Street. He passed the campground and I stared at the place I'd called home for years. Along the main street, campers and RVs filled about half of the spots. There would be an influx of people by Friday. A group of people, two women and five kids, walked toward the swimming pool with towels over their shoulders. In front of the office sat a police car. A man in uniform stood near the door talking with Ms. Birdie. "I think we should—"

"No, we shouldn't," Tony said without taking his eyes from the road.

"I live in that campground. There's a policeman at the office. Do you think someone came back looking for me?"

"If so, that's a bad reason to stop."

I reached for his arm. "How did you know I wanted to stop? Did you know I lived here?"

Instead of answering, Tony shrugged away from me and passed the car in front of us. Dozens of questions rushed through my head. What happened to Dad and why were these people chasing me? Was Alfie safe like Dad had promised? Could I trust Tony? "Why *did* you pick me up?"

He glanced in the rear-view mirror. "Now she wants to talk," he said under his breath.

"That wasn't an answer."

"I knew you were in trouble."

"How?"

"The look on your face."

Thinking back, I remembered the day I met Tony. He'd made a joke about 'checking out' Robbie, but what if he wasn't joking? "Do you work for the people who took my dad?"

"No."

Somewhere inside of me was a strange desperation to believe him. Should I trust Tony? The first answer that came to mind was how none of this made any sense. I was on the run from a man who'd promised to hunt me down. No, *we* were on the run. If I'd avoided the school and drove straight to Atlanta, I'd be alone right now.

But Tony kept a gun in his glove box. What seventeen-year-old carried a loaded gun and shot at people from a moving car?

"Still not scared?" he asked.

That's when the answer hit me. Maybe I could convince Tony to drive me to Atlanta.

If only I hadn't promised Dad not to tell anyone about Sylvia.

* * * * *

About twenty minutes later, we'd followed State Street through the center of town and now buildings to our right and left were older and in need of fresh paint. Some were abandoned, like an old bottling plant that had burned years ago. Only one brick wall still stood with the company's red and blue logo.

Ahead, a light turned red and Tony slowed to a stop. He turned to me. "There's something I need to do before we leave town."

I sighed with relief. He'd planned for us to leave town. "What?"

"Make a stop to get my stuff. It'll only take a few minutes."

"Do you think those men are still looking for us?"

"I'm sure they are, but right now I think we're fine. We've just got to keep track of the time. I've noticed three cops but none have tried to stop us. We're obviously not on the city's radar yet."

"What if the police try to stop us?"

"Let's don't worry about that right now."

"Dad told me to get the truck and leave town." I thought about the F-150 parked in the lot back at school. "It's parked in the sophomore zone. Should we sneak back and get the truck?"

"We're not going back."

"What if my dad—"

"I can promise that wherever he is, your dad is not worried about that truck. This is a one-way trip." Tony turned on his blinker and I recognized the auto parts store to my right. He pulled the car into the entrance of the Twin Pines Motel. We bounced on the rough driveway as he passed the office and stopped in front of door number eleven. He killed the ignition and climbed out of the car.

"Are you at least going to tell me who you are?"

His answer was a slam of the door.

The sound reverberated through my entire body. "You weren't joking about borrowing this car."

Tony stared at me through his open window. "What do you mean by that?"

"You slam the door like you don't care what happens to it."

"It's just a car. Why do you care if I slam the door?"

"My dad drove a Nova years ago, when we first came to Wynder."

"We?"

"Me and my mom."

He leaned down and met my eyes while trying to fight a smile. "I actually want to hear this story, so hold that thought."

Tony put a key in the door and opened the motel room, disappearing inside before I could think about getting out. Next to me was the pool with chains on the gate. Beyond the pool was the breakfast restaurant. I thought about the sausages I ate on my run from the campground and my stomach rumbled. An eighteen-wheeler roared through the parking lot behind me, headed for a stretch of gravel where other trucks had parked.

I looked back at the white door with the number eleven in black. The curtains, pulled tight at the center of the window, prevented me from seeing what Tony was grabbing. I'd have to remember to ask him about this place.

A knock sounded on my window and I jumped. Next to me stood a woman wearing a flowered night-gown that went to her feet. She stood barely as tall as the car, with glasses and a toothy grin.

I rolled down my window. "What is it?"

"Where is your boyfriend? I need my weekly rent."

"I don't have a boyfriend."

"The one who owns this car owes me rent. I intend to collect before he races off again to god knows where. Probably spends the day riding the streets. Wouldn't be surprised if he sells drugs. Don't care as long as I get the rent."

"He goes to school with me. He's in my AP physics class."

The woman raised an eyebrow. "Are you high on something? Don't be rude. We share around here."

I looked at the window with curtains closed tight, silently begging Tony to hurry up. "Rent? Isn't this a motel?"

"That can be bought by the week." She giggled. "Or by the hour if you're low on cash."

"I'll keep that in mind." Was she for real? I glanced down at the plush shoes she wore, in the shape of cats.

Sirens sounded from State Street and the woman raised her head. "What did your boyfriend do, rob the bank on the corner?"

"He hasn't robbed anyone."

A smile crossed her face. "He's not who he says, believe you me."

The sirens came closer, two SUVs with flashing lights and an ambulance. Traffic stopped as the emergency vehicles passed and then restarted as the sirens began to fade.

"Well," she said, "you dodged a bullet this time."

Tony appeared at his window. "Good to see you, Mrs. Benson." He opened the door behind his and tossed two black duffel bags into the backseat.

"I told you I'm not your grandmother. Call me Nati."

"Okay, Mrs. Benson."

She threw her hands up in the air. "Are there any body parts in those bags? You didn't use your tub to chop someone up, did you?"

He laughed. "Where do you get these ideas?"

"I watch *C.S.I.*," she said. "I could spot a killer a mile away."

"You think I've killed someone?"

She shrugged. "You fit the profile. You pay in cash. You're a loner." Mrs. Benson looked down at me. "Until now. I'm glad to see you've found a girlfriend. I hope you've also found some money."

Tony pulled a wallet from his back pocket and took out three crisp hundred dollar bills. "Will this cover me?"

She walked around the car and reached for the money. Mrs. Benson tugged the collar of her nightgown lower and slid the money into her bra. She patted the money. "For now. Next time you show up this time of morning bring me some breakfast."

With a shake of his head, Tony dropped in behind the wheel. He watched as she shuffled in the direction of the office. "What did she say to you?"

"Just that she was looking for the rent. Then police cars raced by and she wanted to know if you'd robbed a bank. Oh, and she thinks you might be a drug dealer."

"I heard the sirens but I doubt they're on our trail yet." He glanced at his watch. "She managed to say all of that while I was inside? I was gone four minutes max." Tony pulled on his seat belt and cranked the car. "Is there anything else you need before we hit the road?"

I shook my head as the engine roared to life. He revved the motor and the whole car shook. "Have you been living at this motel?"

Tony didn't say anything until he'd maneuvered the car back onto State Street. "Yes."

"Where are your parents?"

"My mom died when I was three. My dad disappeared when I was nine."

"So, you live alone? In a motel?"

"That's right."

Tears crept into my eyes. "That's sad. My mom died three years ago. At least I still have my dad." When he wasn't spending every night drinking his life away. Instead of telling Tony about his alcohol problem, I bit my tongue. "I have a little brother; we call him Alfie."

"Where is he?"

"I don't know. My dad said he was somewhere safe." A tear slid down my cheek and I wiped it away. We stopped at the last light near the edge of town. Next to us, a man in a truck revved his engine. Tony answered by keying up the Nova's engine. Would they race?

The man in the truck slammed the gas and shot out in front of us. Tony smiled as the road before us cut down to one lane and the truck merged into our lane. Ahead of us were miles of road with forests and the occasional house to either side. I rarely had a reason to drive outside of town.

"Are you okay?" he asked, barely above the rumbling engine.

"It's hot in this car."

Tony answered by rolling up his window. He turned two dials on his dash and cool air began to pour from the vents. “Let me know when it’s cold enough for you.”

“You’ve got air in this car? Dad’s Nova didn’t have air. I remember Mama cursing in the summertime when her sweaty skin stuck to the seat. One time my crayons melted and I cried.”

“This car went through a retrofit and one of the things the owner added was an air conditioner.”

I laughed. “The owner added air but not a working radio?”

He shrugged. “Everyone has different priorities. When I took the car, the owner was in the middle of an upgrade. The new radio he ordered wasn’t in yet.”

“Tell me why you were living at a motel. Don’t you have any family?”

“Not around here.”

“Do you have a job?”

“Yes.”

Before I could ask what kind of job, a ringing came from my purse. I pulled out my phone. *Piper.*

“Who is it?” Tony asked.

“Piper.”

“The girl you usually eat lunch with?”

“Remind me to ask what else you know about me.” I reached for the green button on the screen, but Tony snatched the phone from my hand before I could answer. “Hey, what are you doing?”

With my phone in one hand, he pointed at the rear-view mirror. “Whatever you see in that mirror is now behind us.”

The phone stopped ringing. “But—”

“No buts. As of now, you’re on the run. We’re on the run. You can’t put our lives in jeopardy by talking to anyone back there.”

“Piper will worry. She’s still on suspension, maybe we

could—" I reached for the phone, which began another round of ringing.

The Nova rolled across a bridge, each section of concrete causing the car to bounce. Tony held the steering wheel with his knee as rolled down his window. He threw the phone out of the window and over the concrete rails of the bridge.

I stared in shock. "That phone cost a hundred dollars and it didn't have any insurance."

"No need to worry about anyone calling now."

"How will Dad get in touch with me?" Anger burned inside of me. "You threw my phone out of the window? Who do you think you are?"

"Someone who doesn't want an armed man on his trail. Anyone with halfway decent tracing software could use that phone to find our location."

I crossed my arms over my chest. "You had no right."

After we reached the end of the bridge, Tony pulled the car onto the shoulder. "What do you think happened at the school this morning? How did Mr. Andrews act when you entered the office?"

"He was angry that I came in. He told me to leave."

"Why do you think he did that?"

Red burned in my cheeks. "Because it was dangerous. Dad told me to leave town and not tell anyone."

"Why do you think he said that?"

"I guess he thought someone might come to the school looking for me."

"Which is exactly why you should have left town."

"You're taking his side?"

Tony sighed and slammed the wheel with his palm. "Damn it, do I have to spell this out?"

"Spell what out?" I yelled. "You haven't spelled anything out. Who are you and why did you pick me up at the office?" I reached for the door. "I'll find my dad and brother without your help."

His voice lowered and all of the frustration disappeared. "What happened in there? Before you ran out?"

I closed my eyes and thought about the scene from Coach Andrews' office. Coach had insisted I leave before the man in gray, Max, took him down with one hit placed below the knee of his bad leg. That was where Coach Andrews was shot in Iraq. How did Max know about his injury?

Max's face appeared in my mind, clear as if he was standing before me. His spiked gray hair seemed out of place; Max was older than Dad, maybe fifties. I could only imagine one word to describe the hard lines of his face—evil. He'd offered me a gun. This man must work for Louis; why else would be looking for me? Max looked into my eyes and filled with excitement when he saw no fear. He jumped at the opportunity to hunt me down.

The comment about my lack of fear reminded me of Dad's conversation from the night before. Louis demanded to meet me, to look into my eyes and see if fear stared back. Somewhere he and Dad were traveling—driving or flying, I wasn't sure. Dad had mentioned a house in Portland. He must have been buying me time to get out of town, but what would happen when they reached Portland? Would Louis kill Dad when he found out I wasn't there?

If the thought of a terrorist killing Dad didn't make me shake, what else could?

Maybe there was something to me not feeling fear. Dad had called me fearless over the years, but I never thought much about his words. So what if I didn't feel the same fear as others? Did that make me weird? If it made me special, I'd feel special. At the moment, I felt nothing close to special.

I thought of the dream with Mama. She'd warned me that not feeling fear wouldn't keep me safe. Glancing down, I stared at the green ring that always made me feel calm. Her ring, the only piece of jewelry I'd ever owned and the only thing Dad warned me never to take off. Emerald green, like Tony's eyes. Was that why I felt so calm around him?

"There was a man in a gray jacket," I said. "His name was Max."

"Max?" Tony stared at the wheel as if deep in thought.

"After he knocked Coach Andrews to the floor, he got all excited. You see, I never feel fear."

"I've noticed that about you."

I turned to him, wanting eye contact, but Tony stared straight ahead. "Max made a big deal about me not feeling fear, but it's not a big deal. How could it be?"

Tony's eyes met mine. "You're looking for an answer?"

"Mama warned me that not feeling fear wouldn't keep me safe."

"I agree with her."

"Then it's a good thing you picked me up. Now I have you to keep me safe."

Tony's expression darkened. "You're delusional. You think I'm the one who can save you? You know nothing about me."

I reached for his gloved hand, but he pulled away. "I bet you don't really have skin allergies."

He laughed bitterly. "You don't want me to take off these gloves."

"You might think I'm crazy. Right now, I think I'm crazy, but at least I have one friend who I can talk to."

"You consider me a friend?"

The emotion in his words caught me by surprise. "You're the only one I have left."

Tony shifted the car into drive with the handle to the right of the steering wheel. The road sat empty before us; no cars had passed while we talked on the road's edge. "Where to now?"

"I want to find my brother."

"Did your dad leave any hints on where he might be?"

I shook my head. "Dad said he was somewhere safe. He said the men after him were terrorists but they weren't after Alfie."

"Why do you think these terrorists were after your dad?"

"I think they're really after me."

He was quiet for a moment. "Why would they want you?"

"I don't know. None of this makes any sense."

"Let's say that they're after you and no one else. Do you think finding your brother would make him safer?"

"No." I slid lower in the seat. "It would make him a target."

"Then we leave Alfie out of this. Did your dad give you any directions in case something happened?"

I thought about the card with the name Sylvia Greene tucked inside my wallet. Dad had insisted I tell no one. He'd made me promise, along with not taking Mama's ring off. He knew that would never happen. "He said go to Atlanta."

"And do what when you get there?"

Breaking my promise to Dad didn't feel right, despite every promise he'd broken for me. "I'll figure it out along the way."

"Someone will be watching the roads between here

and Atlanta. That's an artery for this region and the most likely place for you to show up."

"What do you suggest?"

"Hiding out for a few days. We'll get another ride and make sure our trail is clean."

"Tony—"

"Do you trust me?" he asked.

I hesitated. "Yes, but Dad had a plan. He specifically told me to take his truck and drive to Atlanta first thing this morning."

"To meet him?" Tony asked. When I didn't say anything, he sighed. "You dad's plan might have worked if you'd listened to him and hit the road for Atlanta. Now it's kind of late for that."

"Who are you?"

"Well, I'm not really a student at Palm County High."

"If you're not a student, why were you there?"

"To watch out for you."

Shock sped through my veins. "Do you work for the people chasing me?"

"I work for someone who knew your dad years ago. Someone who wants to keep you safe."

"Coach Andrews?"

"No," he said.

"Someone from the Army?"

"You could say that." Again, his emerald eyes met mine. "We got word the bad guys were after your dad."

"Then you consider yourself one of the 'good' guys?"

"Yes."

With a deep breath, I sighed. "I kind of guessed something was off when I realized you lived in a motel. I saw you at the gas station on Friday night. I was curious where you lived on State Street and decided to follow you."

His eyes widened. "You followed me to the motel?" Again, he seemed lost in thought. "I never noticed you tailing me."

"I'm sorry, Tony."

"Don't be. That was a compliment." He cleared his throat. "Tony is not my name. It's really Travis."

"Travis? Are you joking?"

He held out a gloved hand. "Travis Payne. Nice to meet you."

"That isn't funny."

"Do you hear me laughing?"

I took his hand in mine, disappointed that I couldn't touch his fingers. "Rena Mason. Nice to meet you."

"I think you can consider us friends now."

CHAPTER EIGHT

I opened my eyes and held up a hand to block the sunlight that cut through the rows of pine trees and blinded me in bursts as we drove. The familiar smell of exhaust from this tank of a car surrounded me. Air still blasted from the vents, but Tony had rolled down his window and propped his arm on the door. He still wore the black outfit—jeans, a long-sleeved shirt, and gloves that gripped the steering wheel where his right hand rested on the bottom rim.

With his left hand, he tapped a steady beat as if the radio actually worked. I peered closer and noticed a thin wire that dropped from his ear into his shirt.

"What are you listening to?"

He jumped a little and pulled out the earbud. "Mostly rock, but I'll listen to anything with a good beat."

"No wonder you don't need a radio. Isn't that illegal?"

He shrugged. "I only keep one ear in while I'm driving. I suppose the police could pull me over."

I noticed two drinks in the cup holder between us, both sweating. "You probably wouldn't be worried."

"Not likely." He pointed to the drink on my side. "I got you a coke when I stopped for gas. You look like you could use a cold drink."

Tony—no he wasn't Tony. His name was Travis Payne. He wasn't a student at Palm County, he was… I wasn't quite sure. All he'd told me was that he worked for someone who knew Dad from the Army. His job was to protect me, which would explain why he kept a loaded gun in his glove box.

I would have found our whole situation impossible to believe, except that my dad left town with a terrorist who was determined to find me. And Travis had picked me up in front of the office, ready to speed out of town. It all seemed a little too perfect.

"Who did you say you worked for?"

"I didn't."

As I took a sip of the drink and thought of what to ask next, a wonderful smell made my stomach growl. I looked around for the smell, which reminded me of the burger place Dad took us on special occasions. They had a junior burger, but I'd never ordered it. I always got the Beef Willy, which came with two slices of cheese. "Did you get lunch?"

Travis grinned. "I thought you might appreciate a good burger. No wheat bread, I promise."

He got points for remembering my utter disdain for eating healthy. Well, for eating healthy when it came to beef at least. "Where are we?"

"One of Florida's largest national forests."

"We're still in Florida?" I asked with disappointment.

"I told you we've got to fly under the radar."

"Don't you mean drive under the radar?"

He laughed. "I never thought you'd be joking at a time like this. Running away from everything you've ever known has got to suck."

"I'm trying not to think about it."

"Understood."

"How long before we stop?"

Travis glanced at his watch. "A good forty-five minutes."

"You're killing me. That burger is making me feel like I haven't eaten in weeks."

"Reach behind the seat and you'll find the food."

With a laugh, I took off my seatbelt and reached over the seat. I grabbed the bag with grease leaking out along the seam.

When I took the first bite of greasy beef and oozy cheese, forty-five minutes didn't seem so long.

* * * * *

Travis drove the Nova down a dirt road that went for miles with no houses, only evenly spaced pines to either side. Dust flew into the air like a great cloud around us. He swerved to miss several deep treads left from large trucks and slowed to a crawl as we drove through a small creek that flowed across the road in a shallow trench.

"This looks like a great place to hide," I said. "We haven't seen another vehicle for miles. What's your plan? We camp out?"

"That's funny." He turned to the right, down an overgrown path and through an open gate I hadn't noticed. "But camping isn't a bad idea. At least you'd feel at home."

"If I was home, I'd be taking care of my brother."

"Do you resent having to care for him?"

"No," I said. "When Mama died and my dad started drinking, taking care of Alfie wasn't a choice. It was either keep up appearances or someone would call child services."

"But if you had another choice…"

"I want out of Wynder. I want a life of my own. Is that selfish?"

"I'm not the one to make judgments on people being selfish. My parents made choices I still don't understand." He stopped the car in front of a shed, to the right of a roll-up door. "Look on the bright side. You're out of Wynder."

"Why doesn't it feel that way?"

Travis climbed out of the car and grabbed the duffel bags from the backseat. "This is the end of the road for this car." He pointed toward the shed. "Behind door number one is our replacement."

"An upgrade?" I opened my door and lifted my backpack and purse from the floor. The air felt like a steamy shower despite the trees stretching long shadows over us. I slapped a mosquito on the side of my face. "You're going to leave this car here?"

"That's right."

"But we're in the middle of nowhere."

"Why are you so worried about this car? It's just a car. There were thousands of these made and from what you've said, it sounds like the Nova you remember wasn't in much better shape."

"Won't the owner be mad?"

"He'll get his car back." Travis patted the hood. "It's been worth every bit of the five-hundred dollars he paid for it." He walked around the car and pulled his gun from the glove box. In an easy motion, he slid the gun in the back of his pants. Travis opened his wallet and took out a key, which he used to open the padlock on the roll-up door.

As the door slid up, I squinted in the sunlight to catch a glimpse inside of the shed. At first, I only made out a dark green tarp and the outline of a car. Travis pulled the tarp down, exposing slick chrome. My eyes adjusted to the sight of a car straight out of a racing magazine.

"Are you coming?" He opened the driver's door and got into the seat. When I didn't move, he fired up the motor. Where the Nova had blasted like a jet engine, this car purred with a defiant yet powerful sound. Maybe like a race car before they threw the flag to start. Slowly, the car backed out and stopped by my side. He got out and came around to open the door for me.

"Wow." I stood in utter shock. "What kind of car is this?"

"A Ferrari."

"I've never seen one of those."

"You probably have, just never paid attention." He waved me inside and I, still gasping in shock, dropped into the seat. This car sat lower than the Nova had, almost scraping the ground. "You'll never get down those dirt roads without bottoming out."

"I'll manage." Travis lowered into the driver's seat as if he'd memorized the exact angle to fold his legs into the tight car.

I glanced over my shoulder to where he'd tossed the duffel bags in the backseat. As I arranged my purse and backpack in the small space at my feet, he reached across me and opened the glove box. There he placed the gun and closed the door.

Travis turned the car around in the grassy area and I watched as the Nova faded to a speck in my side mirror and then disappeared completely. Back on the dirt road, the sun had dropped to the perfect blinding angle. I pulled down the visor and caught sight of a picture that hung from the back.

In the picture, Travis had even shorter hair. The girl next to him had reddish-brown hair. They were both smiling as they sat on the hood of this car. She looked to be almost as tall as Travis. "She's pretty," I said.

His eyes cut over to the picture. "Her name is Angel."

My throat felt thick as I met his eyes. "Angel must be really special to you."

"She is."

"Did you shave your hair?"

"I used to, but she convinced me to let it grow out. Something about me looking like a biker dude."

I forced a laugh. "I can't see you riding any kind of bike. Is she your girlfriend?"

Travis looked straight ahead. "Let's talk about something else."

The absence of humor in his voice chilled my insides, despite the heat where my head rested on the window. Until now, he'd been easygoing and willing to be my friend no matter what I asked.

Maybe some subjects were off-limits.

* * * * *

For the next two hours, I said nothing. After twenty minutes on the road, Travis had turned up the radio. Beyond his occasional tap on the wheel when a fast song came on, he barely made a sound.

"I can't take this anymore," I said.

"What?" he asked with no emotion.

"The silence."

"The radio's been playing ever since we left the woods."

To either side of the highway were exits at regular intervals. Food. Hotels. Gas. The sun had faded to a soft beacon of light along the horizon. Streetlights were beginning to turn on. This Ferrari, despite the cramped interior, drove like it barely touched the road. I'd thought the low profile would mean we'd feel every bump. And the smell was nothing like exhaust. This is how Piper's car smelled when her stepdad first bought it.

Piper. I wondered if she knew I was missing by now. Had the cops started looking for my family yet? Was Coach Andrews okay and would he tell them the truth about Dad?

More importantly, how could I get Travis to explain his role in all of this? He seemed like a girl's best friend until I asked the wrong question. Then up went the wall.

"Are we going to drive all night?" I asked.

"Ready to stop?"

"I'm tired." Maybe I'd find a bed to sleep off this nonsense. In the morning, I'd wake up from this nightmare and everything would go back to normal. Except I didn't want normal anymore. I was out of Wynder and I never wanted to go back to that existence.

He checked his phone, which sat on the console between us. "Any suggestions?"

"Not a campground," I said.

"That narrows our options, but I'm hopeful." After fifteen more minutes of uncomfortable silence, Travis turned off the highway at an exit with tall hotels. He pulled up at the entrance to one at the edge of a golf course.

I counted seven stories of rooms that opened to the inside. Through the sliding glass doors, I spotted an elegant chandelier. "Are you joking? People like us don't stay in places like this."

He raised an eyebrow. "People like us? How much do you know about me?"

I reached for my door. "I saw the dump you lived in until this morning. Are you saying you could have afforded a place like this all along?"

"Get out of the car."

The edge of anger in his voice sent me stumbling to my feet with my purse and backpack in hand. The valet stopped halfway to me, scratching his head as Travis parked the car in a nearby spot. I wasn't an expert on cars, but his Ferrari had to be more expensive than most of the vehicles in this half-empty lot.

The valet retreated to his podium and nodded as Travis reached my side and escorted me through the glass doors. At the desk, the attendant surveyed my outfit and his, her face twisting into a smirk as her eyes met mine.

"Do you have any rooms?" Travis asked.

"Our standard rate for the night is two-ninety-nine. Two queen beds or one king."

Travis laid his arm across the counter like he owned the place and leaned closer to the attendant. Mandy was her name; her badge said guest services. "I don't want the standard room. I want the suite."

Her smirk disappeared. "Our suites come with full kitchens and two separate bedrooms. The rate for tonight is four-fifty."

"That would be great," he said. "My little sister likes her space."

I rolled my eyes and Mandy gave him a knowing look.

"Can I see some identification?" she asked. "And a credit card to secure the room?"

"No problem." Travis opened his wallet and handed her two cards.

Mandy typed on the computer, careful not to meet my eyes. When she'd finished with his I.D. and swiped the credit card, she handed both back. She also programmed two cards and handed them to Travis in a cream envelope. "Our restaurant is still open if you'd like a meal delivered to your room. Do you need to purchase any golf time?"

"Maybe tomorrow," he said.

On the elevator to our room, I thought of the two hundred dollars in my purse. "This place is expensive. I can pay for part of the room."

"Money is not an issue."

"Money is always an issue unless you're rich." I turned to him. "I'm sure you don't make boatloads of money working for… whoever it is you work for." I could have kicked myself for saying something that stupid.

"I make enough."

I didn't bother saying anything else until we found the room. As Mandy promised, this room contained a full kitchen and two separate bedrooms. "Why spend almost five hundred dollars on a room for one night?"

"Because the people on our trail will never look for us here."

"Why do you say that?"

"I'd never stay in a place like this."

"Except for tonight," I said, irritated by the tone of his voice.

"Enjoy it while you can." Travis tossed the two duffel bags on one of the beds. "Are you hungry?" He reached for a leather-bound folder on the desk near the TV. "Look this over and order whatever you want."

I put my purse and backpack on the other bed and took the folder from his hand. "This food costs more than what Dad gives me to live on for a week."

"For once enjoy it."

Shaking my head, I went to the window and looked out over the parking lot. "This whole day feels like a dream. I keep thinking I'll wake up at any moment. The fact that we're here together, in a hotel room, when I only met you last week…"

"Don't get any ideas that I might want… This is work

for me."

"You still haven't told me who you are. You said you work for someone who knew my dad from the Army."

"Let's order some food and then we'll talk." He picked up the phone and made an order to room service. When he'd finished his order for a fillet mignon, he motioned to me.

"Whatever you ordered," I said.

When he finished the order, Travis walked into his room and flipped on the light. Through the open door, I watched as he unzipped one of the duffel bags.

I thought of the woman from the motel. "What's in the bag? Body parts?"

He turned up the bag and dumped the contents on the bed. More black clothes, two more guns, a laptop. "Fresh out of toes. Want to see what's in the other bag?"

"Not really," I lied.

Travis waved me into his room. "It's all yours. Literally."

With shaking hands, I unzipped the bag. To my surprise, the bag held an array of clothes—jeans, t-shirts, even underwear in my size. "What is all of this?"

"I bought clothes for you. For the day it was time for you to run."

"How did you know I'd run away with you?" My head spun. "How did you know I'd need these clothes?"

"Part of my job."

"Did your job involve stalking me?" My voice shook. "Do you know where my dad is?"

"After everything that happened today, you're finally scared?"

I lifted a brand new pair of sneakers from the bag, with a price tag that made my eyes widen. In a fury, I threw the shoes at him. "Stay away from me," I yelled. Before he could respond, I ran into my room and locked the door.

For the next hour, I sat on the bed and wondered what to do next.

* * * * *

Staring at the walls of a fancy hotel room was nothing like watching rich people on TV. Instead of being excited about my first night outside of Wynder, I felt trapped. The room smelled sterile, reminding me of the hospital stay the night Mama died, despite the white satin comforter and fifteen pillows on the bed. Yes, I had my own bathroom with an assortment of soaps and lotions tucked neatly in a towel on the counter.

Wall-to-wall of this room was longer than our entire camper. The ceiling was higher, giving the effect of luxury with the ornate trim along the junction of the walls. A long window stretched from floor to ceiling with what appeared to be a balcony though the latch was locked in place. I slid the heavy curtains aside and looked for Travis's car in the parking lot.

Travis. He'd gone from the new guy I invited over to study for the physics test to a mystery that should have terrified me. I'd heard stories of girls disappearing after climbing in the wrong car. About ten years before, Wynder was home to a strangler who had most parents locking their doors and windows at all times.

Some part of me felt excitement at what might happen next. Some part of me felt dread for learning the truth about him. No guy at Palm County High had ever reached 'invite over after school' status. Instead of being a normal student, someone sent him to Wynder to keep me safe.

The black duffel bag was the strongest evidence yet. He'd planned for me to run away with him. If Piper could see me now, she'd give a lecture on how stupid I was to place my trust in someone I barely knew.

She'd ask if I'd lost my mind.

I'd think she was on to something.

A fist slammed against the door. "Your food is here," Travis said as if holding back a temper.

"I'm not hungry." What a lie. My stomach growled loud enough he probably heard it through the door.

"Rena, don't do this."

"Do what?" I asked. "Keep you out of my room? I have no intention of listening to any more of your lies."

He swore. "Open this door."

"No," I said. "If you want in, you'll have to break down the door."

"If I want… Do you hear yourself? What do you think is going on here? I picked you up at the school with one goal—to protect you. That's from anyone and anything that might cause you harm. Even yourself."

"I don't trust you."

"I thought you said we were friends," he yelled. "What happened to all of the progress we made?"

I walked to the door. "Is that what you want? A friend? Friends don't lie to each other. They don't act like stalkers."

"I never stalked you."

"You knew where I lived. You knew who my dad was. You bought a bag of clothes in my size just in case I ran away with you."

"Last time I checked, *I* ran away with you."

"You tricked me," I said. "I wanted to go back for the truck, but you said this was a one-way trip. I could be in Atlanta by now."

Travis hit the door with what sounded like his head. "I thought we could hang out," he said in a lowered voice.

"Let the heat die down. You probably think all of this is crazy, but I really wanted to get to know you."

"You already know all about me," I cried out. "Now I'm stuck with you."

"Is that how you feel? You're stuck with me?"

"I had no choice." Seething, I turned off the light and went to the bed, throwing back the comforter with a mixture of anger and sadness. I kicked off my shoes and climbed under the comforter, into the cold sheets. The sheets on my bunk had never made me shiver.

"Rena, no joke. You really should eat. I'll bring in the food and you don't have to look at me."

"Go away, Tony. Or Travis. Whoever the hell you are."

Travis swore under his breath and stomped across the floor. As I watched the light peeking from under the door, I wondered if Travis really would break the door down. A door slammed and the sound of Travis's shoes faded. That had to be the door to the hall, but where was he going?

And when would he be back?

I climbed from the bed and tiptoed through the darkness. One tug on the door handle proved it was locked. Travis kept a gun in his glove box. He drove a Ferrari instead of the old Nova he'd used to pick me up at school. He wasn't even a student; instead he worked for one of Dad's Army friends.

But what if his employer wasn't Dad's friend? From the moment we met, nothing about Travis was as it seemed, except for what he told me about his dad being a hunter. He taught him how to shoot. For some reason, that was the line that haunted me the most.

No doubt Travis could pick any lock. He'd be inside this room in seconds if he chose. How could I sleep while wondering if he was out there waiting?

I remembered Dad's multi-tool and reached for my purse at the edge of the bed. Slowly, I slid the zipper open. The first part I folded out was one of the knives. Careful not to slice my hand, I cut a sliver of material from the edge of my sheet. I felt around the nightstand until I found the TV remote.

Wrapping the remote in one end, I made a loop and double-knotted the fabric as Dad taught me to do back when Mama thought joining Girl Scouts would teach me survival skills. He'd laughed. If only Dad could see me now. I tied the other end of the fabric to the door handle and balanced the remote on the top ledge of the door frame.

If Travis came in, he'd better have another round of cussing ready.

Satisfied, I climbed back into the bed and marveled at how my entire body felt as if every ounce of energy had been drained. Even though my stomach growled, I closed my eyes and faded far from the hotel and worrying about Travis Payne.

* * * * *

Somewhere in my dreams, the smell of steak made my mouth water. I opened my eyes and tiptoed to the door where only darkness drew a line along the floor. Above, my makeshift alarm sat silent and ready.

On the table beside my bed sat a tray. I slid open the curtains for more light. The tray held a plate with a metal lid that opened to reveal the steak from my dreams. Next to the steak were potatoes and a piece of Texas toast.

Again, I checked the door. No way could Travis have opened the door and placed the remote back above without me hearing. He couldn't have closed the door.

And yet, here was a plate with food tempting me to eat.

It wasn't possible and yet there had to be a way. I crossed my legs and took a bite of the steak. Science told me this food couldn't be in my room. My stomach rumbled in appreciation.

I went to sleep with a full stomach and the vague sense that something had been wrong since the moment I met Travis. For the first time that night, I worried about waking up and facing him.

* * * * *

I opened my eyes to the trickle of light between the curtains. My eyes shot to the door where the remote still waited patiently for Travis. Next, I glanced at what remained of the food on my night stand. Goosebumps rose on my arms; I'd forgotten to turn down the air. I rose and walked to the window, sliding the curtains apart. Outside, the Ferrari waited in the morning heat. Beyond the parking lot, people drove carts toward the entrance to the golf course.

After removing the section of sheet and tossing the remote back on the nightstand, I slowly opened the door. On the long, plush couch in the living room sat Travis, eyes glued to the TV.

He looked up as I walked in and turned down the TV, which showed a commercial for cereal. "I'm sorry about last night."

"Thanks for dinner."

Travis straightened and slid away the bag that sat to his side. He motioned for me to sit, but I held back.

"I won't bite, though after how I yelled last night you're probably thinking I might."

I took a deep breath and walked to the couch. Instead

of sitting next to him, I moved the bag between us. "How did you get in my room?"

"You don't really want to know."

"Did you come through the door?" My voice rose. "No more lies, Travis. If you want us to be friends, you've got to trust me with the truth."

"No."

"How did you get in?"

"What if I tell you I have a power that allowed me to send the food in without opening the door?"

"A power?" I asked. "Like magic?"

"Not exactly."

"I'd say you were still lying. You know I don't believe in anything without a scientific explanation."

He leaned forward. "What if you learned that science can't explain everything? Would you run out of here in a panic?"

I shook my head. "You're wrong. Science *can* explain everything."

"Why are you so stuck on science?"

"Science is my comfort zone. I have to know that everything can be explained."

"Why?"

"Because," I said, "it explains why the rain falls and the moon doesn't spin out of control. It shows us how to make this world better. And it proves that Mama dying wasn't just the senseless act of a man who had too much to drink and climbed behind the wheel. Everyone dies."

He sighed. "I came through the window. Check the lock—it's still open."

The show returned on the TV, an old episode of *MacGyver*. Travis reached for the remote.

"Don't change it. I've always liked this show."

"You've watched *MacGyver*?"

"My dad always watched reruns of *MacGyver* and *The A-Team*."

"So did mine when I was a kid."

For the rest of the show, we watched in silence. When the credits finally rolled, Travis got up and returned with two bottles of water.

I took the bottle he offered. "Tell me the truth. Why did you pick me up from the school?"

Travis lifted the remote and turned off the TV. "Believe me when I say lying to you is not something I enjoy."

"Go on."

"If at any point I start to freak you out, stop me. I want us to be friends. If nothing else, I want you to feel comfortable talking to me. I have no intention of hurting you." He took a deep breath. "If I didn't grab you from school yesterday, the man you described—"

"Max."

He nodded. "Max would have taken you to a black car with tinted windows no one could see through. His next stop would have been a plane owned by a man named Louis Castillo. Once that plane was airborne, any chance of ever finding you would have disappeared. My job was to keep that from happening."

"What job?"

"I'm an agent for the government."

"Like an F.B.I. agent?"

"Kind of," he said. "My mission in Wynder was to find you and protect you."

"Do you know my dad?"

Travis watched me as if trying to figure out what to say next. "He and my dad were partners years ago."

"Dad worked for this agency? Before or after the Army?"

"After. I knew him up until he retired. That's when he moved to Florida."

"You said you were working for someone who knew Dad."

"Our agency's director. She knew Donald Mason for years. He saved her life twice."

I laughed. "Your director is a woman?"

"What's wrong with that?"

"Nothing, just unexpected. How do I know your name is really Travis Payne?"

He opened his wallet and handed me a driver's license. Next to his picture was the name Travis Payne. The license bore the logo for the state of Georgia.

I looked at him and then at the picture. "Don't you have a middle name?"

"No."

"Don't you think that's weird?"

"My parents had issues. Nothing they did was normal."

I gasped when I noticed his birthday. Just to be sure, I counted the years on both hands. "You're twenty-one?"

He drew a long breath. "That's right."

"You attended high school as a senior and you've been out of school since—"

"I never went to a public school. All of my education was handled by the agency, which is where I grew up after my dad disappeared."

"Disappeared?" I asked.

"During a mission in New York. They found his car and his phone. That was twelve years ago."

"You said you lost your dad when you were nine."

"I also said I don't enjoy lying to you. Please don't make this harder than it has to be."

I handed the license to Travis. In the space of our

conversation, he'd managed to move the bag and slide close enough for his knee to touch mine. "What do we do now?" I asked.

"You said you wanted to go to Atlanta."

"That's where Dad told me to go." While hiding the fact I was looking for a woman named Sylvia Greene. "A man named Louis kidnapped him. He told me never trust Louis Castillo."

Travis rubbed his chin, rough with stubble. "Are you sure he didn't say anything else?"

I shook my head and looked down at my hands. "You said your dad and mine were partners at this agency. The F.B.I., right?"

"You said F.B.I. I didn't agree or disagree."

"How many government agencies are there?"

"Hundreds." He laughed. "But don't make me name them all. I'd probably fail that quiz too."

Something still bothered me about Travis's dad. "You said your dad disappeared."

"When I was nine. The agency pretty much raised me after that."

"But he didn't die."

He shook his head. "No one ever found a body. Maybe science can't explain why, but I have a feeling he's still alive."

"Where do you think he's been all these years?"

"I'm not sure, but I won't stop until I have justice for what happened. One man saw my dad the night he disappeared. When I find that man, I'll find answers."

"You know who it was?"

"Donald Mason."

CHAPTER NINE

Travis refused to answer questions about my dad until we were in the Ferrari and headed for the highway. I didn't argue when he threw me the duffel bag and insisted I get dressed. The shirt I chose fit me perfectly and the jeans flared around the ankles like the ones I normally wore to school. Except those jeans were from a thrift store and these still had the original tags.

The way Travis chose all the right sizes didn't put me at ease.

Finally, when we were back on the interstate, Travis set the cruise control and relaxed in his seat. A steady stream of cars passed the Ferrari as we drove toward the sunlight.

"Why set the cruise control below the speed limit?"

"In a hurry?" he asked.

"Just wondering why you have such a fast car when you don't like to go fast."

"Who said I don't like going fast?" His phone vibrated and a message came up on the radio's screen. He quickly cleared the message.

"Someone looking for you?"

"It was a reminder for the morning meeting. Our director expects everyone to attend, even when working a remote case."

"Do you need to pull over and call in?"

Travis glanced at his watch and seemed to consider. "I think she'll forgive me this time."

"Tell me more about my dad. You said he worked for this agency? How long?"

"Years. He had a rough mission while in Iraq most wouldn't have survived. He caught the attention of the director."

"The woman you mentioned?"

"Back then, the director was a man. He hired your father for a government agency that most people have never heard of."

I laughed. "A secret government agency? This keeps getting better."

"Don't laugh. Half the planet would be dead right now if it wasn't for this secret agency. We've saved many of Earth's citizens."

"Secret like double-oh-seven? You know how crazy this sounds? Earth's citizens. Travis, this isn't a movie."

Travis set his jaw. "Laugh all you want. My job is the reason people can sleep soundly at night, even if they never know why."

"What's the name of this agency?"

"Earth Under Fire."

"Now I know you're not one of the terrorists." I laughed between each word. "They'd never tell me a story that silly. What kind of name is Earth Under Fire?"

"You said you trusted me."

"That was before you told me you were a secret government agent. I'm going to start calling you double-oh-seven. At least until I meet someone who can confirm your story."

He looked my way. "That could be arranged. Will it help us be friends?"

"You said this mission was to be keep me from being kidnapped by terrorists. Why is us being friends so important?"

With a glance in the mirror, Travis went ghost-white. "Rena."

"What?" I asked, trying to calm my laughter.

"Grab my gun from the glove box."

Instantly, the laughter died. I looked over my shoulder. Two black cars were approaching from either side. I opened the box and pulled out the gun, this time grabbing the handle with my full hand. "Here."

He took the gun from my hand and tapped the gas, which slowed the car. The other cars crept closer.

"How did they find us?" I asked.

"I'm not sure, but I have a plan ready for them. Is your seatbelt on?"

Before I could answer, Travis floored the car and began weaving between the lanes as he passed the chain of cars and trucks in front of us. He swung in between two semis with barely enough room to squeeze our little car. Looking up at the guard that kept us from sliding under the truck made my stomach turn.

Travis placed a gloved hand on mine. "Are you going to be sick?"

"Afraid I'll ruin your car?"

"Rena, get down."

As soon as his words were out, glass shattered behind us. Air rushed in, an explosion of heat within our envelope of comfort. Travis swerved into another lane as one of the black cars made his same move between the semis. With a twist of the wheel, we slid onto the shoulder, but Travis immediately tugged us back into traffic.

"We've got to get out of this traffic." He slid a finger across the screen of his phone and tapped a button. "Pull up this map and see what kind of roads are up ahead. We need an exit with a good road and some wide-open space."

My hands shook as I scrolled through the roads. "Take exit fifty-five. It leads to a highway that heads north." To my left was a sign that showed exit forty-six.

"I don't think we can make it nine miles." Travis swerved toward the exit and both cars followed. "The last thing we need to do is cause someone to wreck on this highway."

I thought back to the accident. "That would bad. If we hurt someone…"

Travis took the exit ramp at three times the speed limit. A series of lights flashed as he rounded a curve. The sign above said, 'If lights are flashing, you're going too fast.'

"Grab the wheel." As we came to a stop at a red light with cars across all lanes, he reached out the window and fired at both of the cars. "Put your head down. *Now*." Travis fired six shots in total and ducked back in the car. He took the steering wheel and eased over the raised divider to our right. This time his car did scrape and he cringed.

"I knew you were worried about this car."

"How can you still not be afraid? People are shooting at us."

"And you're shooting back. I'm just hoping you're the better shot."

When he'd cut through the grass and landed us back on the pavement, I didn't have much time to look for the cars. Travis floored the accelerator, sending me back against the seat. I reached for the seatbelt, which had locked in a choking position.

"Don't take that off yet."

"I've got to fix this if you want me to breathe."

Travis took his foot off the gas as I unhooked the belt and loosened the strap before re-clicking the buckle. In the mirror to my side, the two cars approached as if we were barely moving. "Hurry up," I screamed.

"Hold on." Again, he floored the accelerator, then slammed the brakes in time to make a sharp turn and propel us through the back parking lot of a huge shopping center.

I noticed the empty mirror and glanced over my shoulder. "You lost them."

Travis pointed behind one of the larger stores, at two rows of semi-trailers. He slowed and cut between the trucks. "No. No." He seemed to be scoping out the contents of the few trailers that were open. Finally, we reached a trailer with only one row of cardboard boxes at the back. "That's a roger."

"You're going to hide us in the trailer? What if it leaves the parking lot with us?"

"We'll save on gas."

Travis made a circle, leaving enough room between our car and the truck to get a running start. He hit the gas and we bounced as the tires hit the ramp, sliding slightly to the side before gripping the top and taking us into the trailer. After turning the car off, he raced to the back of the trailer and closed the doors.

"How did you get those doors to close from the inside?" I asked when he returned to the car.

"Practice. I've been at this agent gig for a long time. Well, what do you think of our new hideout? You didn't seem to like the hotel."

"It's dark in here," I said. "And it smells like

popcorn."

"Probably a delivery for the movie theater at the end of the shopping center." Travis touched his phone and the screen lit up his face. He opened the glove box and put his gun away. "At least we won't have to go out for lunch."

"This is your idea of keeping me safe?"

He smiled. "Looks like we'll have time to become friends after all."

* * * * *

For hours we talked about everything but what had happened in the last two days. Travis wanted to know the kind of music I liked.

"Fast," I said. "I don't like to listen to anything that makes me cry. Life is too short." And it made me think about Mama.

He wanted to know all about my childhood and what it felt like growing up in a campground. Surprisingly, Travis seemed open in describing his experiences growing up on a government base. Maybe he made up the story for my own benefit, but the thing that touched me the most was how lonely he sounded. Sure, there were people everywhere. As in my life, he'd known what was expected of him and never argued, like all the times I fed Alfie and got him through a bath before bedtime.

His life sounded secure… a world full of grown-ups all telling him what to do when no one had a clue what kids on the outside did for fun. No other children lived at the base for most of his teen years. He only interacted with people his age when out for a training mission. Even then, no one Travis met knew who he really was. I wondered if I was getting a rare glimpse inside the head of the real Travis Payne. Or maybe it was all an act.

Still, the pain in his voice, the longing that I recognized from the deepest part of my soul felt real. Despite the gloves he never took off, I wanted to touch his hand. If only I could feel his skin against mine, maybe I'd know for sure he meant every word.

Somehow, figuring out Travis Payne had become the center of my world. I never planned for him to weasel his way into my thoughts. Nor could I figure out the exact moment he locked himself in place. Every time Piper had been 'in love' with a new guy after less than a week, I'd laughed and told myself I'd never be so stupid. Even a month or two seemed ridiculous. You didn't find the kind of love my parents had on a shelf at the store. You couldn't buy it and you definitely couldn't grow the seeds in a matter of days.

And yet, there we were, sitting side-by-side in a sports car with a busted back window, talking in the warm darkness of a trailer. As if the world could stay away forever.

The sounds of doors opening came from behind us, along with a light that crawled over our car. Travis opened his door and jumped to his feet next to the car.

"There they are," said a male voice.

"Stay here." Travis walked to the back of the trailer and faced the two men who'd climbed inside, both holding a gun.

"Max wants to see you," the man to Travis's left said.

"This isn't a good time," Travis said.

"If I kill you, it might get better." The man waved a gun and the other approached the car to my side.

"Get out, sweetheart," he said.

I climbed from the car and he grabbed a fist of my hair. "No running away."

"She's cooperating," Travis said. "Take us to Max. I'm

sure he doesn't want to see her hurt."

The man, whose breath made me choke, released my hair and shoved me forward. "Keep walking and don't look back."

I met Travis's eyes as I reached the back of the trailer. He nodded toward the exit. "Just do what they say and don't hide your fear."

Easier said than done, I thought. The men forced us down the trailer's ramp and across the parking lot. Sweat poured down my face from the short walk to the back entrance of a store. Inside, I realized this wasn't a store yet; it was more of a renovation project. Only a few lights overhead glowed. Shelves to either side of the room were covered with tarps. Paint buckets and crusty brushes lined a tarp at the center of the room.

"Agent Payne."

I spun to see Max leaning against a scaffold, watching us with a smile like a viper ready to strike. "He knows you?" I asked Travis.

"He knows my last name," Travis said. "That's all he knows about me."

"I wouldn't bet on that." Max looked over me. "Glad to see you're still alive. You should have taken the gun I offered."

"I don't need your gun," I said. Probably couldn't shoot straight if I tried. "Where is my dad?"

"Yeah," Max said, "about that. Louis wasn't happy when he realized Donald lied about you. He decided to take a fishing trip."

"Fishing?" I asked.

"You don't want to know." Travis reached behind his back and pulled out his gun, pointing the barrel at Max.

Max merely laughed and glanced at the two men who wore looks of shock. "Can't find good help anywhere. Did you even bother to check him?"

"We roughed him up good. That gun wasn't in his pants."

Thinking back, I couldn't remember Travis grabbing the gun. After we'd ended up at the trailer, he'd placed the gun back in the glove box. As much as that fact bothered me, his words bothered me more. I turned to Travis. "You never told me you knew Max."

"Everyone at the agency knows Max the Detonator. He's number fifty-two on the list."

"Come on, man," Max said. "I thought I'd be in the forties by now."

"What kind of list?" I asked.

"The world's most powerful people. The agency I work for monitors people all over the world with special gifts. If you can imagine a power, we've seen it."

"Like superhero powers?" My skepticism kicked in. "You know I don't believe—"

"If you've ever read the comics," Travis said, "you've been exposed to the truth. People with special powers live all around us. That's the purpose of my agency—to track those with powers and protect all those without."

I turned to Max. "Why are you on that list?"

Travis frowned. "Max likes to set off bombs."

"That's not all I like to do," Max said. "I also get off on hunting down anyone worth tracking. You, my dear, have been an interesting target. When Louis asked me to take this job, I didn't hesitate."

"Rena," Travis said, "get down."

I hit the floor as Travis raised the gun and fired. First, he brought Max's helpers to their knees. Then he fired above Max's head and the scaffold toppled, dropping several cans of paint, one of which hit Max.

Anger flashed in Max's eyes. "I respect no one who

interferes with the hunt." He reached for Travis, but Travis spun and hit him over the head with the gun. Max fell forward, into a can which flipped over and spread purple paint across the floor.

Travis put his gun in his pants and grabbed a stack of tie-down wraps near the paint. He looped three of the tie-downs around Max's wrist, which brought back the memory of Dad wrapping my hands with duct tape. I looked around the room and found a silver roll on the floor near the glass front windows. People walked down the sidewalk in front of the windows, never bothering to glance into the frosty glass.

I handed the roll to Travis. "This will do a better job."

He raised an eyebrow but took the tape without a word. He wrapped Max's wrists with the same precision Dad used to wrap mine. Travis then wrapped the wrists of the other two men; one groaned but didn't have the strength to fight.

"Payne," Max growled, "this isn't right and you know it. That agency of yours trumped up charges to keep me locked away."

Travis stepped back to survey his work. "They do take repeat offenders seriously."

"I have rights, just like any other citizen of this country. If Noah were still alive—"

"Don't bring my father into this," Travis said through gritted teeth. He drew his gun.

"Noah Payne stood up for what was right, even for those with powers." Max looked at Travis's gloved hands. "It's a good thing for you he set a high standard."

"Shut up about my father." Travis stormed out of the room.

I followed him into the store's back room. "You never told me why you don't take off your gloves."

"I did tell you. Skin allergies."

"I thought we agreed to be honest."

"Yes," Max yelled in a fit of laughter, "tell her about your hands."

Travis stuck his head inside the room and raised the gun. "I didn't ask for your opinion."

"Opinions are like assholes," Max said. "You should know."

"You should do this for a living," Travis said. "Give up world domination and go after a challenging career as a stand-up comic."

Max's eyes shifted over me. "We have your brother. If you run, my counterpart has orders to kill him."

"He's eight years old," I said. "You'd kill a kid?"

Max smiled. "I don't discriminate."

"You don't have him," Travis said.

"How would you know?" Max asked.

I glanced at the concern in Travis's eyes. Did he know where my brother was? I wanted to ask, but I didn't trust my shaking voice. Instead, I fled to the back of the store. Tears burned in my eyes as I considered Travis might still be lying. He'd never told me he actually knew Max.

Travis had tried discussing special powers that morning and I'd blown him off. He'd thrown around the suggestion he'd used a power to get my food into the room. I didn't believe him, of course. That would go against everything science had taught me.

Now Travis works for an agency that monitors people with powers. Comic book type powers. Max's performance only seemed to validate his words. Had everyone lost their minds?

Behind me were Travis's soft steps.

I spun to face him. "Do you know where Alfie is?"

"Don't listen to Max. He's powerful, but he doesn't

have your brother."

"How can you know for sure?"

His eyes met mine, those green pools that seemed to calm me. "Do you believe me about the powers?"

"I don't know. I haven't seen any proof."

"You've seen more than you realize." He moved closer. "Rena, I need you to trust me."

I looked at his lips with the crazy idea he should kiss me. Or I should kiss him. I stood on my toes and leaned against his chest.

For a full minute he stood, close enough I could feel his short breaths on my skin. My stomach burned, sending heat to the tips of my fingers. My body shook with an electricity that I'd never anticipated feeling around any person, much less Travis. He'd lied. He'd studied my most intimate details, trying to get into my head.

And here he was. He'd bypassed my head and went straight for the heart, which pounded as his lips almost touched mine. If going crazy felt this amazing, I wondered why more people weren't locked away.

He pulled back. "I can't do this."

My throat burned as I fought the tears. "Why?"

"Because…" He groaned. "I can't think of a good way to answer you."

"Do you hate me that much? Is it because of my father?"

"No."

"Why won't you touch me?"

"I have a special power," he finally said, in a voice that floated through the air like a gentle breeze. "More like a curse."

"What do you mean, you have a special power?"

"You know, one of those things your science can't explain?"

"What kind of power?"

"When I touch a person's skin… Maybe it would be better to show you."

Travis turned and walked back into the store. He kneeled next to Max and took off his glove. Max's smile disappeared. He grabbed the man's arm above his wrist.

Max screamed in agony as a huge welt appeared on his skin, fanning out the longer Travis held him.

"One, two, three," Travis counted and released Max's arm.

Jerking away from him, Max crawled across the floor in an effort to escape. "Stay away," he said in a voice that sounded more like a pig squealing.

Travis stood. "There's your proof. Skin allergies."

I stared in disbelief. "You burned his skin."

"My skin secretes a chemical like the acid in your stomach. It doesn't take long to burn through human skin, which is why I always wear the gloves. Imagine if I shook your hand without them."

"You could have burned me."

"Thirty seconds and I could have killed you."

I backed away from him. "Why are you doing this?"

He replaced the glove and grabbed my arm, pulling me through the back of the store and into the bright sunlight.

"Let me go," I said.

Although I fought his grip, Travis didn't release me. "For the short time we've known each other, I've felt normal. I wanted to hang onto that…" He sighed. "Now you'll watch me like everyone else and think about what kind of freak I am."

The pain in his words stopped me from fighting. "I'll never think of you as a freak."

Behind us, the building burst into flames, shaking the

ground beneath our feet. Travis's eyes never left mine.

"What just happened?" I asked.

"Max must have found a way to cut through the tape. We've got to get out of here." Travis ran to the truck and climbed inside.

I followed, dropping into my seat as the car roared to life. He backed us out of the truck and down the ramp into the parking lot. Sirens sounded in the distance. Flames rose from the section of the building with the abandoned store. Part of the roof collapsed, sending sparks dancing through the air like a circus show.

Travis typed a text on his phone before hitting the gas and driving past a group of people watching the front of the store in horror. A man took a video of the blaze with his phone, but Max and his men were nowhere to be seen.

Neither of us spoke until our car cruised along the highway. "Do you think Max is following us?" I asked.

Travis glanced in his mirror. "I hope not, but I sent a message for backup. Someone from the agency will come to help clean up the mess. Max will be on everyone's radar."

"Do you think everyone made it out of the store alive?"

"Unfortunately, yes. You do understand what Max meant about being a hunter? Once you're on his radar it's either him or you. Eventually you living will probably mean him dying."

"Doesn't sound like I have much of a choice." After we drove for several minutes in silence, I turned to Travis. "Tell me about your dad."

He glanced in the mirror again and cleared his throat. "My mother never had a power. She died when I was three and there was no way to save her."

"I'm sorry."

Travis nodded. "After she died, my dad never stayed away for more than two days at a time. He and Donald were close. I used to watch TV while they sat up talking late into the night. I still remember the taste in my mouth when I stole a sip of the whiskey they drank. Dad laughed when he found out why I felt sick."

"What do you remember from the night he disappeared?"

"Not much. He tucked me in and wanted to read me a book, even though it had been years since he'd done that. He mentioned going to see his old friend, Donald Mason. Then he handed me a coin and did the same magic trick your father taught me years ago. Only he was faster, and I really believed the way he made the coin disappear was magic."

I lifted a quarter from one of the cup holders and flipped it over in my hand. "Is this the one?"

He looked at the quarter and nodded. "The next day, he never returned. A week later, someone from the agency found his car on a deserted road in New York. His keys were still in the ignition and his cell phone sat on the dash, unused since the night he left. After twelve years, he's still listed as M.I.A. Not wounded, not dead, but missing in action. Those three letters have eaten me away inside ever since."

In his eyes, I recognized the loneliness I felt after Mama died. "You had nowhere to go."

"I had the agency. The director kept me there and raised me like her own son. Other agents were jealous when she allowed me to start training earlier than anyone had before." He closed his eyes. "I learned to fight. I perfected my aim. And I spent my nights dreaming of the day I'd get revenge."

"Revenge?"

His eyes opened wide. "Look, I didn't mean—"

"Are you after my father?" I asked. "Is that why you were at the school?"

"I was at the school because of you."

"Because a terrorist group would have kidnapped me like they took my dad, right? But you were there to fight. You alone."

"The director thought I could handle the job."

"What did my dad do to make a group of terrorists mad?"

"He protected your mother."

"What does she have to do with anything?"

"What do you remember about her?" he asked.

"I was six when my parents got married and Mama moved us to Florida. Mama told me Donald Mason was my father, but I was never sure. He took care of me back then and that's all that mattered."

"Do you remember the night your mother died?"

"Of course. It was only three years ago."

"Can you tell me what happened?"

"Dad drove us to eat after church. A new buffet restaurant had opened downtown and Mama insisted on trying it, even though Dad hated to eat out. They argued. I put my earbuds in so I didn't hear them fight. They rarely ever fought but, when they did, I always got worried."

"Worried about what?"

"That Mama would pack me up and leave. I overheard them one night back when I was in elementary school. Dad wanted to move and Mama said there was nowhere left for us to go. I decided she must have been thinking about leaving. I mean, we moved there when I was six. I cried to Dad and begged him to make Mama stay. He promised to make her stay."

"What about your brother?"

"After Alfie was born, I didn't worry as much about leaving. We had the most boring life filled with Mama's cooking and Dad's talent for fixing everything and I loved it. I swore I'd never leave Wynder. Ever."

"But that changed," he said.

"A drunk driver hit our car. I woke up in the hospital with a broken hip. The accident twisted Dad's hand into a bloody mess. He wouldn't let any of the doctors touch his hand until after they worked on Mama. After that night, Dad said he'd never buy another car. He bought a huge truck and taught me to drive it as soon as I was old enough."

"I'm surprised he let you drive at all."

"He always told me I couldn't live in fear. He's the one who made me drive. I tried to tell him no, but then he turned into a drunk and I had to…"

"Had to what?"

"Drive everywhere. The car wreck became a fear of mine, but he made me face it. He's always made me face every fear and find a way to stay strong."

Travis cleared his throat. "Years ago, there was a woman on the list with a power the agency had never seen. Your dad and mine were assigned to protect her. She was powerful—top five."

"Wow, top five? What happened to her?"

"She died eighteen years ago." Travis handed me a picture. "Her name was Rosanna."

Rosanna. She'd died by my father's hands, according to Louis, if this was the same Rosanna. Her long hair glowed with a brilliance that still took my breath away.

But how could she have died all those years ago? The woman in the picture raised me. "Are you sure this is Rosanna?"

"You recognize her, don't you?"

"Yes," I whispered. "This is my mom."

CHAPTER TEN

When I woke and stretched, the sun had drifted lower in the sky and now glowed in the mirrors. "My mother had a power," I whispered as if merely saying the words might convince me.

"Yes," Travis said. "Enjoy your nap?"

How could he act like my life hadn't changed with learning the truth? "Is all of this normal for you? Guns, special powers, bad guys chasing us…"

He smiled. "You have no idea. I've learned to play it cool, even if I don't feel that way. Since you only believe in science, and we've already established you have no fear, playing it cool should be easy."

Maybe he was right. I'd have to think of this logically, even if my mother having a power didn't fit with any logic. I glanced in my mirror. No black cars. "I guess riding makes me tired. I could drive."

"As tempting as that sounds, I think it's best I stay in this seat."

I thought about the scene with Max, how he'd known Travis and his father. "If you were watching me at the campground, why not grab me after Dad left? Why wait until I showed up at school?"

Travis shifted in his seat. "Because I didn't know your dad left."

I glared at him. "If you're such a great agent, how did you not know?"

"I've watched you for four weeks, Rena. Every night except for Sunday."

"Why not Sunday?"

"Because I went to my sister's wedding on Sunday. That night, I drank until I couldn't walk straight and ended up passing out in a hotel. When you saw me at the school, I was getting a late pass."

My voice cracked. "You drink?"

He ran a hand over his hair. "Not often. Look, I shouldn't have told you…"

"I can't be around you if you drink."

"But—"

"No." I wiped a tear from the corner of my eye. "Alcohol has made my life hell."

"There's nothing wrong with drinking. I'm twenty-one for god's sake. It's when all you can do is drink… I know about your dad's drinking. I can't say I understand him wasting his life away, but it's his choice. I'll never let drinking become that important. I promise."

Something in the way he said those last two words brought another tear. I wanted to believe Travis, even tell him so, but I turned to the window and tried to wipe my eyes with all the privacy a tiny sports car could offer.

I was used to tiny. Living in a camper had shown me how to do more with less. At that moment, all I wished for was more space between us.

"You asked about your mother's power."

Quickly, I wiped my nose and turned back to him. "What was it?"

"Rosanna had the power to stop a nuclear bomb or cause one."

"Nuclear… bomb?" My eyes doubled in size. "Did you say bomb?"

"Yes, as in a nuclear explosion."

"How is that possible?"

"I'm not the best one to explain the science of how Rosanna's power worked, but I've seen pictures."

Rosanna. Mama had always gone by the name Jackie. "It seems strange to hear that name. Are you sure this Rosanna and my mother were the same person?"

"They both knew Donald Mason," he said dryly, "which raises the odds."

"What did her power look like?"

Travis pointed to the glove box. "Reach inside and open the folder."

I opened the box and a manila folder sat under Travis's gun. "That folder wasn't here before."

"Are you sure?"

Thinking back to the confrontation with Max, I peered at the gun. "How did you get the gun out of here?"

"What do you mean?" he asked.

"Back in the store, you pulled the gun from the back of your jeans. When you left me in the trailer, you never took the gun out of the box. Last time you asked me to grab it for you. I would remember if you took it out."

"You're rambling. Is there something you want to know?"

"How did you do it?"

"Me explaining would collapse your belief in science like a house of cards. Open the folder."

Arguing with Travis Payne was pointless. I sighed and opened the folder, which showed more pictures of Mama, but this time with black hair. She couldn't have been much older than me.

"She was twenty when the agency saved her," he said as if reading my mind.

"Saved her from what?"

"A terrorist group called the Black Dawn. Louis Castillo was their leader. He manipulated Rosanna into using her power to threaten governments around the world. He took the phrase 'for the people' to a whole new level."

I thumbed through the folder, which held reports and also included a picture of my father next to Rosanna. To her other side stood a man with the same soft brown hair as Travis.

"My dad," Travis said. "Their job was to keep Rosanna safe while the doctors found a way to control her power."

On the next page was a picture of a woman's hands which glowed with blue. I thought of the day in the cafeteria when blue appeared in my hands. For the briefest of moments, I imagined inheriting this power from her. Something that would connect us forever. Then I thought of the cold reality, of seeing the blue laser light dance across the wall. Wanting to be like her was impossible and wishing didn't make it any more likely. I never believed people could have special powers before meeting Travis.

"She always had this power?" I asked.

"She got it around her eighteenth birthday."

I closed the folder. "My friend Piper believes in that stuff but not me."

"Let me guess. Blue sparkles shooting out of your hands goes against science."

"Science has never let me down. People don't have magical powers."

"Who said anything about magic? Do you think magic

is the reason I burn people by touching their skin?"

"Weren't you born with this power? You said your mom didn't have a power, but I figured your dad—"

"I was given this power, which is where the science part comes in. The person who had this power wanted to get rid of it and an expert in genetics found a way to make that happen. Turns out, I ended up in a coma and everyone thought I was brain dead."

"How did you end up in a coma?"

"I was shot, fell off a bridge, and was under water for thirty minutes."

My eyebrows shot up. "You're lucky to be alive."

"That's what everyone keeps telling me, but some days I wonder. Since I was brain dead, guess who drew the short straw when it was time to pick another host for this power."

"Can you give the power to someone else?"

"Maybe, but it's not as easy as it sounds. First, I'd have to find someone willing to take on a curse that means not touching anyone ever. Second, I'd have to find someone who could perform the procedure."

"What about the person who gave you this curse?" I asked.

"She died."

"Oh."

"See my problem?"

"If this power really does exist, is there a way I could have inherited what Mama had?"

"You have the main indicator—lack of fear."

"What happened to Rosanna?"

"Some say she disappeared. Others believe she died. It appears she might have faked her own death and changed her name to stay with your dad. After he retired from the agency, he went to Florida and married her a month later.

Different name and different look, but it could have been the same woman."

"You think they were able to fool everyone at a government agency?"

"Maybe not everyone." Travis moved the car into an exit lane leading to a rest area. "Stranger things have happened."

When we'd finished at the rest area, he insisted on walking a path down to a lake at the edge of the grass. "Not everyone was thrilled with Rosanna's power," he said. "Many people feared her."

"Did she ever hurt anyone?"

"She never caused a major nuclear event. She helped us avoid several."

"Then she's a hero."

"A hero who may have realized that kind of life isn't for everyone. Especially not for raising a family. It's definitely not free."

I watched as several ducks fought over a loaf of bread someone had tossed near the shore. "Does anyone know about me and Alfie?"

"Only a few. Unlike you, most people are naturally afraid. They'll want to know how to keep you in check if this power does appear."

"Keep me in check? Max mentioned being locked up because of his power."

"Comes with the territory. If you have the power, it's up to you to show the agency you're not a threat."

"You have a power, right?" I asked. "And you work for the agency."

"So do others, plus the agency knows my history. Not many people know you exist. When the truth gets out, things will get interesting."

"But you'll be there with me, right?"

He nodded. "Nothing could make me leave your side."

* * * * *

After another nap, I woke to see signs for Savannah. Next to me, Travis sat stretched out with the cruise control on. A wire hung from his ear and he nodded his head to an invisible beat.

"You can turn up the radio."

He pulled out the earbud. "Thought I'd let you get caught up on your sleep. Probably didn't rest in the hotel last night."

"Are we going to Savannah?"

"Yeah, why?"

"I thought we were going to Atlanta."

Travis shrugged. "We'll get there eventually. I think you still have doubts about trusting me."

"Can you blame me?"

"No," he said with a laugh. "I want you to meet someone in Savannah. Maybe she can convince you to trust me."

"I've been thinking about what you said, about Rosanna's powers. If this really was my mom, maybe I did inherit her power. You said the main indicator was no fear." I took a deep breath and exhaled. "I've always been fearless."

"Doesn't this go against science?"

I held out my hand and concentrated. Inside, I felt a rush of excitement at the prospect of having a power. Her power. This would make me different. Special. However, nothing blue came from any part of my hand. "Nothing happened."

"Good thing. The warranty on this car doesn't cover

nuclear explosion."

My cheeks reddened. "I guess that was a bad idea."

"I'm all for figuring out your power, but there's a huge difference between burning someone's skin and blowing up half the state."

"How did Mama's power work?"

"According to the file, the only way to access this power was to—" His eyes stopped on the rear-view mirror.

"What?"

"We've got a tail."

I glanced in the side mirror but couldn't see any black cars. "Are you sure?"

"Burgundy Blazer, six o'clock."

The Blazer stole through traffic and ended up a car-length behind us. "You think that's Max? Or could it be Louis?"

"Louis would never drive himself. He would get someone from the embassy to drive him."

"He was alone the night he came to the camper."

Travis shot me a sideways glance. "How did you hide from him?"

I thought of the wooden bin under the bench seat at the table. Of the smell of mothballs and the sensation of tiny legs crawling through my hair. I licked my lips, remembering the sticky film left from the tape. "Dad knew Louis was coming. He hid me beneath the table."

"Beneath?"

"Campers are full of places to hide. I heard them mention the embassy. He accused my dad of killing someone he cared about. Her name was Rosanna."

Travis bounced between cars as he tried to distance us from the Blazer. "What else did he say about her?"

"Nothing other than how they found a body that

couldn't be her. She had a purple rose tattoo on her ankle."

"Do you remember your mom having a rose tattoo?"

"No. His voice sounded foreign, with a rhythm like poetry."

"Sounds like Castillo."

"Maybe they were talking about a different Rosanna." Even as I said the words, the thought of this Louis knowing Mama made my skin crawl. He'd wanted to see me…

Travis left the highway at an exit for Savannah. The Blazer kept its distance, but didn't hesitate to take the same turns we made.

"Can you lose him?" I asked.

I thought about Alfie, about how Dad told me he'd be safe. "What about how Max threatened Alfie? Do you think he'd really try to kill my little brother?"

He sped through a red light that left the Blazer stuck between a power truck and school bus. As soon as we were out of sight, Travis turned down a road that led to a pier. "No one will take a chance on killing him, not when he could have your mother's power one day. I'm sure he's in a room filled with video games and ice cream. Now your father, on the other hand, probably isn't faring so well."

The idea Louis might kill Dad made me cringe. "What will they do to him?"

"What won't they do to him? He was an agent, a damn good one who made many enemies over the years. Louis likely blames Mason for your mother's death."

I grabbed Travis's arm. "How do you know that?"

He hesitated. "You told me, remember?"

"Why did Louis care if my mother died?"

"He needed her power to fight the governments of the world. Without her, he wasn't even a good terrorist."

Travis approached the pier. "You know Max will

follow this car, no matter what happens." He glanced in the mirror. "He'll come around that corner at any moment."

I pulled my purse strap over my head. "What do you have in mind?"

"A distraction. When I tell you, jump out of the car."

"Wait, what?"

"No fear, remember?" He slammed the gas and we flew toward the pier. The force threw me back against the seat. My heart pounded as the last rays of light glimmered on the water before me. The power of the engine surged through every pore of my body. The metal rails of the pier came closer. Beyond the pier, I spotted boats of all shapes and sizes. The car would probably rip through one of those boats if Travis didn't reach for the brakes first.

"Is this a test?" I screamed. "Is this how you see if I have any fears?"

"Jump," he yelled.

I opened my door and leaped from the car. My feet hit the ground first and then my knees. The force sent me forward and I reached out to brace myself. My wrist came down with a loud crack, bending one of my fingers completely backward and shooting pain up my arm to my shoulder. I collapsed on my side and watched helplessly as the car rolled down the pier and did a nose-dive into the calm waters below.

Travis grabbed my arm and yanked me to my feet. He half-helped, half-dragged me to an alley and around a corner before any other vehicles appeared on the road to the pier. Screeching tires sounded from somewhere behind us. Around the next corner, Travis pointed me in the direction of a yellow cab.

"Perfect timing," he said.

I tripped and he grabbed me. He looked at where I

held my throbbing hand.

"Are you okay?" he asked.

"Fine," I said, biting my lip. "Let's just get out of here before Max shows up."

Travis opened the back door of the cab. The stench of cigarette smoke hit me and I choked.

A woman looked back at us and covered the speaker of the cell phone she held. She placed her cigarette in an ashtray. "Can you give me a minute?"

From his wallet, Travis pulled a hundred dollar bill and handed it to the woman. "That should cover your minute."

She looked over him and then at me before ending the call. "Where are you going to?"

"House on the beach." Travis held up his phone. "Here's the address."

The woman read his screen and turned around, putting the car in gear as Travis helped put my seatbelt on.

"How bad does your finger hurt? You must have twisted it pretty good when you fell."

"You mean when I jumped? It hurts pretty bad, but I don't think it's broken. Why don't you have any scars?"

"Do you need a hospital or can we wait?"

I swallowed the pain. "Let's wait and see if it stops hurting."

As the cab sped along the road, we once again passed sirens and flashing lights. "This is getting to be a habit," I said.

"Hang around. It only gets better from here."

I leaned into Travis, thankful nearly every inch of his skin was covered with the black outfit that seemed a living, breathing part of him. "What were you going to say about my mom's power?"

"When?"

"Before the Blazer found us, you started to tell me how to access her power. Remember the file?"

His green eyes met mine. "To unlock her power, she had to feel fear."

CHAPTER ELEVEN

The sun had set by the time we reached the address Travis suggested. Our cab stopped in front of a two-story wooden house with an old stone drive. Deep carvings lined the wood along the roof. Red metal fell from a sharp point to form the roof. Moss hung from the trees to either side of the drive, dropping like waterfalls along the edge of the lawn. Travis helped me out of the car, into the humid air that smelled of salt.

Even in the darkness, I could feel water peeking out from behind the house. I pictured a sandy beach, stretching for miles and filled with shells and moonlight, and gentle waves that crashed along a wooden dock. Seagulls cried overhead as they swooped down and disappeared behind the house. In the distance, lightning flashed and thunder rumbled with the last breath of day.

Travis gave the driver another hundred and she gifted him a genuine smile before driving away.

"You must be rich," I said.

He rubbed my upper arms and a chill shook me despite the heat. "I told you not to worry about money. From this day on, you'll never worry about money again, understand?"

I looked up into his eyes, which shined as he smiled. "I'll hold you to that one."

Travis collected my hands in his and pulled me to the door. A small light burned to the right of the wood, throwing shadows across the red and yellow stained-glass window.

"What time is it?" I asked.

He checked his phone. "Seven-thirty."

"Does this person know we're coming?"

Instead of answering, he knocked on the door. A light came on, along with a loud voice and what sounded like someone running down a set of stairs. The door opened and a girl stepped out into the night, dressed in a lacy black nightgown.

Despite her appearance, I recognized her as the girl from the picture Travis kept under his visor. The picture that was now lost with his car.

"You're kidding me, right?" She put her hands on her hips. "Please tell me there's a good reason you're on my doorstep." She gave him a critical look, but her expression softened when her eyes stopped on me. "Who is this?"

"I want you to meet Rena Mason. Rena, this is my sister, Angel, and," he pointed to a guy who appeared in the doorway behind Angel, "her husband, Skip Greene."

"Didn't you two just get married on Sunday night?" I asked.

She raised an eyebrow and shot Travis a wry grin. Next to Travis, she stood at almost his height, only outdone by Skip who towered above everyone. "So, you told her about us. Didn't realize things had moved that fast." Angel held out a hand. "Nice to meet you."

When I hesitated, Travis gave a nervous laugh. "Go ahead. Angel doesn't have the same skin condition as me."

I reached for her hand, but shivered when our skin touched. "Your hands are really cold. It's like holding an ice cream."

Angel shot Travis a knowing look. "I get that a lot. Travis told me about you on Sunday. He said he'd met a girl but I never thought we'd be introduced this soon."

Skip held out a hand for Travis. As he leaned forward, I noticed his t-shirt and shorts were the same shade of black Travis always wore. "Hey, man. Is everything okay?"

Angel slapped his chest with the back of her hand. "What kind of question is that? We're on our honeymoon and my brother can't go two days without seeing me."

"Actually," Travis said, reaching forward to shake Skip's hand, "I came to see you."

Skip laughed. "We were just talking about going to eat. There's an Italian place downtown—"

"No Italian," Angel said. "And you know exactly why."

Travis glanced at the hand I'd held back, throbbing at my side. "We need a ride to Atlanta."

Angel looked around as if someone might jump from behind a tree and let her in on the joke. "You need a ride? To Atlanta?" She bent over in laughter. "When has the great Travis Payne needed a ride anywhere?"

"I need a ride tonight," he said. "Please, sis."

The laughter died. "You're serious, aren't you? Why did you show up in a cab?"

"My car is at the bottom of the harbor."

Angel put a hand over her mouth. "Your Ferrari? I thought you loved that car." She looked at me. "Did Travis say he was bringing you to Savannah to meet me?"

"No, but I've seen your picture. He keeps it behind the visor of his car." I slapped my forehead with my good palm. "You left the picture in the car. It's at the bottom of the ocean."

Travis reached in his back pocket and handed me a picture. The same picture from the car. "You didn't grab this," I said, shaking my head. "I never saw you pull the visor down."

"Can we eat first?" Skip asked.

"We're in a hurry," Travis said.

Angel nodded. "Let me get dressed."

* * * * *

Angel's idea of getting dressed was a black suit that looked sleek and expensive. Powerful. Skip, wearing a similar suit, climbed into the driver's seat of a black SUV. His large frame made the front seat seem small as Angel took the seat next to him. Both looked like they belonged on an elite crime squad. Maybe this agency really was like the F.B.I. Skip pulled away from the beach house and found the highway without making a single wrong turn. No G.P.S. necessary.

I leaned forward from my spot behind Angel. "Skip, are you from Savannah?"

He laughed. "No, I'm just really good at remembering directions."

"Where is he taking us?" I asked Travis.

"To the agency," he said. "That's always been our destination."

"I need you to stop at the airport," I said. "That's where my dad told me to go."

Angel and Skip exchanged a glance. "That can be arranged," Skip said.

"Do you guys work for this agency too?" I asked.

With a pointed look from Angel, Travis nodded. "Everyone works for the agency. Can you get us going,

Skip?"

"How far is Atlanta?" I asked.

"With Skip behind the wheel," Travis said, "probably two hours."

Angel groaned. "Didn't realize you were in that big of a hurry."

"Hello?" Skip said. "He said no to dinner. Who says no to any meal?"

I laughed despite the throbbing in my hand. Travis's family was cool. Maybe I'd been wrong about him having a lonely life like mine. "We can eat."

"No," Travis said, "keep driving."

Glancing over Skip's shoulder, I was surprised to see the SUV had topped a hundred. "Finally, someone who knows how to drive."

"Hey." Travis pushed my arm. "My driving was perfect… until I drove off the pier." He reached for a strand of hair that hung over my eyes. Travis pushed the hair behind my ear, which was no easy feat wearing gloves.

I turned to stare out of the window and the conversation lapsed into silence. When the road merged into two lanes, Angel broke the silence.

"So," she said, "how has your mission been going? Did you find the answers you were looking for?"

A motion caught my eyes and I spun to see Travis waving his hand under his chin. He stopped immediately and Angel looked from him to me. The SUV hit a bump and my elbow slammed against the seat. I gripped my aching hand where my finger shot currents of pain through my arm. My pinkie finger had swollen larger than my thumb.

"Are you hurt?" Angel asked.

I nodded. "My hand hit the pavement when we jumped out of the car."

"Wait," she said, grabbing Skip's arm, "pull this SUV over." Angel turned and glared at Travis. "If she's hurt, why didn't you just use your power to—"

"Because," Travis said. "I didn't want to scare her."

As if he could scare me. "Travis got rid of his car to save us. It's my fault Max was after us."

Skip stopped the SUV on the shoulder and swung around. "Max the Detonator?"

Travis rolled his eyes. "I had it under control."

Angel shook her head. "Sylvia is going to have an emergency meeting about this one. Maybe two."

I patted the purse that hung at my side. Inside my wallet was the card Dad gave me with the name Sylvia Greene. I hadn't thought about it before, but Skip's last name was Greene. Could they be related? "Who is Sylvia?"

With a confused look, Angel opened her mouth.

"It doesn't matter," Travis said, his eyes burning into me as if he'd touched my bare skin.

I leaned between the seats. "Her last name wouldn't happen to be Greene, would it?"

"How do you know Sylvia?" Skip asked.

"Travis is right," I said. "It doesn't matter. I just need to find her."

Angel cleared her throat. "You know, this would be funny if Rena wasn't hurt." She turned around to face Travis. "She must be really special. Is all of this worth her being in pain?"

"No." Travis gave a long sigh and turned to me. "I need you to keep an open mind, Miss Science."

"An open mind about what?" I asked.

"We'll be at the base in a matter of seconds," Travis said. "The same base that's under the airport, which is where I'm assuming your dad sent you."

I nodded. "He said go to the airport and ask for

Sylvia. I'm supposed to tell her my name and Dad said she would protect me."

Travis held out a gloved hand. "I wish you'd told me that before."

Instead of arguing about something I knew was impossible, I put my hand in his.

He closed his eyes and the world around us changed. We no longer sat in the backseat of the SUV. In fact, there was no seat to keep us from—

Travis put his arms around me to keep me from falling. I stared up into his eyes, caught off-balance by the intensity that radiated from the endless green. He steadied me until I got my footing back.

"Agent Payne?" someone said.

"She needs medical attention," he said to the nurse that approached.

The nurse nodded and I looked around us. We were in the hall of what looked like a hospital. The walls were white; nurses and doctors rushed around in white. She led me into the only empty room and Travis followed.

"Sorry, Agent Payne. We've been dealing with a case of radiation poisoning."

"Are we in danger?" he asked.

"No," she said. "The base is secure, but we've been seeing fallout from an increasing number of cases." She looked over me. "Does she have clearance?"

"She will," he said.

The nurse shook her head. "You know Sylvia doesn't approve of you entering the base without passing through security."

"This was an exception." He pointed to my hand. "She was hurt because of me and I want you to heal her."

"I'll start the paperwork." She left the room and Travis stood next to where I sat on the bed.

"Paperwork," Travis said under his breath.

I glared up at him. "How did we get here?"

"I teleported us."

"Another power?"

"It's how I moved the gun without you seeing, and the picture." He held a hand to the side of my face and the picture appeared between his fingers. "It's how I got the food in your room without opening the door. I never stepped foot in your room."

"You mean you could have brought us here all along? Why didn't you tell me before?"

"Why didn't you tell me why you wanted to get to Atlanta?"

I gripped his arm with my good hand. "My dad made me promise not to. I'm sorry."

"No, I'm sorry."

"How many powers are there?"

"Hundreds that we know of."

Hundreds? "Where do the powers come from? I can't believe a scientist hasn't studied this and written a book for the world to read."

"Some of the powers are inherited; some appear because of evolution. And people have written all of this down in the form of comic books. If you can dream it, this agency has seen it."

I thought of the man filming the fire at the shopping center with his phone. "If all of these powers exist, why aren't there videos all over the Internet?"

He shrugged. "This agency keeps things quiet. Besides, another superhero movie comes out every week. If people see a video online, most think it's just a CGI hoax. People don't even think about the difference between real and movies anymore." Travis stepped into the hall and left me alone in the room.

In a few minutes, the nurse returned and made an x-ray of my hand, with a device about the size of a tablet.

"Her bone is fractured," she told Travis when he returned.

"Then we'll do this off the books," he said.

The nurse left and a moment later a doctor appeared. He held up a device that reminded me of a glow stick. At the end was a circle of lights.

"What is that?" I asked.

The doctor gave Travis a look. "It's called a re-generator wand. The disclaimer is it's not FDA approved yet and I can't actually use it to heal your hand."

"A re-gen what?"

"It's technology that can heal bones," Travis said. "Pretty basic."

"No," I said. "Pretty basic is off the shelf at a corner pharmacy. I've never seen one of these hanging next to a register."

Travis reached for the wand. "I'm sure on the planet it came from they're everywhere."

"Planet that it came from…" I stuttered. "Are you saying this is alien technology?"

"Aliens should be in your comfort zone. Those textbooks don't preach against life out there. No magic necessary, right Miss Science?"

"Quit calling me that."

The doctor cleared his throat.

"Look, Rena," Travis said. "The doctor can't legally use this healing device, so I'm going to use it under his supervision." He held the wand near my hand and the tip began to glow. A soothing mixture of hot and cold wrapped around my hand. A blinding flash of light expanded through the room and then faded as quickly as it began.

"Move your fingers," the doctor said.

To my surprise, the pain and swelling had disappeared entirely. "What happened?"

"You're cured." Travis handed the wand back to the doctor.

I looked around, disoriented. Beside me, the doctor marked on a chart. "Where are we?" I asked.

The doctor glanced at Travis and he nodded. "We're at an underground government base," the doctor said. "This agency is called Earth Under Fire."

Same as what Travis told me before. Maybe he didn't lie. "And we're near the airport?"

The doctor looked at me strangely. "Beneath it. Why do you ask?"

"If you're finished," Travis said, "please give us some privacy."

"Don't be long," the doctor said. "We'll need this room." He left the room and shut the door behind him.

Travis sat next to me on the bed. "Tell me everything your dad said. All of it this time."

Before I could respond, a knock sounded on the door. The door opened and in walked a woman with a black suit and hair tied back in a bun. As she moved closer, I noticed the wrinkles around her eyes and decided she must be older than Dad. A badge hung from her suit. Sylvia Greene.

Travis stood.

"What have I told you about the importance of security?" she asked.

"Always use the approved entrances," he said.

"Perhaps you need further definition of the word approved." She looked over me. "You're not a member of this agency. At the least, you should be wearing a security pass."

"This is Rena," Travis said. "Mason's daughter."

"And you felt the need to bring her here because…"

"I was hurt," I said. "Plus, my dad sent me here."

Sylvia pressed her lips. "As far as this agency is concerned, upon leaving his job here, Donald's memories were erased. There would be no reason for him to send anyone here or even know of our existence."

I reached in my purse and showed her the card from Dad. "He was taken by a man named Louis. Dad told me to go to a car rental office and ask for you by name."

Travis's eyes widened. "You had this with you all along?" He rubbed the back of his neck.

Sylvia gave him a critical look. "You let your feelings get in the way of this mission. Perhaps I erred with my choice in sending you to recover Miss Mason."

"Recover?" I asked.

"His job was to bring you in," she said. "We needed to know if you've developed your mother's power and if you're a danger to this planet."

"Danger to the planet?" The words burned my throat. "I think Agent Payne did a great job. Exceptional."

"That's yet to be seen."

I stood and moved away from the bed. "What happens to me now?"

"Now," she said, "we find out how to access your power."

*****

Travis led me down a hall, into an elevator, and to another floor that stretched with offices as far as I could see. Each office had a similar brown door and a window with blinds. Most were closed. "How big is this place?" I asked.

"Twenty-five floors at the center."

"My dad used to work here?"

"Not in this building," Travis said. "When he left, the agency was just starting plans to build underground."

He stopped before an office with the name Dr. Joel Greene on the nameplate.

"Another Greene?" I looked at Travis. "Have I met all of them yet?"

"Joel is Sylvia's son. Skip is her grandson." He knocked on the door. "Dr. Greene has only recently joined the team."

"Great, I get the newbie."

"Take this seriously, Rena. His job is to determine your threat level."

"You mean I might get my name on the list?"

"Not if you don't find your power."

I stepped away from him. "I thought you said no one knows if I have the power." Travis reached for me but I ducked. "Don't touch me, double-oh-seven."

"Don't call me that." He pointed a finger in my face just as the door opened.

"Agent Payne?" said a deep voice.

To his credit, Travis lowered his hand and appeared to be embarrassed. "Dr. Greene, this is Rena Mason."

Dr. Greene held out a hand. "Nice to meet you. Sylvia told me you were on the way up."

"Does everyone call her Sylvia?"

"She wouldn't have it any other way." He nodded to Travis. "Leave us."

"I can stay if—"

"No," Dr. Greene said. "You can't stay. This is about Rena, not your search for justice." He waved me into the office and shut the door firmly in Travis's face. "Take a seat, anywhere you like."

I dropped down on the couch, which was softer than

any couch I remembered. "Dr. Greene?"

He sat in a chair next to the couch and opened a folder. With a pen in his hand, he wrote as he talked. "Please, call me Joel."

"Joel, why are we having this meeting?"

"My job is to make sure you're okay. Not just here," he pointed at my head, "but here." He pointed at my heart. "From what I've heard, you've had a rough two days."

I took a deep breath and let it out slowly. "I've given up on trying to figure any of this out."

"That sounds like a good first step."

Glancing around the office, I wondered why the walls were bare. Then I remembered he only recently started the job. "What made you come to work at a government base?"

"I was needed."

I thought of how Coach Andrews always gave the same calm answers. "You remind me of my principal back in Wynder. He was a friend of Dad's."

"I spent fifteen years working for a public school, mostly as a principal."

"Do you miss that job?"

He smiled. "Not as much as you would think. What can you tell me about your father?"

"I'm sure everyone here knows more about him than I do. He left town on Sunday night and told me to go to Atlanta, find Sylvia Greene, and not tell anyone."

"Why did he send you here?"

"For my protection. He said a group of terrorists were after him. He told me he'd sent my brother somewhere safe."

"Donald didn't tell you where?"

"Dad didn't want me to worry."

"But you are worried."

"I've spent the last three years taking care of Alfie while Dad… He loves to drink more than he loves us."

"I've read Donald's file. I think that's a bit of a harsh assessment."

"You haven't lived with him for the last three years."

"Noted." He wrote in the folder. "What can you tell me about your mother?"

"When you're done asking questions, can I have a turn?"

His eyes rose. "Asking questions?"

"You want to know about my mother, but so do I. Can I ask *you* questions about her?"

"I want this to be as informal as possible. My questions might be about other people, but the objective of this meeting is to make sure you feel safe here."

"What if I don't?"

"Let's assume you do."

"I always hear that when you assume, it makes—"

Dr. Greene held up a hand. "Like I said, your safety is my primary objective."

"The agency is worried, right? That I might be dangerous? That's why we're talking."

"In that case, you could make my job easier by answering my questions. Do you feel safe?"

"I've heard this agency locks up people with powers."

"I can't say that hasn't happened. Rena, this is fluid situation. We're in an underground government base, home to an agency that acts as the world's first line of defense against people with powers that could harm others. But powerful people also work here and understand where you're coming from. Your cooperation is ideal. Do you think it's possible to trust me?"

I looked into his eyes. "Maybe."

"Did Agent Payne describe your mother's power?"

"He said she had the power to make a nuclear bomb. Do you think I have her power?"

"Do you?"

"I think I might. Travis described it as glowing blue light coming from my mother's hands. I believe it's happened once before."

"When?" he asked.

"I was in the cafeteria eating lunch. I was looking around for Travis, feeling like I might actually get sick if he noticed me looking for him." Then I'd thought of Alfie and how the truck almost slammed into our side.

"You were afraid of Agent Payne?"

"Agent… I've got to get used to that name. When we were at school, I met him as Tony. After he almost…"

"Almost what?"

"Kissed me," I finished. "I felt this energy inside of me, but no blue sparkles."

His eyes widened, ever so slightly. "Do you have feelings for Travis?"

Red crept into my cheeks. "Maybe," I said again.

Dr. Greene closed the folder. "I think we're done for now."

"Am I getting locked up?"

He smiled again. "Not yet, but the night is young."

* * * * *

When we finished, Dr. Greene took me to the security level and got a badge made with my picture. "Temporary," he said. "You'll need another agent with you at all times."

"That won't be a problem," Travis said as he walked up with Angel and Skip.

Dr. Greene narrowed his eyes. "That was a short honeymoon. I thought I told you both to take the entire week off. That was an order, not a suggestion."

"I liked you better when you were principal," Skip said. "At least then I just got grounded."

"I have to consider the mental health of everyone with powers. After all, it's my job."

Angel stepped forward. "We're not on the clock. My brother wanted us to meet Rena and he invited us to dinner."

"He didn't have to ask us twice," Skip said.

"Dinner?" Dr. Greene asked. "I should have known." He turned to me. "Well, Rena. I'll leave you in good hands."

As they led me out through security—I had some strange looks since I didn't come in through security—I wondered what Dr. Greene meant about people with powers.

We walked through two large doors and into a car rental office. I looked around in shock.

"Act normal," Travis said as he nudged me forward.

Two men working the counter nodded as we walked by. The green on their striped shirts matched the green carpet below my feet.

"This is the car rental office where Dad sent me?" I asked when we stood outside of the sliding glass doors. Before me stretched miles of vehicles.

"The perfect cover," Travis said. "Most people will never know what's behind those doors."

Skip pulled up to the curb in the SUV. "We've got to hurry. The pizza joint closes in an hour and a half."

"It will take us an hour to get out of this traffic," I said as we pulled away from the curb. Even at night, cars fought for the right lane while exiting the airport.

"Not with Skip driving." Travis placed his hand in mine. The slick leather of his glove felt warm against my skin.

"What did Dr. Greene mean about taking care of people with powers?"

Travis squeezed my hand. "Everyone in this vehicle has powers. Angel has the power to control people and Skip drives like a maniac."

"His job is to make sure none of us go crazy and try to destroy the planet," Angel said. "The agency has to have a plan B in that case."

"Has anyone ever gone crazy and tried to destroy the planet?" I asked.

Travis only smiled.

CHAPTER TWELVE

The pizza restaurant Skip chose had an outside eating area and an indoor section where we could sit next to a pool table. I knew nothing about shooting pool, but watched with interest as Travis and Skip faced off.

"Hanging in there?" Angel asked from across the high-top table.

I kicked my barstool. "I miss my brother. He's the only person I worry about with everything that's happened. Not me, not my dad. Just Alfie."

"There's nothing wrong with worrying," Angel said, "but don't let it consume every minute of every day. Some things you can't change. I've had to learn that the hard way."

"Are you happy with being an agent?"

"I never really had a choice."

A waitress appeared with the pizza Travis ordered for us. Thankfully, he didn't argue when I asked for banana peppers.

"Anything else, hon?" she asked.

I shook my head and she walked away. "Travis said your power is the ability to control people. That sounds pretty cool."

"It has a good side and a bad, like anything else. If I use my powers on someone, I can feel their emotions. Happiness is like a high for me. Anger leaves a bad taste in my mouth. True evil makes me want to destroy things. What about you?"

I took a sip of my coke. "Travis said my mom had the power to cause a nuclear explosion or stop one."

"The first part screams top of the list. The second part could be useful. Nuclear weapons are an honest fear for most of the world. If you could figure out how to control this power, I'm sure Sylvia would have an immediate opening for you."

"That's the problem. Travis said my mom could only use her power by feeling fear. I've never feared anything."

She sat up straight. "No fear? Ever?"

"That's right."

Angel watched me, seeming to decide. "Can I read your emotions?"

"Do you think that would help?"

"If you've got fear inside of you, I'll find it."

"Okay." I glanced to where Travis and Skip argued over a trick shot that Travis insisted he could make. "Do I need to do anything?"

"No." She took a deep breath and stared into my eyes as if she could see the depths of my soul. My chest tightened as I felt a strange pressure. A tingling came over my body, like a thousand pin-pricks invading my skin. And then, just as quickly as the onslaught began, the pressure stopped.

After taking a sip of her water, Angel opened her eyes. "You're right. No fear."

"How can you be sure?"

"For me, every emotion has a specific signature or to

make things easier a specific taste. It's all very particular."

"What does fear taste like?"

She grinned. "Pineapple."

Travis and Skip finished their game and dropped into chairs at the table. Skip had an entire pizza to himself while Travis and I shared. Angel watched as we ate, but never touched any of the pizza.

"Aren't you going to eat?" I asked.

"I ate earlier," she said. "Besides, pizza's not my thing."

Skip gave her a look of sympathy. "I'm sorry you've got to miss out. This pizza is better than anything we had back home."

"What's with the black?" I asked. "Even when you're not at work, you're all still wearing black."

"A good agent is always on the clock," Skip said.

Travis shook his arms, loosening the long black sleeves. "You'll get used to the black." He finished the slice in his hand and leaned into me. "I want to show you something."

I stood and he led me to the back of the restaurant. In a dark corner sat an old Pac-Man video game.

"Think you can beat me?" he asked.

"Does this thing still work?"

"Of course it works." He placed two quarters in the slot and the machine came to life.

"So," I said, "you're into video games?"

He grinned. "Only the classics. Let's see what you've got."

* * * * *

After I beat Travis three times and he beat me twice, he finally gave up and found a nearby table for us. He watched the jukebox that sat across the room, silently waiting to be played. Some kids about Alfie's age put coins in a pinball machine. The smallest one cried when it took her money.

Travis flicked his hand and the balls fell down, ready for a game to start. "Hey," she said as she jumped around, "it's working now."

"I guess you do have a heart," I said.

"It's in there even if no one can touch it." He raised his eyes to meet mine. "Have you ever feared anything? Anything, during the whole time you were growing up?"

"I don't think so."

"People have all kinds of fears. Maybe you haven't been exposed to the right trigger yet."

I put my hands in my lap to keep from touching him. "What do you have in mind?"

Travis tapped on the table. "Did you ever watch *Fear Factor*? It used to come on TV years ago."

I shook my head. "We never watched much TV other than old episodes of *MacGyver* and *The A-Team*. Dad always said you can't trust anything you see on TV."

"Yeah, that sounds like Donald Mason—suspicious of everyone and everything. He did a great job of staying off the government's radar, but he knew all of the tricks and even created some of his own. I hope you didn't inherit that gene."

"The only person I'm suspicious of is you."

He grinned. "Okay then, at least we know where to start."

* * * * *

That night, Travis led me to a room that the agency assigned me, near the end of a long hall. It was larger than the camper but smaller than the hotel room. I wanted to ask Travis how far his room was from mine, but I didn't.

He left me a folder with information about my dad. "Nothing too classified," Travis said, as if there was a line in the sand when it came to secret documents. Seeing Dad in those pictures, dressed as an agent with a gun at his side, made this whole nightmare seem real. Dad was once an agent here, a respected one from the sound of the reports.

On some of the reports, several names were marked through with black ink. I wondered what or who the agency felt they needed to protect. None of the reports included specifics about my mom. In fact, I only saw the name Rosanna listed once and that was for a routine follow-up after she diffused a bomb in New York City.

Wow, New York City. She saved lives, though no one in the country probably ever heard the truth. Her work was important, but it was also an intelligence risk.

If not for that listing, I'd have thought Travis made up the part about my mom having a power.

The next morning, Travis knocked on my door at seven. When I opened the door, I stepped back and looked over his outfit. He now wore a black suit that proved he could walk and talk the role of agent. The suit hugged every angle of his body like it was made for him. My heart welled with pride as I remembered this was the same guy who sat with me at lunch only a week before.

He brought me a black t-shirt and black jeans to wear, again a perfect fit. "Just breaking you in," he said. "From now on, black will be your color."

I wasn't so sure about that, but at least Travis didn't seem out of place within the walls of this agency. He'd seemed weird at school with his all-black outfit including black gloves. Now that I understood he wore the gloves to keep from touching anyone, I'd developed a strange respect for him.

"Has anyone found a lead on my brother?" I asked.

He shook his head.

"What about my dad? You said last night the agency is looking for them. I want to help."

Travis gripped my arms. "There's nothing you can do that the agency isn't already doing."

"Nothing?"

"Well, there is something. I've got a meeting this morning, but after that we're going on a mission to help you find your power."

"Really?" I asked.

"Skip is making a list of all known fears, even the strange ones that only show up on the Internet. If there's a way to make you feel fear, we'll find it."

*****

At nine o'clock sharp, Travis showed up at my door. He'd changed out of the suit and back into the black jeans and black polo shirt. I shook away the disappointment of not seeing him in the suit.

"Ready?" he asked.

I nodded. "Where are we going?"

"Everywhere. Skip has the list ready and we're going to start working on finding something you can fear. We've got a team of people on board for this mission. Sylvia gave us all the resources we'll need."

"What's first?" I asked.

He reached for my arm. The room around me changed to open air. Below my feet was a bridge with gaps that showed trees and bushes below. Way below.

"Where are we?"

"On a bridge in Alaska. If you've seen a lot of old

movies, you've probably seen this bridge. The ground is a thousand feet below us."

I peered through the gaps closest to my feet. "That's a long way to fall."

"Not scared, are you?"

Shaking my head, I looked out over the valley, to the side of a mountain where a train bounced along a track, seeming to circle the mountain. "That looks like fun."

With a sigh of frustration, he grabbed my arm. "I think we'll move on to number two."

The air around us changed to humid, ocean air, with a killer breeze. My foot slipped and I grabbed the orange mass in front of me.

"Easy," Travis said, his hands touching mine as he held tight to the buoy, which flopped from side-to-side within the ocean waves. "Fear of water."

There wasn't a boat or hint of land as far as I could see. "I don't think this is it."

Travis's phone rang and he reached for his pocket. Halfway there, he changed his mind and reached for my hand. The world around me changed to a jungle. Birds screamed overhead. Rain pelted my face. "I think this still qualifies as number two."

"No." He pointed above my head. A snake longer than the camper coiled around a branch and held its head down, tasting us with a forked tongue.

Travis's phone rang again and this time he answered it. "Not the snake. Got it." He gripped my arm and pushed down my head. Before I could breathe, we crouched inside the glass casing of a zoo exhibit. A chemical smell tickled my nose, along with the smell of grass. Near our feet crawled spiders larger than my hand. One fell into my hair and I squealed.

"Is that it?"

I looked down at my hands as he swatted the spider away. "Don't think so. What's next?"

Travis took us to a crowded arena. He pulled me onto a stage and waved at thousands of fans waiting for a concert. The people stretched into a sea of glow sticks waving and cameras flashing.

"What's going on here?" a man asked from behind. "Someone call security."

With a laugh, Travis whisked me behind the stage and through a band practicing for the show. I giggled when he pulled me into an empty dressing room and took us out of there, to a place made entirely of ice.

"South Pole," he said.

I gripped my arms, stinging with the blast of cold air. "That's just wrong."

"What's next?" Travis chattered into his phone.

"How… do you… get service… here?"

Breathing a sigh of relief, I relaxed when I realized the ice had disappeared. The relief faded when I noticed we were in a hospital storage area. Travis opened a stainless drawer and lifted a needle sealed in plastic. It was an empty syringe.

"Needles never bothered me," I said. "But hospitals do. It's not a fear, though."

"We can also try the fear of blood while you're here."

I took the needle from his hand and peeled back the plastic. I removed the plastic cap from the end and aimed the needle for the tip of my thumb.

Travis grabbed the needle. "That's not necessary."

Laughter came from his phone. "Are you afraid of blood, man?"

Travis groaned. "What's next?"

"Claustrophobia," Skip said.

"You can scratch that one," I said. "I grew up in a

camper."

With a smile, Travis hung up the phone. "I want to try number one again."

Within an hour, we stood in the belly of an old airplane that bounced with every gust of wind. Travis had suited up with a parachute. He tightened the straps on mine.

"Ready?" he asked.

I looked out of the open door, at the world below us. Cars crawled along the streets like ants.

"On three," he said. "One…" Before Travis said two, he'd pushed me out of the plane.

Spinning uncontrollably, I tried to remember the quick lessons from one of Travis's fellow agents. An Army guy like my dad. I knew normal people didn't do crazy stunts like this. When did he say to pull the cord? To my side, Travis fanned out his arms, enjoying the drop as the world rushed closer. He motioned when it was time to pull my cord and the parachute opened like a flower with every color of the rainbow.

When we reached the ground, I dropped to my knees.

Travis approached, holding the bulk of his parachute. He put his goggles on top of his head. "Why weren't you scared?"

I stared up at him, the sun at his back. "Because I knew you could save me. You could have teleported us to safety if anything bad happened."

He dropped to the ground next to me. "I could have saved you anytime today."

"That's why this isn't working."

Travis bowed his head in defeat. "You've got to be afraid of something."

I swallowed. "Not being able to save my brother."

He raised his head and reached for my arm. "We'll

find your brother. I promise."

Something inside of me loosened as if a trap was about to snap but was stopped just in time. "Thanks."

Travis reached for my hand, but this time held up my fingers. "Where did you get this ring?"

"It was Mama's ring. Dad made me promise not to take it off."

His eyebrows rose. "Is there some special significance?"

"Dad always said the ring kept her calm."

"Can a ring keep a person calm?"

"You're asking me? I'm Miss Science, remember? I don't believe in any of this."

"But you accept that people have powers now, right?"

"If I didn't, how could I accept you?"

Travis moved closer, until his lips were as close as possible to mine without touching. "Do you fear the truth?"

My palms tingled as his gaze deepened. "No."

"Take off the ring."

I reached for the ring, ready to do anything he asked, but stopped when his phone rang.

He swore and answered the phone.

"Hey man," Skip said. "I found a listing for someone who's afraid of lunch."

With a defeated laugh, Travis stood and pulled me up. "Lunch it is."

* * * * *

We met Angel and Skip in one of the restaurants at the base. It was Italian, even though I remembered Angel saying no Italian the night before. Skip ordered enough for two; Angel only ordered a water. I decided on a pasta dish

I couldn't pronounce and Travis motioned for two.

Travis was going over the rest of our fear list when Skip's phone rang.

Skip finished his last bite of food and answered the phone. "Yeah, I'll be there."

"What's up?" Angel asked.

"Some foreign dignitary is in town and a threat has been made. We've got to get him moved through the streets to a safer location. No collateral damage. Up for a mission?"

Angel shook her head. "Your driving skills are always in demand, but I think I'll sit this one out. I want to talk with Rena."

Skip stood and kissed her before heading to the door. He'd been gone for less than a minute when another agent took his seat.

I looked at the man who held a dark drink in his hand. An alcoholic drink, which lost him several points before he even opened his mouth. I turned to Travis, who nodded to the man.

"Agent Lockhart," Travis said.

"Agent Payne," the man threw back.

Angel turned to me. "This is my dad, Jon."

Her dad? He and Angel looked nothing alike. "Is everyone here related?"

Jon shrugged. "For the most part. We're like one big happy family."

Angel rolled her eyes. "One day I'll tell you the irony of that statement."

"You came for lunch?" Travis asked.

"No, I came to meet Rena. Since you're inviting me to lunch, I wholeheartedly accept." He watched me with a careful smile. "It's not every day you meet someone who can hide an emotion so powerful as fear."

"From what I hear," Angel said, "lots of people want to meet Rena. Including Louis Castillo."

"Old buddy Louis." Jon tipped up his drink and took his time downing half of the glass of liquor, which radiated a sweetness I could smell. "Haven't heard much out of him lately."

The waiter appeared with a menu, but Jon waved him off.

Travis checked his watch. "I hear he's in the company of Donald Mason."

"Oh?" Jon took another sip of the drink. "That's got to be an interesting conversation. I wonder if either is dead yet."

"I hope you're joking," I said.

Jon gave me a look of sympathy. "I'm putting my money on Mason. He was born wired for battle and, if that didn't make him deadly, the incident in Iraq honed his skills to a new level."

"Did you know his friend?" I asked. "Jacob Andrews?"

"He was the only survivor other than your dad. They were part of a special forces team that became a closet operation for senior officials. No one stateside ever heard about it."

"No surprise there," Angel said.

With a raise of his glass, Jon nodded. "After their team received intel about a defector with knowledge of secret uranium trials and moved on a safe-house, they found themselves facing machine guns and outnumbered five to one. Our own government cut ties and nuked their exit, if you don't mind my play on words."

"I heard they were attacked at a market," I said, "and Jacob took a bullet for someone on the team."

"They took every mission knowing it could be their

last. Mason was the one who shot Jacob in order to save his life. He then proceeded to take down every man who had the unfortunate luck of facing him."

I frowned. "That's not the story I heard."

With a shrug, Jon motioned the waiter back to the table. "The past is the past. But after all these years, you don't stop being that kind of agent."

* * * * *

After lunch, I sat in my room as Travis paced the floor. "I don't know what else to do."

"Me either," he said. "I never considered the fact we'd fail. That's a tough word for me."

"Have you gotten any word on my dad or brother?"

"They've both vanished," he said. "Which is a good sign. Bodies turning up is always a bad sign."

"Is that supposed to make me feel better?"

He stopped pacing and sat next to me on the couch. "I told you before—I don't enjoy lying to you. If there was something I could do… It's best that you wait this one out. I have a feeling everything will turn out for your brother."

I looked around the room and considered the lack of windows. "This life seems lonely."

"More than yours?"

"You've got me on that one. My dad always insisted on keeping a low profile. Now I understand his intense hatred of the government."

Travis nodded. "He didn't want to be discovered."

"Have you ever had a real friend down here?"

"For a while. His name was Tyler Greene."

"Another Greene?"

"Yes," he said, laughing. "He was Skip's older brother."

"Was?" I asked.

"He was in the Army when the agency discovered his power. Sylvia brought him here for training and insisted we 'hang out.' At first, I was skeptical, but we got tight pretty quick. We became partners and took on cases together, like my dad and yours did all those years ago."

"What happened to Tyler?"

The laughter faded from Travis's voice. "He was my partner. He knew about my search for the truth about my dad. I told him almost all of my secrets…"

"Almost?"

"He didn't know about my powers. No one ever knew about my powers."

"Where is Tyler now?"

Travis stared at the floor. "He betrayed me, he betrayed his family, and ultimately he betrayed his country."

"Did he die?"

"No. I saw him the night of Angel's wedding."

"Sunday night? What happened?"

"We talked. He asked me to forgive him."

"And?"

"I told him some things can't be forgiven. Then I downed half a bottle of crown."

Despite admitting to drinking more than he should have, my heart still hurt for Travis. "He made a mistake."

"He lied to me." Travis stood and walked to the door. "He's the reason I almost died."

"But you never told him about your powers."

Travis looked back at me. "No."

"So, you lied to him."

"I couldn't tell anyone the truth."

"Not even your best friend?"

"You're not making this any easier."

Travis's phone rang and he ripped it from his pocket. "Payne here." His eyes lifted to mine. "Be there in ten."

"Time to go back to work?"

"That was Sylvia. She's holding a meeting on the hour. She wants you to come."

"What is this meeting about?"

"A nuclear bomb threat."

CHAPTER THIRTEEN

I walked to Sylvia's meeting in a daze—to the elevator with stainless panels and down a hall lit with warm lights along the wall's edge. Blinds sealed all six windows of the conference room where Travis stopped. Although my hands didn't tremble with fear in the wake of his mention of a nuclear bomb, the thought of facing my supposed power this soon did make me hesitate. Travis gripped my arm and forced me into the room.

According to Travis, Sylvia had insisted on him treating me like a guest at this underground base. I'd remain in the dark until the need for a security clearance could be determined.

Or, it seemed, until they needed me to diffuse a nuclear bomb.

Rubbing my palms together, I thought about Travis's suggestion to take off the ring. Since Mama died, that ring had never left my finger. Could it be keeping me from feeling fear?

Inside the room, Sylvia sat at the head of a metal table that seated eight, glancing through a folder I stretched my neck to see. If only I could have read the pages. To her left sat Jon and next to Jon sat Angel. When Travis motioned for me to take the seat next to Sylvia, I skipped that seat and reached for the one across from Angel. Travis took the next seat, leaning back in his chair as if he attended a meeting like this every day.

"Thank you for coming, Miss Mason," Sylvia said.

I crinkled my nose. "Call me Rena, please."

"From what I hear," she said, "we've put you through an intense search for your power. I think you would benefit from an explanation of how your power should work." Sylvia checked her watch and glanced at the speaker phone at the center of the table. "We're waiting for a call from someone who can provide this explanation."

They needed tech support on explaining my power? That couldn't be a good sign. "Have you found my brother?" I asked. "Or my dad?"

"At the moment," she said, her eyes firm, "your power is our main concern."

"My brother has asthma," I said. "If he has an attack, he'll need medicine."

Sylvia glanced at Jon. "Has your search yielded any results?"

Jon shook his head. "Nothing concrete, but I'll put another team on the trail of Mason's son." He looked at me. "That's all I can promise for now."

Travis propped his elbow on the table and leaned over. "Has anyone figured out where Max is?"

I looked around the table. "Can someone tell me why Max came to my school? Or why Louis took my dad?"

"Max is working for Louis," Jon said. "Louis took your dad because he wants your power."

"I got that already." When I was sure no one planned to finish, I pushed back from the table and stood. "If you can't trust me with the truth, why am I here?"

Sylvia gave a slight smile. "Sit down, Rena. Ask your questions, whatever you'd like to know."

With a glare at Travis, I sat back down. He made no movement. "Who is Louis Castillo?"

Angel looked around the table. "I think she deserves the truth."

"Louis Castillo is leader of a terrorist group called Black Dawn," Jon said. "Years ago, he exploited your mother's power to shift the balance of nuclear weapons in governments around the world. She could cause an explosion, but she escaped the group before Louis was able to make good on that threat. She came to this agency and used her power to help prevent several nuclear events."

"Does Louis have a power?" I asked.

"No," Jon said.

"What about Max the Detonator? He said he was on your list. What's his power?"

"Party favors," Jon said. "He can rub his fingers together and light a fire. Max used to carry dynamite with him at all times—probably still does. That's how he got the nickname Detonator."

"Lighting dynamite is a big deal," I said. "He could blow stuff up. Kind of like what you're asking me to do."

Angel laughed. "He wishes. Max is nowhere near as powerful as you."

The phone rang and my heart began to race. Was I feeling fear? I looked at my empty palms.

As Jon answered the phone and introduced a scientist named Presley, I looked from Angel to where Travis stared at the far wall. The two looked nothing alike.

Angel had said Jon was her dad, but Travis's dad disappeared when he was nine. If Angel was Travis's sister, they must have the same mother but different fathers. I sat back in the chair as I thought of two men loving the same woman, at this same agency. That must have been strange. It also must be what Jon meant about everyone being 'one big happy family.'

The call broke up and Presley's voice sounded as if he stood at the end of a long tunnel. A click sounded and the call ended.

"I apologize," Sylvia said. "Our expert had planned to explain the physics behind a nuclear event."

I laughed. "I actually understand the physics. A neutron, which is the particle of an atom with no charge, collides with an atom." When I noticed the looks on the other faces, red filled my cheeks. "I wrote an essay on the difference between nuclear fission and nuclear fusion."

Sylvia gave me a look of surprise. "They're teaching nuclear physics at your high school?"

"It was for a scholarship," I said. "A college in Florida offered an engineering scholarship for the best essay on fuel sources for future space missions. I wrote about how to harness this energy safely."

Smiling, Sylvia leaned forward. "You are full of surprises, my dear. There is irony in that statement to be sure."

I groaned. Would I ever get a shot at a scholarship now? "When you find my dad, please don't say anything since he has no idea. I probably won't get the scholarship anyway."

"You think he would be upset?" Angel watched me with a look of sorrow. "That's pretty messed up. After everything I've heard about Donald Mason, I'd love to finally meet him."

"You mean get a read on him," Jon said.

"If you understand the physics behind a nuclear event," Sylvia said, "then you've probably already figured out how your power should work."

No, I'd been too busy trying to figure out how to *use* my power and find my brother. "The neutron hitting the atom starts the event. In less than a second, other neutrons hit other atoms and cause a chain reaction. Like a domino effect. My power must be to affect the neutrons."

"Sounds plausible," Sylvia said. "You might have a future here after all."

I frowned. "Knowing the physics doesn't tell me how to flip the switch and make it work. How do I slow down the neutrons?"

"I understand your hesitation. You deserve the proper time to figure out how to flip the switch. If only we had time."

"What do you mean?" I asked.

Jon tried again to get the scientist back, but eventually shoved the phone away. "Louis has declared war on this agency. His weapon of choice is nuclear."

I thought back to his conversation with Dad. "Because of what happened to Rosanna?"

"Do you know where your father is?" Sylvia asked.

I shook my head. "He told Louis he had a house in Portland and I was on the way there."

Jon made a bridge with his hands. "A distraction. Too bad I couldn't see Louis's face when they arrived."

"Dad told me to run here but he didn't say why other than I'd need protection." I held up my hand for Sylvia. "Dad told me to show you this ring, that it was my mother's."

Sylvia nodded. "Yes, I've seen the ring before. It belonged to Rosanna."

"That proves it then." I spun the ring around my finger, amazed at the mixture of happiness and dread I felt with her confirmation.

"Three days ago, Louis detonated a small device at one of our remote facilities as a warning," Sylvia said. "This is not public knowledge. Our doctors have treated several people with radiation poisoning. No one has died, but we fear he has more bombs waiting."

"He has my dad," I said, glancing at Jon. "Do you think Louis will kill him?"

Sylvia turned to Jon. "Three years ago, I paid Donald a visit off the books. He recognized me, which means his memory was intact."

Jon met her eyes and then looked down at the table. "You've known for three years?"

"Did you erase *any* of his memory?"

"No."

She looked at me. "We have rules for people who leave this agency with knowledge of our operations. Those select few who choose to leave do so without any memory of their work here. However, Donald might be one of those rare exceptions Jon and I agree on."

My eyes widened. "This agency has a way to erase memories?"

"I have the power," Jon said, raising his eyes. "Like your power, mine has a dual purpose. I can erase a person's memories but also bring them back."

"Will you erase my memory?"

"In a hurry to leave?" Angel asked. "The fun is only beginning."

I glanced at Travis, but he merely shrugged.

Sylvia closed the folder in front of her. "As much as I would like to welcome you to our agency and offer you a comfort zone to explore your power, we simply are out of time. We need your gift to stop this impending attack."

"Louis knows about her gift," Jon said. "He's only threatening us to draw her out."

"It's working," Angel said. "People are on edge waiting to find out where he'll hit us next."

"I don't know if I have this power," I said. "And if I do, I have no idea how to control it. What if I blow something up by mistake? Or someone?"

Sylvia sat back in her chair. "Are you afraid of your power?"

I looked down at my hands. "I don't know, but it's not helping if I am."

She stood. "You don't sound sure of anything. Perhaps another session with Joel might help you decide."

* * * * *

Travis remained silent until we reached the elevator.

"You're not trying hard enough," he said as soon as the doors slid shut and we began to rise.

"Whose side are you on?" I asked.

Travis pressed a red button and the elevator stopped. "This agency is my home. This suit represents a job to protect everyone who can't protect themselves."

I crossed my arms and looked at my reflection in the panel above. "You don't have to be so blunt. At least you could have tried to make me feel better. In that room, you never said a word."

He gripped my shoulders. "Believe it or not, I'm on your side. If you'll just give this a chance, everyone comes out a winner."

Hot tears burned in my eyes. "What if I can't control my power?"

"Does the thought scare you?"

"Ha." I shrugged him away. "Why did I think you could understand? This power is huge. It's deadly."

Travis leaned against the slick metal panel. "And you

think my touch isn't?"

"You got stuck with easy powers. Mine can cause massive destruction."

"Easy? You call what I was stuck with easy?" Laughing, he grabbed my arm and the elevator walls faded.

My feet sank into red sand, which stung my eyes as it swirled around us. Dunes of the same red sand stretched to infinity in every direction. "Where are we?"

"Can't you tell with all the sand?" His voice cracked with bitterness. "We're in a desert. Which one doesn't matter, but we're halfway around the world from Atlanta."

I took a deep breath of the dry air, which made me cough. "Why did you bring me here?"

"The agency is up against the clock and so far, we're not on the winning end. You're the only one who can stop these bombs."

I held out my hands. "If I had the power, it would have made an appearance by now."

"I know that look in your eyes because I've seen it in the mirror every day since we met. You're scared of failing."

"You're lying. Travis Payne is not afraid of anything."

He took my hands. "My job is to help you find your power. If I fail you, I fail everyone."

I swallowed the pain in my throat. "I don't know what to do."

"Show me your power."

"Here?"

"Yes, here. Now. Use your power. Show me you can. Since we've met, you've done nothing but prove you can do anything you set your mind to."

I pulled my hands away. "There's not exactly a manual for this, unless my mom left instructions."

"You have everything you need. You're stubborn

enough to make this happen; you've just got to believe in yourself."

Closing my eyes, I held out my hands and tried to concentrate. Harder. Stronger. Deeper. My palms tingled. I opened my eyes in anticipation, but no blue sparkles came from my hands.

"You're not trying hard enough," he said.

"You're mad at me."

"The people in that room were my friends, Rena. My family. The agency raised me and I'd do whatever it takes to save them. I don't think you feel the same."

"I can't take this pressure." Shouting into the howling currents of wind, I put my hands over my face to block the sand. "I find out I may have this power and in twenty-four hours, I've suddenly got to find it and become a master. How long did it take you to figure out your powers?"

Gently, he lowered my hands. "You're not in this alone. Don't ever forget that." His gloved hands felt soft against mine, bringing us closer despite the fabric between us. "Do you know why I didn't show you my power to teleport sooner?"

"You didn't want to scare me."

"To complete my mission, I needed to gain your trust. After we met that morning in the office, I wanted to earn it. How could you trust me when you only believed in science?"

"You said you wanted us to be friends, but it was all a lie. You already knew who I was."

Travis released my hands and took ten steps back. The loss of his touch twisted my insides. He raised his hands and slammed his fists together. The ground beneath my feet began to shake. I stumbled, trying to catch my balance with feet that felt like weights in the sand.

"What's going on?" I screamed.

"An earthquake I caused. You think you're the only one with destructive powers?" He slammed his fists again and the shaking brought me to my knees, which sank into the sand.

"Stop, please." My body shook with the ground. I looked down at my hands, which were beginning to glow. Tiny blue lines appeared along my palms, first in branches like my veins, and then shooting out along my fingers.

"There," he said.

Before I could ask again, the shaking stopped. The blue sparkles faded and the tingling disappeared.

Tears slid down my cheeks. "You're still lying. All along, you've lied to me."

Travis held out a hand.

I stared up at him. "Is that everything you've been hiding?"

"I have one more power. I can see a person's future by touching their skin."

Laughing, I fell back on my butt in the sand. "That's real irony. You could see their future, but you'd also kill them." Reluctantly, I put my hand in his and he pulled me to my feet. "If I added correctly, you've got four powers and I have one.

"Two, actually."

My laughter died. "What else can I do?"

"Well, there's a reason they gave Rosanna the nickname Firebird." He pointed to the sky. "She knew how to travel in style."

"I can fly?"

"How does that fit with your science books?"

"It doesn't."

He chuckled and returned us to the elevator. "I guess you'll just have to figure out what you believe."

I took a deep breath of the sterile air and wiped sand

from my eyes. "I believe I'll focus on one power at a time. Just don't lie to me anymore, Travis. It hurts."

Before the doors opened, Travis faced me with a dark look in his eyes. "When you think about me lying, you need to understand one thing. This agency raised me. They are my family and I'll do whatever it takes to save them."

* * * * *

Dr. Greene sat in his chair for twenty minutes as I sat on the couch, neither of us willing to break the silence. When his phone vibrated, we both jumped.

"Sorry, I should take this." He answered the phone. "What's wrong? No, I believe the milk and butter go in after you cook the noodles. Haven't you ever seen your mother cook macaroni and cheese? This doesn't constitute an emergency."

I laughed as he hung up the phone. "You're right, it goes in after."

"I apologize. My youngest son is having a sleepover or whatever they call it these days. He's decided to cook dinner. Hot dogs and macaroni and cheese."

"That sounds like something my brother would ask for."

He coughed and took a drink of water from the bottle on the table beside him. "You spent a great deal of time caring for him, didn't you?"

A sick feeling washed over me. "With Dad drinking, I didn't have a choice."

"Maybe it's good for you to have a break."

"You call this a break? I ran away from home, spent the night with a guy I just met last week, and found out most of my life was a lie. Except for the part about Dad drinking. Why couldn't that have been a lie?"

"I've been thinking about what's between you and Travis."

"What's between…" I laughed again. "He can't touch me. That kind of rules out anything between us."

"You said you spent the night together."

"You know what I mean. I locked myself in the bedroom and he did whatever secret undercover agents do for the rest of the night. Now that I know about his power to teleport, he could have been halfway around the world."

"Go back for a second. Did you say you locked yourself in the bedroom?"

"Yeah, why?"

He scribbled in the notebook on his lap. "I think we're making progress. You seemed rather stressed when Travis brought you to the door. He wouldn't make eye contact."

"Is discussing Travis necessary?"

"Are you scared of him?"

"He took me to a desert and made the ground shake with some kind of earthquake."

Dr. Greene stopped writing and glanced up, concern on his face. "To my knowledge, he's never used that power."

"Never?" I asked, stunned. "I guess he wanted to make sure I was scared."

"Did it work?"

"For a minute. The blue lit up my hands and then faded."

"Are you scared of using your power?"

"I think I'm more scared of not being able to use it."

He nodded and went back to writing. "So, what if you can't use it?"

"Without me, people could die."

"With or without you, people die every day."

"But I could stop these attacks. I have the power." I spun Mama's ring around my finger. "This ring belonged to my mother. I think it's keeping me from using my power."

"Have you tried taking off the ring?"

"Should I?"

Shrugging, Dr. Greene opened the bottle and took a long drink. "You should do what you feel is right."

"Aren't you on the agency's side? Travis said the agency raised him and he'll do whatever it takes to do his job and keep his family safe."

"Like Travis, I grew up at this agency until I was a teen. Now I also have a job here, which is to maintain the mental health of those with powers. Despite what happens to everyone else, my job means making sure you have a support network. You've lost your dad and your brother. Travis is no substitute."

Dr. Greene's words lingered in my thoughts long after I returned to my room. After a careful decision, I removed the ring and placed it on the wooden dresser in my room.

My skin felt naked without the ring, exposed, as if my support network had been wiped away all over again. Dr. Greene had managed to get into my head. What did I normally do when people got into my head?

I fought back.

Before leaving the room again, I found Dad's multi-tool and slid the cold metal into my pocket.

* * * * *

That evening, Travis returned with the offer of dinner. I told him I wasn't hungry. Instead of taking me to dinner, he reached for my hand and sent us both to the top of a building, looking out over a city alive with every color of light imaginable.

"Where are we?" I asked.

"New York City," he said.

I walked to the concrete barrier and looked over at the streets below. A steady stream of red lights dotted the streets. The muted sounds of honking and screeching tires rose to greet us. The air clung to my skin, amazing me that even New York suffered the same intense heat as Florida. "This is a special place?"

"I found it when I was looking for my dad. Years ago, I decided the agency must have buried the truth about his disappearance. I didn't trust Sylvia when she said he'd disappeared into thin air. My dad would have never left me without a reason. When I was old enough to gain access to the files, I decided to do my own investigation. An address left in his deserted car on the back of a receipt led me here."

"The agency didn't realize?"

"The agents only saw a series of numbers. It was a special code me and my dad made up back when I thought it was cool to play a secret agent. The only other person who would have known was Donald Mason."

"What did you find at the address?"

"A secret apartment, as if he was leading a double life. I never told anyone at the agency."

"Why are you telling me this?"

"Because I want you to trust me. I want you to know what you mean to me."

Mean to him? My throat felt thick with all of the words I couldn't say. "What hap… happened to the apartment?"

"It's still here. The apartment was paid in full, left in a name I'd never heard of. The taxes are paid through a trust so there's no reason for anyone to come here." He pointed to a set of glass doors behind us. "It's the penthouse suite, so this person had more money than my dad could have ever made working for the agency."

"Thanks for telling me."

Travis moved closer, pushing back the hair that blew around my face. "I want you to help me find the truth. It's only been me on this for years…" His voice lowered. "It will be good to have a friend who understands. I'm still hoping your father knows the truth."

I barely noticed the glove against my skin as his hand drifted down the side of my face. As I leaned into Travis, the scent of him made me warm inside. His head bent closer to mine.

"Kiss me," I whispered. "I don't care about the pain."

"We can't do this, remember?" Travis's breath tickled my cheek.

I brought my lips to within an inch of his, but he gripped my chin, holding me back. "Two seconds won't kill me," I said, "but you not kissing me might."

"I won't hurt you, but I needed to know how you feel."

My pulse quickened until I could barely breathe, barely think. "What good is *knowing* if you won't kiss me? How can that ever be enough?"

"It's enough to know that you want me."

I shivered at the raw anger in his voice. "That's great, but how am I supposed to know how you feel?"

"I want to kiss you, more than you'll ever know."

"Then show me."

He pulled back and held out his hands. "Because of this power, I can't. Nothing good will ever come out of a relationship with me. When you figure out your powers, you should run the other way, as fast as you can."

First, he showed me a secret no one knew, then he

told me to run. At least I wasn't the only one confused here. Or maybe it was the agent inside of him, still playing me to achieve his mission. Either way, my heart had decided and there was no going back.

"Then my fear will be of never knowing." I held out my hand and tiny blue sparkles appeared as if glitter had been thrown into the air. The sparkles rose up to form a small fountain above my palm. In the semi-darkness, blue light reflected in Travis's eyes.

"I'm your fear?" he whispered.

"I think it's been that way ever since we met."

"Can you control it now?"

I focused and the blue sparkles rose higher into the air. I waved my hand and the blue light disappeared. "I think so."

Travis's phone rang and he stepped away. "Hold onto that feeling. Payne here," he said into the phone.

I touched my lips, which tingled even though he never touched me. Tears threatened in my eyes and I didn't trust my voice, not when my whole body trembled.

He hung up the phone. "Sylvia needs us back at the base. We're out of time."

"What's going on?" I managed to say.

"It's time to show them what our newest Firebird can do."

CHAPTER FOURTEEN

We appeared in a conference room with a long wooden table, surrounded by dozens of men and women dressed in black suits. Their conversations died as all eyes focused on where we stood, at the back of the room behind where Sylvia sat. Some people covered their mouths as if they'd never seen someone teleport. Angel, sitting about halfway down the table, shook her head as Jon whispered in her ear.

Sylvia turned around. "That was fast."

"You said immediately." Travis watched the other faces. "This is the Centennial room," he said to me. "Around this table are the agency's senior personnel."

"Take a seat, Agent Payne," Sylvia said.

Travis led me to an open seat in a row of chairs against the outer wall. He took the only open seat at the table. Angel left her seat at the table and sat next to me along the wall. She linked our hands; the cold radiating from her skin felt oddly comforting.

Above us, the ceiling seemed to be lined with rows of dark windows, the first I'd seen in this place. I wondered if we were close to ground level. I peered at the screen on the far wall, which showed a list of names. Highlighted at number fifty-two was the name Max the Detonator.

"Is this the infamous list of people with powers?" I whispered.

Angel nodded and put a finger to her lips.

A woman at the other end of the table gave an update on a sighting of Max the Detonator. "He was in Atlanta," she said, "about five miles from this base. We also have Louis on camera at a mall north of the city."

"So, they're knocking on our door," Sylvia said. "Has anyone spotted Mason?"

"No," a man to her right said. "If he's with them, he hasn't showed up in any of the footage. Louis hasn't exactly been hiding."

"He's taunting us," Jon said.

"And with Donald he could have the upper hand," Sylvia said. "Agent Payne, have you been able to tap into Miss Mason's power?"

"Yes," he said.

Whispers began around the table. Someone scrolled upward on the screen, taking us through the forties and then the thirties. As the numbers lowered, I noticed Jon's name, Skip's and Angel's, and Sylvia. Almost all of the people who I'd interacted with since arriving. The family Travis was determined to protect. My breath caught as I noticed my name at number seven.

Angel felt me tense and leaned close. "A placeholder for now. If you're after an upgrade, make sure to show your powers today."

I choked when I saw the name at number one. My gaze landed on Travis; his eyes were fixed on me as if judging my reaction. "You're number one?"

The voices around the table stopped and every eye turned to Travis. His face hardened. "I have four powers.

Right now, that's a record."

"Four important powers," Angel said.

"You called us here for a reason." Travis's eyes shifted to Sylvia. "Can we get on with this?"

Sylvia's phone rang and she answered the call. Everyone watched as she listened, her eyes stopping on me. "Have a team ready in twenty minutes." She hung up the phone and shot Travis a dark glare. "No need to get upset, Agent Payne. We've received a message from Louis directing us to send Regina Mason to an address in Atlanta." She read the address and an agent pulled up a map of the area. A street-level view showed the front of a store called Mission Thrift.

"There must be something wrong," the agent said. "This is an actual store."

"It's a trap," Travis said. "She can't go alone."

"Let me guess," Sylvia said. "You'll volunteer to go with her."

Travis leaned forward and took a long look around the table. "That store is on the other side of town. Louis will expect the full agency treatment, probably so he can get the biggest bang for his buck when it comes to casualties. I can teleport Rena there and catch them off-guard. They won't be expecting us so soon and they won't blow up anyone until Louis has her out safely. If there's a bomb, she can diffuse it."

I released Angel's hand and stood. "I'm not ready for this." My voice shook as the world around me blurred.

The only sound was the collective intake of breath. Travis looked at his hands and shook his head as if he'd never been so disappointed. Then his eyes met mine, shooting like icy daggers through me. "Louis doesn't have to know you'll fail."

"Fail?" I said.

"I've known all along," he said in the clear voice of resignation, "but maybe you're right. It's time I stop lying to you. There's no way you have the power to stop him. We've wasted our time trying to find your power, time that could have been spent finding another way to save lives."

My stomach churned. Would I puke in front of all these people, on the spotless carpet at my feet? "If that's true, why did you save me? Why bring me here?"

Travis laughed in a way that brought the sick feeling to my throat. "Isn't that obvious? This mission is all about justice for me. Justice for what happened to my father. For the last twelve years, finding the person responsible for his disappearance has been my only mission."

I felt the eyes of every person burning into me. If they didn't know I was a fraud before, they knew now. "But your job as an agent—"

"Means nothing," he said. "I came to Florida to find your father. Donald Mason was the last person to see my father alive. He's the only one who can tell me what I need to know."

"What about me?"

"You're a lost cause. I've tried to help you find your power, but I don't think anyone can. I think if you do have Rosanna's power, you've buried it so deep that everyone on this planet will die before you figure out how to stop Louis's bombs."

Tears filled my eyes. He'd seen the blue in my hands, seen my pain. Was this payback for pushing him to admit feelings for me? "You're a real ass."

"I've never pretended to be anything else."

"I thought you were my friend."

"Great illusion, huh? Sylvia gave me a mission to find you and be your friend. She wanted me to assess your power and determine if you were a threat to the planet. My job was to bring you in and that's what I did." He looked at Sylvia. "Tell her the truth."

Sylvia pressed her lips. "I'm not sure this is the time—"

"Tell her," Travis yelled. "You wanted me to be her friend, to bring her over to our side. You said I was the master manipulator. Well, I got her here, but now what?"

He was telling the truth, I could see in the way her eyes avoided mine.

Anger and embarrassment oozed from every pore of my body. I raced from the room, into the hall and slammed the door behind me. My heart pounded as I realized I would fail at this. Travis could lose everyone he cared about. I'd already lost him; he'd lied and could never take that back.

He didn't want to take it back—he hated me.

Travis opened the door and stopped behind me. "Are you running away?"

Blue sparkles appeared in my palm and I spun, holding my hands out to Travis. "You were wrong. I have the power and I can control it." The blue light rose from my hands and formed a glowing ball above our heads. With a flick of my hand, the ball collapsed and radiated a circle of energy that shot out at the speed of light. In less than a second, the windows of the conference room shattered and a black ring appeared across the wall around us. The force of the blast knocked us to the floor.

Inside the conference room, agents began to pick themselves up from the floor and shake off the glass. Sylvia was the first to recover and meet us in the hall.

Travis pushed himself up to stand and reached for my hand.

"I've got this," I said, standing on my own. My ribs throbbed from the force of slamming against the tile.

"Can you do that in reverse?" Sylvia asked, her eyes wide with excitement.

I wiped my hands on my black jeans. "If I didn't stop the blast when I did, everyone would be dead. So yes, I can."

She eyed Travis. "I don't always agree with your methods, but this mission was right for you. You knew what it would take to help her."

I froze as I realized Travis had played me again. Some part of me felt anger at his display in front of the other agents, at purposely trying to hurt me. Some part of me felt a special pride that he'd gone this far to help those he cared about.

Would that part of me ever be able to trust him?

* * * * *

Travis teleported us to a dark alley, a few streets down from the thrift store. He pulled his gun from inside his suit jacket and gripped the handle as he led me along the sidewalk, tiptoeing through the shadows and crossing the streets after the cars had passed.

"How far?" I asked.

"Hush," he said in a tense voice. Travis waved me against a wall and leaned around a corner. "The store is up ahead. Are you ready?"

I followed his gaze around the edge of the brick building. The front windows greeted us with darkness. The sign above hung slightly to the left, with the glowing letters 'Mission Thrift.' "Do you think Louis is in there?"

"We're about to find out. Stay close to me. Just because you have a power doesn't mean you can't die if someone shoots you."

"Louis is after me, right? Who would risk making him

angry?"

Travis stared at the building. "None of this feels right. Stay close enough that I can teleport you out of there if needed."

On his heels, I followed until we reached the store's front. "I don't see any cameras," Travis said, "but I'm sure he's watching us. Louis is a movie fanatic that gets off on recording every angle of his victim's pain."

"How do we get in?" I asked.

Travis reached for the door handle. The door slid open with a simple tug. "It's worse than I thought. Somewhere Louis is laughing at us, probably with a bucket of popcorn."

"What if my dad's in there?"

Instead of answering, Travis waved me inside of the dark store behind him and closed the door. My eyes adjusted to the faint light from the street. Shelves filled one side of the store and racks of clothing the other. Travis held his gun close as we crept down the main aisle toward the back of the store. Through huge double-doors was a room filled with gray donation bins with every household item imaginable.

"This looks legit," I whispered. "I've seen the back of one of these stores. It's called the sorting room."

A lone light hung at the center of the room, casting a halo of amber light across the floor. I wondered how they managed to get only one light to come on, when usually a dozen or more of the lights above should be on the same circuit. When we reached the end of the donation bins, I realized the purpose of the light.

In the center of the floor was a metal chair. On that chair sat my dad, his face bloody and hanging forward at a painful angle. I ran to him and Travis stayed close by my side. Dad's eyes were closed; one looked as if it had been beaten and then glued shut. Dried blood trailed down his face in even strokes as if painted on. His shirt, the same black t-shirt he'd worn on Sunday night, was stained with blood and ripped across his stomach. At his feet, blood also stained the floor. Behind his back, his wrists were bound with thick plastic ties, similar to the ones he used for repair around the campground.

Travis pressed two fingers against Dad's neck. "This is hard to do with gloves." He crouched down and held his ear to Dad's face. "He's still breathing."

I let out a sigh of relief.

"Regina Mason," said Max, who stepped into the light with the clicking of his snake-skinned boots on the concrete. "Louis has been waiting."

Travis reached for my arm, but I shrugged him off. "What does Louis want?" I asked.

Max laughed. "Unfortunately, just to talk. As long as you cooperate, he's insisted Agent Payne and your father keep breathing. If not…" He put a cigarette in his mouth and rubbed his fingers together at the tip. Smoke spiraled up from the cigarette. "Next we try the dynamite."

"This is a trap," Travis said, reaching for my arm again.

I glanced down at Dad, who didn't move. "What did you do to him?"

"Louis and your father came to an agreement," Max said. "If Mason ever wakes up, make sure to ask him about the details." He laughed again. The lights above came to life, all at once, and the floor around us shined as if recently polished.

"Rena." Travis moved closer and his hand touched my arm. "Louis will try to steal you away. If you leave the building, they'll kill anyone who shows up to save us."

"Tonight isn't about bombs. If only I could be so

lucky." Max pulled a gun from the holster in his jacket and pointed the barrel at Dad's head. "Give me your gun, Agent Payne."

Travis handed over the gun, his expression calm. "I expect that back when we're done here."

"Sure, man, keep on believing that." Max's eyes slid over me. "Agent Payne might escape, but your father's not going anywhere. Talk to Louis, and Mason walks out of here alive." He pointed to a set of wooden stairs leading to a small room over a pair of bathrooms. "There's only one way in or out of that room."

I pulled away from Travis. "There's no reason I can't see Louis. I want to know why he's doing this."

Travis eyed the stairs and nodded. "Be careful. If Louis tries to hurt you, scream. I'll be right there."

Maybe Travis could see there was no harm in me meeting Louis. Maybe he'd teleport in there, but I hoped to learn some of Louis's secrets before he showed up. If Louis tried to capture me, I'd scream and run from the room. Travis could save me from anything; he'd proved that much in the last few days. I'd finally get answers about my mother.

I walked to the stairs and each gave a low creak as I stepped higher. At the door, I looked back to where Max still held a gun to Dad's head. Travis stood next to him with his arms crossed over his chest, tapping his foot with impatience.

As I turned the handle, I prepared myself for Louis to attack, maybe hold a gun to my head. What I didn't prepare for was the beauty before me.

Paintings lined the wall with colors ranging from soft pastels to hungry reds and blues. A clothesline hung across the center of the room, holding pencil drawings of a face I'd known every day growing up. Above the line of drawings was another rope holding pictures snapped in black and white. A smile… dancing eyes… this young woman looked so much like Mama, my heart hurt from the onslaught of memories.

At the center of the room, along the far wall, sat a man leaning over a drafting table. His hand drew long arcs over a sheet of paper almost as tall as me. For a moment, I watched the back of his slick brown head as the arcs became like words while he hummed a low tune that brought tears to my eyes.

It was the same song Mama once sang at my bedside.

The jagged strokes stopped. He put down the charcoal pencil and turned slowly to look at me.

I swallowed the catch in my throat. "Are you Louis?"

Focusing on his eyes was impossible at first with all of the pictures, but pain in the deep amber drew me closer. Even with the dim light over the table, I could see his face was tanned, as if he belonged on a beach, basking in the sunshine instead of this tight room. Louis reminded me of an actor from a popular TV show with his toned arms and AC/DC t-shirt that hugged his abs. His face was etched with a rare, sensual beauty and without a single shadow left by time's careless touch.

A smile stretched across his lips. "I've waited a long time for this."

His voice was the same poetic sound I remembered from the camper. Dad had mentioned an embassy, but I'd never bothered to ask which country Louis was from. "How do you know I'm—"

"Regina? With a face like yours, there's no hope of fooling me." He waved a hand around the room. "As you can see, I was Rosanna's biggest fan."

Although the pictures made him seem like a stalker, the softness in his voice convinced me he'd cared for her.

"Rosanna—"

"Castillo," he said.

"Wait." My head spun. "She wasn't… no way was she…"

"Rosanna was married to me at the time of her disappearance." He smiled. "You didn't know."

"No."

"I'm not surprised Donald never told you, but the agency should have been honest."

I turned and walked to the door.

"Where are going?" he asked in an innocent tone. "Running back to those thieves already?"

My hand rested on the handle. "I don't believe you."

"You don't believe Donald Mason lied or that the agency hid the truth?"

I spun around. "Why bring me here?"

"With your power, we'll make every government either prove their worth to their citizens or bow down before them. Every person should have the power to hold his—or her—government accountable."

His words became a jumble in my head. All I could think about was Mama. Rosanna. Her name was Castillo and no one ever bothered to tell me. "I don't care about your fight. Donald Mason is my dad. Mama told me so."

"Did she ever tell you her real name?"

I shook my head and put my hands over my face. Travis said something about this place didn't feel right. I was starting to agree.

"It seems Rosanna lied to us both. After losing her, all I had left was my pledge to free every person on this planet. When a governing body becomes like a cancer, it's revolution time. You're American. You've studied the schism of your country from British rule."

The last thing I needed was a history lesson. "They

threw tea in the harbor, not nuclear bombs."

"With changes to technology, our methods of fighting must also undergo a material change. We must, in effect, keep up with the times."

I lowered my hands and met his eyes. Louis leaned back against the table. His last words had the sound of someone fighting to keep a straight face. "You don't care about taking down governments." I reached for the door and turned the handle.

"Wait." Louis sat up straight.

"Tell me the truth or I'm out of here."

Louis sifted through the drawings on his table and held up a photograph. "Do you recognize her?"

Stepping forward, I reached for the picture. My stomach churned as my pulse sped with panic. "That's my mom." At the bottom of the picture was a date and time. Two weeks ago. I dropped the picture and covered my mouth. "I watched her die."

"I've been through this," Louis said, "the nightmares, the agony of not knowing. Rosanna's no more dead this time than she was eighteen years ago. With your help, Rosanna will return to me."

The thought of her being alive, the wonderful 'what if' brought tears to my eyes. My throat closed making breathing impossible. A tingling sensation crawled across my palms, bringing the blue sparkles to the surface like a raging fire.

Fear. Knowing Mama might be alive, that Louis might be telling the truth, brought a panic I'd never known. I closed my palms to hide the blue.

"There," he said. "I knew she didn't die that day at the ocean. Your power proves she didn't die."

"You're sick," I managed to say.

"I was sick for years after she left, but now I know

how to make her love me again. You will help me."

"No." I ran to the door, this time not hesitating to throw it open and race down the stairs.

All the lights were still on. I glanced across the storeroom, but no one stood on the concrete below. When I reached the bottom, I spun around. Which way to go? Halfway across the room, Dad's chair sat empty.

"You'll be back," Louis called after me. "You'll want to know the truth as much as I do."

A donation bin tipped over along the far wall. I ran toward the noise. Someone grabbed my arm and I wrenched myself away. I spun, thinking Louis had caught me, but it was Travis's gloved hand that reached for me.

"Did you know Louis was married to Rosanna?" I asked.

He opened his mouth but couldn't seem to find the words.

"Of course you knew." I shook my head. "Everyone at the agency knows Rosanna was married to Louis. I was so stupid."

"We need to get out of here," he said.

"Were you hoping I wouldn't find out?"

His voice cracked. "I was hoping Donald told you the truth. Before we left Wynder, you told me that your mom moved you to Florida when you were six. I just assumed you must know Mason wasn't your father."

"Mama told me he was my daddy and that was good enough."

"You never stopped to wonder where he was for the first six years of your life?"

"Don't give me the double-oh-seven routine," I shouted. "Back then it didn't matter."

"Why should it matter now?" he shouted back.

The click of a gun brought me back to reality. Max

stepped out from behind the bin and pressed his gun to the back of Travis's head. "Hands in the air."

Travis frowned and raised his hands. "This is really a bad time."

"Don't let me interfere with your spat," Max said. "Go on."

I glared up at Travis. "What do you know about my mom?"

Max pressed the gun harder. "She asked you a question."

Travis sighed. "Sylvia thinks Donald and my father helped Rosanna fake her own death. She disappeared for several years and then showed up in Florida after Donald retired from the agency. She changed her name and stayed off the radar. I told you all of this before."

"But you left out the part about Louis. She was hiding from him?"

"Why do you think Donald lived in a campground? No bills in his name. Records show he dodged paying any income or property taxes. As far as the government was concerned, he was a ghost. He knew that's what it would take to hide from Louis."

Anger flared inside of me. "Why hide this?"

"I've changed my mind," Max said. "Turn around." He placed the gun against Travis's forehead. "I want to see the look in your eyes as you die."

A noise sounded from across the room. I thought of Dad and reached into my pocket. Slowly, I pulled the multi-tool from my pocket and slid open one of the blades.

"Tell your girl goodbye, Agent Payne."

I raised the blade, aimed for Max's face. Before I could strike, a hand shoved the gun aside. My whole body froze as Dad's bad arm stretched around Max's neck. A cry escaped Max's lips as Dad twisted his neck and dropped the lifeless body to the floor.

Dad stared down with a blank expression. "Haven't you ever heard the phrase 'don't bring a knife to a gun fight?'" Before I could answer, he turned to Travis. "You're Noah's son?"

Travis nodded.

"If you have his power, get us out of here. Now."

*****

As Dad suggested, Travis took us back to the base—me first and then he went back for Dad. Nurses approached where we stood in the long white hall. No questions were asked. All anyone needed was one look at Dad's bloody clothes and swollen eye. They took him into a room and began a series of tests, leaving me in the hall.

Travis made a call and returned to my side. "Do you need a nurse?"

"We need to go back for—"

"Other agents are on the scene," he said. "They'll find Louis."

I tried to watch Dad through the gaps in the blinds. "Is this a hospital?"

"We call it the med-level," Travis said, "but it's essentially a fully-equipped hospital."

After a few minutes, a doctor entered the room to check Dad out. A nurse left the room and returned with the re-generator wand Travis had used on me. "I figured you would ask for this since that's Donald Mason."

The fact this nurse knew Dad's name brought home the fact we'd all lived a lie. Travis reached for the wand. "Why not? He knew about my power. This won't shock him."

I followed Travis and the nurse into the room where

Dad sat on the bed. The two nurses had managed to clean the blood from his face. He'd changed into a white t-shirt. He said nothing while Travis used the wand to heal his wounds, each cut disappearing as if his skin had never been pierced. His eye took the longest, but eventually the burst of light faded and the swelling went down to normal.

Travis stepped back and looked over his work. "Want me to fix your hand too? Or does that injury have sentimental value?"

"By all means," Dad said. "I didn't realize the agency's technology had advanced this much in twelve years."

When the light had again faded, Travis lowered the wand. "Good as new."

Dad nodded and flexed his hand. "Travis, could you leave me alone with my daughter?"

Travis's eyes met mine, but he didn't argue with the chill in Dad's voice. He followed the doctor and nurses out of the room, closing the door behind them.

"Max said you made a deal with Louis."

Dad patted the bed beside him. "Rena, I'm sorry for whatever Louis told you."

I sat on the bed. "He told me Rosanna was his wife. Was she really my mother?"

"Yes."

"Louis also said you're not my father."

"I suspected, but I was never sure. Neither was your mother."

"Not sure? How can you not be…" The truth stung like a late frost, with the power to kill everything green it touched. "You had an affair with another man's wife?"

He swallowed. "Yes."

"They were married and you—"

"Broke a sacred trust. Rosanna fled the Black Dawn because Louis forced her to use her power to terrorize the world. After she came to the agency, my job was to protect her."

Tears burned in my eyes. I jumped to my feet and paced the floor in front of him. "You took advantage of her?"

"I loved Rosanna. She made me feel things I'd never imagined. I lost my head during that time, but we managed to hide our love from everyone at the agency. When she found out she was pregnant, Louis was close on her trail. We decided the only way to save her was to make her disappear."

"And Travis's dad helped?"

Dad sighed. "Noah knew there was no way for the government to protect her. Making Rosanna disappear was the best option for everyone involved. As long as she hid somewhere Louis couldn't find her, both of you would be safe. As long as she could control her power, she wasn't a danger to the planet."

"You told Louis she died?"

"As I expected, he didn't mourn her death as much as the loss of his weapon. Louis craved the thrill of performing on the world's stage."

I dropped into a chair next to the bed and put my head in my hands. "That means they never divorced."

"That's right."

"Then the two of you never got married."

"In this life, you make do with what you're given. I loved Rosanna and I was willing to take her any way possible. She gave up a life of luxury to live with me in a campground. That ring on your finger is worth more money than I've made in my entire life." He eyed my hand. "Where is your ring?"

"I took it off so I could use my power. The agency wanted me to… wait, what about Alfie?"

"We're talking about you, not Alfie. There's no doubt he's my son."

"But where is he?"

"Jacob placed him somewhere safe. I told you not to worry."

I looked down at my hand. "Why give me this ring when she disappeared from that life completely?"

"Because some part of her knew you would be like her. From a young age, you were fearless. That ring always helped to calm her, to keep control over her fears. It's hard to explain, but it helped to control her power. She knew you would need at least that much to survive."

"She had fears?"

"A few of them. She wasn't quite as fearless as you, but she was a force in her own right. And she loved you and Alfie. No matter how you feel about me, don't ever forget how much she cared for you. She made sacrifices to ensure you would have a safe and happy life. As far as she was concerned, Rosanna's old life died the night she left Louis."

"What happened the night of the accident?"

"I realized I couldn't save her."

"But she was powerful."

"Even her power couldn't keep her alive. When the truck hit us… I never saw it coming until the lights flashed in my eyes. It came from her side…" Dad's voiced choked. "If she'd been driving, she'd be alive."

"Did she really die that night? Louis showed me a picture—"

"I watched as the doctors took her off life support. You were sedated because of the pain. The truck hit on your side and the seatbelt dislocated your hip."

I rubbed my hip and cringed at the memory of a pain so strong my bones felt as if they were on fire. "Why didn't you call someone at the agency? Maybe someone here could have—"

"And risk them finding out about you? Your mother would have rather died."

"Louis showed me a picture of Mama. He thinks she's still alive."

"Louis Castillo is an expert with imagery and deception," Dad shouted. "He made that picture to get you on his side. He told me his plans, blurted them out as if desperate to make someone else believe he had the power to bring her back. Your mother is dead. Even if that wasn't true, she'd never go back to him."

A silence fell between us. I looked up at Dad, at the tired lines of his face and the tears in his eyes. He stared at the closed door, through the blinds and into the hall where people rushed past. "Did you ever get a DNA test?"

"I didn't want to know the truth. You were my daughter and nothing else mattered."

Which meant the odds were in Louis's favor. "Does anyone know for sure if Louis is my father?"

"Would that have changed you running down those stairs?"

"You saw that?"

Dad smiled. "Looks like I raised you right. Now, give your old man a hug."

I reached for Dad and smiled. For the briefest of moments, he was the same laughing man who'd held me in his arms after falling from my bike. All the sacrifices he made to keep me safe became clear, along with the sacrifices that Mama made to hide me from Louis Castillo.

"Do you think he'll set off more bombs?"

Dad's smile died. "He's planted five around the city, but I got a look at his map. Louis made the mistake of assuming I was as good as dead." He stood. "I need to see

Sylvia."

It was time to show Louis what family really meant.

CHAPTER FIFTEEN

Travis didn't say a word as he led us to Sylvia's office. She sipped a cup of coffee while Dad sat before her and made five markings on a tablet, which he held out for Travis.

"Give Skip the map and leave us." Sylvia waved a hand at me and Travis.

In the hall, Travis walked by my side to the elevator.

"They could be in there for hours," I said.

"They'll be done when we find the bombs." He reached for my hand. "Then it's show-time. I don't want to hear any more doubts."

"That doesn't mean I won't have them."

In a room full of computers, Skip worked with several other agents to determine addresses and find street-level shots based on Dad's map. Jon organized five teams, one for each of the bombs. The closest bomb was somewhere in the airport above.

Concern filled Jon's voice as he addressed the teams. "The airport device might be the trickiest to find. Luckily, it's the middle of the night and the dogs are ready. We've asked for all service to be stopped and the terminals cleared."

"Clearing the airport won't be easy," Travis said. "What's the cover story?"

"Bomb threat," Jon said. He tapped several buttons on the screen of his phone. "Angel's on her way through the terminals as we speak."

Travis reached for my arm. "That's where we'll go first."

I nodded and the room around us changed to the inside of an elevator. Travis pressed several buttons and the elevator moved upward. "This way no one will see us," he said. When the doors opened, he led me up an escalator. People rushed by us in both directions, some calm and some with panic on their faces. He dialed his phone and Angel answered.

"Where are you?" He tilted his head toward a row of gates and looked down at me. "Believe it or not, they've found the bomb. The dogs worked their magic."

"Can it be that easy?" I asked.

He gave me a strange look and hung up the phone. "Finding the bomb *is* the easy part. What happens next is up to you."

We reached the top of the escalator and ran down a long, tiled walkway, to the end of the terminal. At the last gate, Angel stood inside a circle of agents, staring down at a chair that had been flipped upside down. Attached to the bottom was a device about the size of a cell phone, with pulsing red and yellow lights.

"I'd hate to be sitting in that chair," Travis said.

Angel spun around. "We've got to get this bomb under control."

Travis rubbed his hands together. "I can handle that. Where do you want it?"

"No." She pushed his hands down. "Skip said not to let you teleport the bomb. He's afraid of what altering the molecular makeup might do."

I'd never thought of what altering *my* molecular makeup might do each time he teleported us. Travis took my hands before I could say the words. "You'd rather it blows up here?"

"I'd rather Rena diffuse it here," she said. "It has a counter, like in the movies."

"And probably a camera to watch our reactions." Travis eyed the device. "How long do we have?"

"Fifteen minutes. I'll stay, but I think we need to clear out the other agents, just in case…"

Travis turned to me. "Check out the bomb and get yourself together. We might need a little of that fear you felt tonight."

Or a lot. "You guys can't stay here. What if—"

"I'm not afraid of dying," Travis said.

I turned to Angel. "I can't be the reason either of you die. If we fail—"

Angel took my hand. "If the timer gets close, I'll stay while Travis saves you both."

"But you could die."

She shook her head. "I can't die. That's one of my powers."

"You can live forever?"

"That's the price of being a vampire."

"Vampire?" I wasn't sure how I felt about making that trade. Her pale skin, the haunted look in her eyes… Maybe it was time to toss out all of the science books. "That's why your skin is so cold?"

"If I've learned anything since joining the agency, it's that none of us can escape our powers," Angel said. "You've got to trust in your abilities. No one can do that for you."

I dropped to my knees in front of the bomb and held

my hands to either side. If there was a way for me to diffuse it, I'd figure out how. Travis and Angel were depending on me. Their voices faded from my thoughts. Only the bomb existed. I felt the particles inside, dormant as the clock ticked. A tiny explosion inside the pulsing case would set off a chain reaction that could level this airport.

Like marbles, each of the particles cascaded before my eyes. I thought of the phrase Travis had used when he talked about my belief in science. The marbles would all fall like a house of cards. Maybe my knowledge of science could be of use here. I pictured myself slowing the particles on an individual basis. If only I had enough time… but maybe I did. First, I'd set off the bomb. Then I'd stop the particles in their tracks.

Blue tingled along my palms and rose into a fiery ball, like in the conference room. Forget waiting fifteen minutes. I'd nudge the reaction to start the neutrons shifting and the first would collide… just one teeny tiny explosion…

"Rena," someone said from a distance.

The blue radiated as the device began to glow. In slow motion, I watched as the first explosion led to another. The colors brought tears to my eyes. Radiant colors as a third and fourth explosion began an exponential climb in energy. I released the blue ball of fire, blasting the device until it became a hot red and then disintegrated into a pile of crisp black dust.

Travis kneeled at my side. He took my hand when the glowing faded.

I pulled away to wipe my eyes, but he brushed the moisture away himself. "I'm sorry," I said.

"You better be," he said. "If we're going to be a team, you'll at least have to let me help. Next time I'm giving the countdown."

"Next time?" My head felt fuzzy, as if we were under water.

"We've got four more." Travis pulled me to my feet. "Come on. I'll take you to the rest."

* * * * *

The next morning, I woke to find Travis sitting by my bed. After wiping the sleep from my eyes, I noticed the machines to my other side. "I hate hospitals."

He leaned his head forward. "Your dad insisted. He wanted the doctors to monitor you after disarming all those bombs."

I yawned. "I used my power to slow the neutrons affecting five nuclear bombs…"

"And save countless lives," he added.

"My dad has no right to worry about me."

"Everyone is worried about you." A knock sounded on the door and Travis jumped to his feet. "Matter of fact, you've got a visitor who just wouldn't wait a second longer."

The door opened and in ran Alfie. Despite the sheets and the ugly white nightgown, my brother climbed onto the bed and threw his arms around me.

I hugged him tight. "How did you get here?"

"Uncle Jon brought me. We got to see the planes and I've had ice cream with every meal. I like this place."

"Uncle… Jon?" I glanced at the doorway where Jon leaned against the frame. Dr. Greene stood next to him.

"Donald left him with Jacob Andrews," Jon said. "The night he disappeared, Jacob drove your brother to the home of a relative in Tampa. As soon as word got out that someone attacked Jacob, a man who fit the description of Max the Detonator, I went down there. It took some convincing, but Jacob revealed Alfie's location that afternoon."

A mixture of anger and relief flowed through me. "He's been here ever since?"

"I'm sorry, Rena," Dr. Greene said. "I thought it would be better for you not to know, at least until we got this bomb situation under control."

I thought back to my last meeting with Dr. Greene. "The sleepover with your son. Alfie was the friend?"

He nodded. "If you don't mind, I'd like for Alfie to spend more time with us. If you haven't noticed, we're a family here. We help and support each other."

"I've noticed." I glanced at Travis. "You knew Alfie was here. You kept telling me not to worry, that Max didn't have my brother."

Travis nodded. "I also told you how much I hate lying to you."

"You hid my brother from me. Why?"

"When you said you feared something happening to Alfie, I realized we might have to use that as motivation. Sylvia decided it was best to keep you in the dark in case it came to threatening his life."

Would Travis really have made that threat? A voice inside told me 'yes, he would have.' When it came to protecting his family, he was willing to do whatever it took.

I patted Alfie's back and he smiled up at me. "Thanks for keeping my brother safe."

"He's part of the family now," Travis said. "Anything for him."

* * * * *

That afternoon, I attended a meeting with only Sylvia and my father. She showed us a picture of a woman who looked like Mama, from six months ago.

"Where was this taken?" Dad asked.

"At a bank in Russia. Do you think Rosanna could still be alive?"

Dad stared at the wall behind Sylvia. "I watched her die the night of the accident. The doctors had a tube down her throat. Yes, I was crushed by guilt and my hand felt like it took a round in a blender." He grunted as he flexed the hand Travis healed. "I saw them turn off the machine. Her heart stopped."

"Was she buried in Florida?" Sylvia asked.

"Rosanna asked to be cremated. At that point, Alfie was barely old enough to understand what was going on. Rena spent her time comforting him and I knew the longer I waited the more our family would hurt. I had the cremation performed as soon as the hospital released Rosanna to the funeral home. There was no service."

Sylvia's voice lowered. "Did you see her body before they took her in?"

"I couldn't bring myself to look at her cold face. I wanted to remember Rosanna as she'll always be for me—smiling and full of life." Dad looked over the picture again. "I suppose it could be her."

"Wouldn't you want to know?" I asked.

"If she's alive and left Florida with a purpose…" Dad cringed. "I loved Rosanna but I don't want to think of her with evil intentions. If she went back to the Black Dawn—"

"We've interrogated what's left of the Black Dawn," Sylvia said. "Since you removed Max from the equation, only Louis remains in play."

"Louis had a room with pictures of her," I said. "Hundreds of paintings, photographs, sketches…"

Sylvia shook her head. "Our agents tore the thrift

store apart. Although we took four people believed to be helping him into custody, there was no sign of Louis or any artwork."

"That's it?" I asked.

"Louis has fled the country, or so we think," she said. "No one knows where Rosanna is or if she's still alive."

"How can you be sure?" Dad asked.

"Angel has the power to read emotions," Sylvia said. "None of them knew anything about Rosanna being alive. If she's out there, she's not working with them."

"Then we've hit a dead end," Dad said. "If Louis believes she's alive, he'll be back."

Sylvia folded her hands together on the desk. "About our conversation from last night. I'd like an answer as soon as possible."

Dad looked over me. "I need to have a talk with my daughter first."

"Have your talk, but please make the right choice for everyone involved."

After we left Sylvia's office, I wondered what choice she wanted Dad to make. Travis leaned against the wall across the hall, scrolling through messages on his phone.

He tucked the phone in his pocket and stepped into Dad's path. "I think you owe me an explanation about what happened to my dad."

"It's a little more complicated than a simple question," Dad said.

"I have time," Travis said.

For a moment they stood in the hall, staring each other down. The two men I cared about most. "I was with your father in New York," Dad said. "What I saw there is hard to describe. That's the night I found out about his powers."

Travis rubbed his chin. "You never knew before that

night?"

Dad shook his head. "I never knew. That night men with guns came—laser guns that weren't made on Earth. And one woman with a gun that was made on Earth—she could shoot better than any of the others. They were fighting over a girl. They spoke in a language I couldn't understand."

My eyes widened. "Aliens?"

"Why were you there?" Travis asked.

"That's the kind of question you ask over a good stiff drink." Dad glanced at me. "Unfortunately for you, I've given up drinking."

Travis's face fell. "You're not going to tell me, are you?"

"Your father could see the future. He warned me of this day. So no, I'm not going to tell you."

"This isn't over." Travis disappeared, leaving me alone with Dad in the hall.

"What did you say to Sylvia last night?" I asked.

"That I still feel guilty for breaking the trust associated with my promise to protect Rosanna. She was my charge and I let my feelings…" He sighed. "I didn't deserve to wear that suit."

"From what Jon said, you saved lives."

Dad faced me. "While I was with your mother, I was a different person. I wasn't the agent prepared to do whatever it took to save the world. Now I'm in that black box again."

I reached for his arm. "You still have me and Alfie."

He pulled away. "No, it's me against the world. That's the only way I can survive without her." Tears filled his eyes and he wiped them away. Dad lifted his head. "The Army made me a killing machine. For a time, I stifled my raw needs with a bottle."

"What do you need?" I whispered.

"To know everyone I care about is safe. The power to control the looming dangers I can't see."

"Do you have any powers?" I asked.

He shook his head. "Only the strength to do whatever it takes for my country. Dreams of war will haunt me for as long as I breathe. The only way for to balance the scale then was by killing to save lives. My hands are drenched in blood."

"And now?"

"I know life and I know death. Everything in between is useless."

"Does everyone know Louis could be my…"

Dad cleared his throat. "What about that friend of yours from Wynder? Have you talked to her?"

"Piper?"

"She'll want to know what happened to you."

"I think it's safer if she never knows."

Dad took one of my hands in his and examined my palm. "You could be right."

* * * * *

That night, there was a celebration dinner in one of the restaurants at the base. While we were waiting for our food, Travis and I moved to a lounge at the back of the restaurant. Most people there drank and laughed at the bar, but no one said a word as we sat down on a leather couch in a dark corner.

I'd planned to drill Travis about any other lies he might be saving, but Dad walked in before I could start my questions.

"Sylvia has offered my old job back," Dad said as he wedged between us and put an arm around both of our shoulders. "Provided I can stay sober."

Reluctantly, I slid over. "Can you?"

"I think so. Either way, I made a promise to you and Alfie. You deserve a father who cares more about you than the bottle."

"It won't be easy," I said.

He smiled wider than he had in three years. "You and Alfie will live here while I perform my agent duties. Rena, you've proved your ability to keep your powers in check. I imagine, though, Sylvia will want to track your progress."

Despite hearing the words track and progress in the same sentence, excitement rose within me. "Did you accept the job?"

"That depends on you." Dad turned to Travis. "I always imagined Regina would one day bring home a silly boy. I'd put the fear of death in him if he dared treat my daughter wrong. But you are no boy."

"No, sir."

"You're a man who has the power to protect her. Travis, you might have your mother's spirit, but you've also shown your father's resolve to fight for what's right, no matter what. I respect that."

"Thank you," Travis said in a thick voice.

"I'll leave the choice of us staying up to my daughter. If she chooses to stay, I assume your respect for her will be a priority. What's between you and Rena—"

"Dad, this is ridiculous." I shrugged his arm away and stood. "There's nothing going on between me and Travis. He can't touch me. How could there ever be anything between us?"

Travis bowed his head. "You have my word."

"Good." Dad stood. He put a hand to my cheek and left the room.

When we were alone, Travis pulled me down beside

him. "I don't have the right to ask this, but I want you to stay. Rena…"

"My dad wants to stay," I said. "Couldn't you see it in the way he smiled when he talked about Sylvia offering his old job back?"

"But he left the choice up to you."

"I don't know why he insisted on giving you that speech."

"He wanted to know that I'm here for the long haul. After everything, don't you think I should factor into your decision?"

My stomach fluttered as I stared into his green eyes. "I thought I was just a mission for you."

"You know better than that."

"I never pictured you wanting a relationship. You can't even touch me."

"You're right, it's selfish of me to ask."

"But you're really asking?"

He sighed. "I can't let you go."

I leaned into Travis's chest, careful not to touch the bare skin of his neck. Through the black suit, I listened as his heart raced like mine. The smell of him made my insides twist with the need to belong. To have Travis forever. "I'll stay."

He wrapped his arms around me and brushed a lightning-fast kiss against my hair. "Thank you."

"If only you could kiss me in other places." My cheeks burned when I realized what I'd said. "I meant—"

"I know what you meant. I'll find a way. One day, Rena, I promise we'll work this out."

I smiled at the warmth in his voice. His honesty touched my soul in a way no one had ever made me feel with the touch of a hand. Maybe he was right.

One day we'd find a way.

* * * * *

The next book in this series, *Fear Power*, will be ready in August of 2019.

Acknowledgements

Thanks to:

Everyone who has read this book. Please feel free to contact me anytime with your feedback since I love to hear from readers. And please take a moment to leave an honest review on Amazon and/or Goodreads. I do read these and I appreciate the time and effort that goes into each one of them.

The people who read my material and offer suggestions on a weekly basis: Larry, Barbara, Cindy, Robin, Julia, Jennifer, Erick, and Pete. I'm happy I found this great circle of writers.

Tazz for listening to my ramblings over this story and all the others. I loved his list of all the things MacGyver could have done with Rena's multi-tool.

Jodi for the feedback she's given on every book I've written. It means a lot to have someone read these stories early.

Annelise because I'll miss sharing my stories with her.

Tommy for reminding me why I do this.

Sherri for her support.

Christie for working with me during a rough time in my life. She's the reason this book happened and on time.

Fiona—I loved the concept for this new cover and look

forward to showing off the next three.

My husband as always.

About The Author

C.C. Bolick grew up in south Alabama, where she's happy to still reside. She's an engineer by day and a writer by night—too bad she could never do one without the other.

Camping, fishing… she loves the outdoors and the warm Alabama weather. For years she thought up stories to write and finally started putting them on paper back in 2006. If you hear her talking with no one to answer, don't think she's crazy. Since talking through her stories works best, a library is her worst place to write… even though it's her favorite!

C.C. loves to mix sci-fi and paranormal—throw in a little romance and adventure and you've got her kind of story. She's written nine books including the Leftover Girl series, The Agency series, and The Fear Chronicles.

Please visit her website at www.ccbolick.com for updates on future releases.

58378105R00159

Made in the USA
Columbia, SC
22 May 2019